The Dog Show

A Clara

CW00867777

By
Evelyn James

Red Raven Publications
2021

The Dog Show Affair is the twenty-second book in
the Clara Fitzgerald series

Other titles in the Series:

The sort where you take dogs with a pedigree and have them compared to others of their breed and you can win titles. Dear little Ling-Ling only needs one more win to declare him a champion, you know!"

"A champion what?" Clara asked.

"A champion Pekingese!" Mrs Monroe declared, annoyed Clara was not impressed. "And you can qualify for Crufts, which is the biggest dog show in the country! It has only just started up again after being put on hold during the war."

Clara nodded along, not sure what the fuss was all about and why anyone would care if a Pekingese was champion of its breed.

"You really do not understand," Mrs Monroe sighed. "I should have spoken to Mrs Cobb. She breeds whippets, you know."

Clara wanted to ask her why she had spoken to her but thought that might be rather rude. Instead, she smiled politely and hoped to be away from the conversation sooner rather than later.

"I thought I should tell you, seeing as you could attend and the more people who attend, then the greater the chances they shall organise another show for next year. Mr Trelawney at Mulberry Hall is trying this out, you see, to see if it will be popular and worth doing again. I am encouraging everyone I can to enter."

Clara considered this.

"I am assuming this is not like the summer fete show, where any dog can enter?" she asked cautiously.

"Oh no dear! No mongrels or those without papers. But your Labrador pup is a pedigree, is she not? I remember Tommy showed me her paperwork."

That was accurate. Pip came from a long line of pedigree gundogs and Clara recalled there being a few champions noted in her ancestry.

"Then, Tommy could take her and show her?" she asked carefully.

"Most certainly!" Mrs Monroe declared. "In fact, I insist

5

he does so. We want as many people as possible to attend. You ought to get the Gazette, there is an entry form printed inside."

"I shall mention it to Tommy," Clara said, noncommittally.

"I will check up to make sure you do," Mrs Monroe wagged a finger at her.

Clara had to bite her tongue to still her temper. She was not going to be bullied into attending a dog show! Somehow, she managed simply to smile.

"Have a lovely day, Mrs Monroe."

Anyone else would have realised this was a dismissal. Not Mrs Monroe.

"I have been anticipating this for years. When the war broke out it was near impossible to hold dog shows, what with the government not wishing for people to travel and all the restrictions. Some people even said it was unpatriotic to hold dog shows while our lads were fighting in France. People do say some stupid things!" Mrs Monroe held her head up higher and looked as if she expected Clara to be one of those people.

Clara just kept smiling. It was the easiest way to get rid of Mrs Monroe. Let her tell you what she wished to, offer no more feedback than absolutely necessary and eventually she would run out of things to say, as long as you did not encourage her, you should be fine.

"Where was I? Oh yes. It has been years since I attended a dog show, a proper show, that is. Ling-Ling is nearly ten, bless his heart. I thought I might not be able to make him up to a champion, which would be such a shame for the breed."

"Yes," Clara said, really not sure on that front, but not going to delve into the issue and prolong things.

"Then we hear that Mr Trelawney is going to host a show, well, you can imagine my delight. You do know Mr Trelawney?"

"I have heard his name," Clara agreed.

"He inherited Mulberry Hall from his uncle. The place

6

is in need of some serious work, I believe the roof is fit to fall in. Anyway, he is trying all sorts of different ways to raise funds and this dog show is just one of them."

Clara had a vague idea of where Mulberry Hall was. She recalled a sprawling, ill-kept building, largely covered in ivy and set back beyond a brick wall and ornate gates, which had rusted open years before. She had never been to the house. The owner had been quite elderly and rarely went out. There had been something in the paper about his passing back in January. She had not given it a great deal of thought.

"It is all very exciting. I know one of the judges and have found them very keen on my line of Pekes. I am full of hope for Ling-Ling!"

"Well, I wish you the best," Clara said, trying to separate herself from the woman.

Why could people not leave you alone when you were having a nice quiet cup of tea?

"Thank you, Miss Fitzgerald, and I am sure if Tommy was to attend, he would be very successful with Pip," Mrs Monroe cast her eye over the well-behaved pup. "She has sound confirmation."

"Does she?" Clara said, turning to also look and try to see what Mrs Monroe did.

"Remember, buy a paper and get that entry form," Mrs Monroe persisted.

Clara gave her a smile and left it at that. Finally, the annoying woman had imparted all the information she could and headed back to her house to see to her dogs, who were howling at the back door to be let out.

Clara was relieved to return to her two.

"I shall have a tall hedge planted," she informed them. "It looks less rude and more coincidental than a high fence."

Bramble tipped his head on one side, apparently giving this due thought. Clara picked up her teacup and despondently found the contents were now cold.

"Come on," she told the dogs. "Let us escape while we

can."

She headed into the kitchen where Annie was yet again attempting to ice her wedding cake. So far, this would be her third attempt. Each previous attempt, though they had looked fine to Clara, had some minute flaw Annie could not abide and so she had stripped the icing and the marzipan completely off and started again. Clara was not sure this obsession was healthy.

"Mrs Monroe cost me a cup of tea," she told Annie, pouring her cold tea down the sink. "She insisted on talking about a dog show happening at Mulberry Hall. She thinks Tommy should enter Pip."

"Oh," Annie said, completely oblivious to what Clara was saying.

Clara turned from the sink and watched as Annie smoothed a layer of marzipan down over the stacks of rich fruit cake. She worked with the care of a master craftsman, smoothing, and pressing, getting every line perfect.

Clara wished she could convince her this was all unnecessary. That any cake she made would be amazing and, in any case, this wedding was not about fruitcake, it was about sealing a bond between her and Tommy. Clara, however, knew when she was beaten and said nothing.

She headed through the house to the garden room which overlooked the lawn and at least meant she could look at the flowers without being disturbed by Mrs Monroe.

"Clara! Just who I wanted to see," Tommy grinned at her. He had been reading the newspaper.

Tommy was Clara's elder brother and now her partner in her detective business. Clara had promoted herself as Brighton's first female private detective and it had taken a lot of consideration before she had felt able to ask Tommy to join her in the business. She had not wanted anyone to think she could not manage the business alone.

"Have you seen the paper?" Tommy asked her, a big smile on his face. "There is to be a dog show at Mulberry Hall!"

Chapter Two

Clara went for a walk with Captain O'Harris later that day. As they were both very busy most of the time, they found it hard to coordinate themselves to meet up. This was placing a slight strain on their burgeoning romance and Clara was making an effort to see John as often as she could to compensate. O'Harris was doing the same and the result was they were spending much more time in each other's company.

Now they were strolling along the pier which was having something of a refurbishment after the hardships of a long war. Workmen were all over the place with tools and buckets of paint. This was impeding the progress of the visitors walking along.

"Private Peterson is going home at the weekend for a couple of weeks, to see how he fares," O'Harris said as they walked.

Peterson was one of the toughest cases the captain had had in his rehabilitation home for veterans of the last war. He dealt with their mental injuries, rather than the physical ones. He was one of the few to realise how important that was.

"I am glad Peterson is progressing," Clara replied. "He

has had a tough time."

Private Peterson had become embroiled by accident in the gang business that had affected Brighton for a while. He had been stabbed and left for dead, not to mention this coincided with him being accused of murder. Clara was relieved to hear he was doing better.

"And at the end of the two weeks?"

"He will come back to the home and we shall review how things went. In the past, Peterson has been treated and sent back out into the world with no backup. We don't want to be like that."

He was interrupted by a scurry of paws and something brown and fluffy scuttled between their legs.

"Fifi!" a woman cried in a high-pitched voice.

Fortunately, Clara had spent a lot of time around her own dogs when they were intent on escape and her reactions were primed as a result. Without even thinking about it she put out a foot and stood on the escaping canine's lead that was trailing behind it. Fifi came to an abrupt and unhappy halt. She gave Clara an accusing look.

An overweight woman in dark tweed and a skirt that heavily restricted her movement was prancing on kitten heels towards Clara with a frantic look upon her face.

"Thank goodness!" she declared as Clara handed her the lead she had retrieved from beneath her foot. "Fifi is from a line of champions, you know! I dread to think what could happen if she fell into the wrong hands. They might ransom her!"

The woman jerked the lead and escorted Fifi, who proved to be an extremely fluffy and over-groomed poodle with exaggerated balls of fluff around its ankles and tail, towards a group of people at the end of the pier. O'Harris raised an eyebrow at Clara.

"Heaven forbid Fifi would fall into the hands of someone who would actually clip her so she looked like a dog."

Clara tried not to laugh, since she was aware of people watching.

"Oh look, Oliver is down there."

Oliver Bankes considered himself the foremost photographer in Brighton and also subbed as a crime scene photographer for the police. He did not advertise this at his shop, needless to say, as people could be aversive to having their picture taken by someone who had recently shot photos of a corpse.

"Seems to me he is trying to get a picture of Fifi's loving owner and her companions," O'Harris said.

There were five people stood alongside the rail of the pier. Three women and two men. Each had a dog that they were endeavouring to pose so its best side would be caught on the picture. Oliver was having a hard time getting the people to look at his camera and stay still, let along the dogs.

"My knowledge of dog breeds is not formidable, but I believe that is a pug and that an Irish Wolfhound," O'Harris said.

"Fifi is a miniature poodle, I believe," Clara added. "Bramble is a toy poodle, though on the big side."

"And without the haircut," O'Harris said wryly.

"Now, I recognise a bulldog when I see it," Clara said, pointing to a dog held by a man with a round flabby face. "That leaves that tall leggy thing that looks like a fluffy greyhound."

"It is a Russian Wolfhound or Borzoi," a friendly voice said from behind Clara.

She turned around and saw an older gentleman in a smart suit and bowler hat.

"Arnold Jessop," he introduced himself. "I am in charge of the dog show to be held at Mulberry Hall. From your knowledge of dog breeds, I suspect you are dog enthusiasts yourself?"

"I have two," Clara replied. "A poodle and a Labrador."

"Then you ought to come along," Arnold said in a polite fashion which almost made you think you were not being invited to spend money. "The show is open to any dog that has pedigree papers, you know. And you can come along just to look. Many people find their next best friend, of the four-legged variety, by visiting a dog show and speaking to people."

"My brother is already in the process of entering our Labrador," Clara explained.

"Oh, delightful!" Arnold responded, smiling at O'Harris as he thought he was Clara's sibling.

"This is not my brother," Clara explained swiftly.

"Captain O'Harris," O'Harris introduced himself. "I do not own a dog."

"But are you considering it?" Arnold asked eagerly.

"Not really," O'Harris replied to him cheerfully, bursting his bubble.

Arnold was only deflated for a moment.

"You will surely change your mind should you come to the show," he smiled. "You were admiring our top competitors over there?"

Clara could not say she had been admiring anything, rather she had been idly curious, but she decided not to hurt Arnold's feelings further.

"We were," she agreed pleasantly. "Why are they having their picture taken?"

"Ah, well, before the war, the five people you see before you were considered top in their sport and we are making a thing about that to raise publicity for the show. If we can make this hugely successful, we can host it again, you see?"

Arnold waved his hand in the direction of the dog owners.

"Before you are some of the top champions in their breed. From working dogs to toy dogs, these are fine examples of the canine form."

Clara eyed up the bulldog, which was panting hard, and considered that debatable, but said nothing.

"We are going to do a feature on them in the paper," Arnold added. "Between you and me, we are doing a special 'best in show' prize at the event and Nigel Love is pegged to win. He is the one with Brutus the bulldog."

Clara frowned.

"But how can you know who will win before all the entries are in?" she said.

Arnold's face froze and it was plain he had said more than he had intended.

"Well, you know, it is just what people say. Do not let that put you off! You could be best in show!"

Arnold hurried away before he could put his foot further in his mouth. Clara turned back to O'Harris.

"I bet it is like flower shows," he said.

"Flower shows?"

"Yes. My aunt entered them all the time. She said it was not about the flowers but about who knew who."

"Then why enter?" Clara asked.

"Oh, she liked to show off her flowers, that was all. And it amused her no end when her glorious dahlias never took a prize, instead it going to another whose flowers were abysmal but who was having an affair with the judge."

"I do not understand," Clara sighed, thinking she could not enter a competition that was inherently unfair.

"Everyone knew it was fixed and it amused Aunt Flo to display her magnificent dahlias, the best anyone had ever seen and then watch the prize going to a lady who had a pathetic little pot of flowers. It proved her point and Aunt Flo loved to prove her point."

Clara shook her head, bemused by this logic. Oliver had finally managed to get a picture with everyone looking his way and seemed satisfied with his work, or rather he was at the end of his tether and could not bear anymore. He informed his subjects they could depart, and they set off with such haughty looks on their faces you would think they were already in the show ring. They had the dogs prancing along in a show step as if there were a judge to impress.

Clara simply did not understand it all.

"Hello," Oliver said, walking over to them lugging his camera on its tripod. He looked worn out.

"Busy day?" O'Harris asked him.

At one time Oliver had been vying for Clara's affections,

13

but he had resolved himself to never being able to compete with O'Harris. O'Harris was aware of Oliver's sore feelings on the topic and always endeavoured to be friendly to him.

"I have been taking photographs of dogs all morning and now this," Oliver said, trying to stifle a yawn and failing. "This is worse than the Christmas bonny baby photography shoot I had to cover for the newspaper last year. I thought bawling infants and their crooning mothers was bad enough. But dogs take the biscuit, excuse the pun."

"How so?" Clara asked, thinking the dogs could at least be kept on a lead.

"Well, it's not so much the dogs as their owners. Fussing over them all the time, making sure every hair is in place. The amount of shots ruined because the owner has turned their head at the last moment to adjust a tail or a span of fur is ridiculous. They would be a damn sight more cooperative if they were paying for the plates, excuse my French."

"Excused," Clara smiled at him. "Are you done for now?"

"No, more is the pity," Oliver groaned. "I have to go take pictures of more dogs and handlers. This lot are the royalty of the dog world, as far as I can tell. They have won so many prizes between them it boggles the mind. Five people who have made their mark by breeding pretty dogs."

Oliver shook his head thoughtfully.

"I am told their dogs are worth hundreds of pounds," he added in a whisper. "Not to mention stud fees and puppies. Brutus the bulldog is the face of Master's Dog Food, appears on all the adverts and is paraded on stage at company events."

"Well," Clara said, not able to think of what to add. "Well."

Brutus was being marched down the pier when he took a dislike to a mongrel that was wandering along the wooden planks. There was a growl, teeth bared and some ferocious barking as the bulldog lived up to its breed's reputation.

The mongrel gave it a look of pure disdain and marched away; tail held high.

"Delightful creature," Clara said with a smirk.

"Compared to its master, Brutus is a pleasure. I have never known such disagreeable people. Just getting them to stand side-by-side was nightmarish. They all hate one another."

"Whyever would that be?" O'Harris asked. "They all have different breeds."

"Professional discord," Oliver shrugged. "You would think you had asked them to drink poison when I suggested a group shot. A lot of these shows go for overall winners, where dogs from different breeds compete against each other for the top prize, and those five are often up for that award. So, they resent one another, and they resent the judge, unless he or she happened to pick their dog. You would think people had enough strife in their lives without making more for themselves."

Oliver tutted.

"Anyway, got to see a woman about photographing her papillons. See you soon!"

He headed off, his camera tripod banging into him uncomfortably.

"I assume he was still talking about dogs," O'Harris said.

"One has to hope," Clara replied. "It seems to me that the moment there is some sort of 'best of' prize available it brings out the worst in people. It does not matter if it is dogs, flowers or cakes. As soon as people are having to compete based on the quality or appearance of their chosen subject, then the knives come out."

O'Harris smirked at this.

"I think you have a point. It is different when you run a race. It is obvious who wins is the fastest. It is a quantifiable thing. But when you are basing things on the way a creature or object looks, then it becomes subjective and much more open to debate."

"I am very glad I am not a dog judge," Clara said firmly. "I do hope Tommy is not going to open himself up to trouble by entering this show. He thinks the world of Pip, he will be heartbroken if someone declared her a bad example of her breed."

"You could dissuade him from entering?"

"Too late," Clara sighed. "The form has been snipped out of the paper, filled in and posted. In any case, it would seem to me unfair to do that. We have to discover these things for ourselves."

"And he might win," O'Harris added.

Clara was amused.

"I think that unlikely. Pip is delightful, but she is not a show dog."

"How are preparations for the wedding going?" O'Harris changed the subject.

"Annie is fussing over the cake. There is another situation where a person is becoming stressed over the way a thing looks and tastes for no reason. She should be concentrating on enjoying her wedding."

They walked on in thoughtful silence for a while. Then O'Harris opened his mouth, at first words did not come out, he seemed to be reconsidering what he planned to say, then he spoke.

"Do you suppose, one day..." he couldn't finish.

"One day?" Clara asked.

"I was just thinking, what with Tommy and Annie getting married and so forth...," O'Harris coughed anxiously. "Have you ever considered it?"

"Marriage?" Clara asked. "Are you proposing John?"

She had a playful smile on her lips. O'Harris blushed. It was very amusing, he floundered about for a new subject.

"Cake, have you ever considered the complexities of wedding cake?" he said, clearing his throat.

Clara was amused. She slipped her arm into his.

"I have considered that one day I should like to eat a slice of my own wedding cake, alongside a gentleman who has pegged his life to mine, for better or worse."

"Ah," said O'Harris. "You see, I wondered with you being so independent and all…"

"Marriage does not mean losing that," Clara replied to him.

"Well," O'Harris said, his smile now boyish and mischievous. "Now, I better remember that, hadn't I?"

Chapter Three

There appeared to be 'dog fever' in Brighton that week as seemingly every canine owning resident in the town prepared for the big show at Mulberry Hall. Annie spied Mrs Monroe washing her squash faced dogs in an old tin bath in the garden. She had half-expected to see her peg the poor beasts out on her washing line to dry.

"She don't treat them like dogs," she puttered to Clara later on in the kitchen. "They are more like toy dolls."

Bramble, whose experiences of baths had largely been the hasty, cold splosh of disgrace when he had rolled in something despicable, heartily wagged his tail at Annie, as if he understood every word.

Tommy's preparations for the dog show were no less intense and elaborate. He had acquired a book from the library on dog showing and had read it from cover to cover one evening. He then spent every following morning teaching Pip to stand in a presentable fashion, ready for the show ring. Pip, being a loping puppy with uncoordinated legs and a tendency to be easily distracted, was struggling with the concept, though she did appreciate the many dog biscuits Tommy handed out in an effort to teach her.

He also invested in a comb and spent the evenings

attempting to groom a protesting pup, who was far more inclined to bite the offending article then allow it to be used. Bramble watched on with a self-satisfied look. Clara suspected, should he be able to talk, he would thank his lucky stars he did not have a pedigree to speak of. There were some benefits to being found in a bush, after all.

The morning of the show arrived, and Clara dressed in her new summer gown and hat, looking forward to time away from the house and Annie's incessant wedding cake deliberations. She was onto her tenth attempt at icing it. Clara was sure the cake must now have an inch of apricot jam adhering to it from the many efforts to stick marzipan upon it.

She came downstairs and found Tommy dressed in his best suit, the one reserved for formal occasions such as funerals and Christenings, and, of course, the one he intended to wear at his wedding.

"Don't get dog hair on it," she warned him, recalling the time Annie had spent cleaning the suit and removing the musty smell it had acquired from sitting in the wardrobe.

Tommy, who was engaged in a last-ditch attempt to get Pip to perform a stand on cue, grinned.

"It is very important the handler looks as smart as the dog at shows," he informed Clara. "I could not simply turn up in my regular clothes."

Clara could really not see how it mattered what the handler looked like when the point of the show was to determine the finest canine specimen present, but she decided not to quibble the matter.

"Have you convinced Annie to come?" Clara asked.

Tommy pulled a face and that was all the response she needed.

"I am starting to dread this wedding cake. I feel as though it is looming over the whole thing and taking away the gloss of the ceremony," he sighed. "I love Annie and to me the most important part of this wedding is the exchange of vows and us being properly united. The cake is not even secondary to that, it is somewhere down a long list of priorities. I could not care less if there was cake or not. What matters to me is marrying Annie. It wouldn't matter to me if there were no guests at all."

Tommy shrugged his shoulders and some of his joy had faded. Clara wished she had not mentioned it.

"I am sure it will be a lovely day," she reassured him.

"I can't see how if Annie spends the whole time fretting about whether people will like her cake or not," Tommy grumbled. "Well, never mind. Let's head off to this dog show."

O'Harris had offered them a lift in his car. He had opted to drive it himself instead of bringing Jones along. Sometimes a man needed to feel in control of his life and getting behind the wheel of a car was just a little part of that.

He arrived outside the Fitzgeralds' home not long after they had stepped outside to wait for him. Tommy had Pip on a slip lead (apparently this was another necessary item for showing, no flat collars to alter the neckline) and Clara was in charge of Bramble. Though the poodle could not enter the show due to a lack of papers, they were all agreed it would be best to keep him out of Annie's way for the time being. Bramble had a tendency to get under Annie's feet at the best of times.

They climbed into O'Harris' car and set off for Mulberry Hall.

"What do you know of Mr Trelawney?" O'Harris asked them as the they headed out into the countryside.

"He inherited the hall from his late uncle," Clara said. "Moved here about a year ago and has been trying to pull the estate out of debt ever since."

"I heard it said he was something big in London," Tommy added. "An investment banker or something along those lines. Unfortunately for him, Mulberry Hall is something of a money pit."

"I have a vague memory of the place from when I was a boy," O'Harris said, a slight frown on his brow as he dragged out the memory. "My aunt and uncle knew the old man at the hall, his name escapes me. They took me there once to see some old suits of armour the owner had collected. My uncle was considering writing a book about them. You know how he was fascinated by military history. I have this distinct memory of a house that was going tatty about the edges. Even as a boy I saw that."

"We never moved in the circles the owner of Mulberry Hall did," Tommy said. "Old money, I think. The best I can say is I bicycled past the gates of the place once or twice."

"There has been a lot of speculation about Mr Trelawney since the announcement of the dog show," Clara had refrained from using the term 'gossip'. "They say he is determined to save the hall and will attempt anything to reach that end. The dog show is just one example of his plans."

"Well, I know that feeling," O'Harris mused, having spent a considerable fortune saving his own ancestral home from ruin. He knew what debt looked like and how swiftly an old house could eat into a man's financial reserves. "I wish him luck."

They found the gates to Mulberry Hall after taking a wrong turn and having to double-back. The gates had long ago rusted open, the former owner not being particularly concerned about security. They drove up a gravel drive and watched as the hall appeared through an avenue of trees. It had been constructed in the late sixteenth century originally, and it was of red brick with those narrow, arched rows of windows the Tudors liked. However, later generations had added to the building without paying much heed to uniformity. There was a Georgian wing with tall windows and a veranda with classical pillars running along it, and there was a Victorian Gothic addition on the other side that looked like something out of a fantastical story. There were even gargoyles on the roof, which Clara felt was going a touch too far.

There were only a handful of people at the front of the house. Hand painted signs indicated that the guests attending the dog show should walk around to the back.

The trio dutifully followed the signs and found the main event spread out upon the vast lawns behind the house. A large marquee had been set aside for the show ring and also for the judges' dining area. Anyone not immediately needed in the show ring could spend their time as they chose, either walking around the estate or lazing on the grass in the sun. Clara noted that many of the regular competitors had come prepared with chairs and parasols, some had even brought sheets to make crude sun tents for their dogs to ensure they did not overheat.

Closer to the house, on the terrace, were tables where the organisers were attempting to keep control of the event. There was a long queue up to the tables, and everyone in it was holding a dog. In many cases, they were holding several. Tommy joined the queue, while Clara and O'Harris wandered over to a stand selling tea and cakes. A youngish woman behind the table was looking slightly fraught at the demand for her wares, especially when one of her customers began to impatiently tap his foot. Clara recognised this disagreeable individual as Nigel Love.

"I haven't got all day," he said loudly.

This caused the already stressed woman to try to speed up and, in the process, she slopped tea from an urn over the edge of the cup she was filling and scalded her hand. Clara could not simply standby and so went to her aid.

"Get that under a cold tap," she told her.

The woman gave her a grateful look and dashed off. Clara put aside the overfilled cup and saucer and made a fresh one, pointedly ignoring the huffing and tutting of Nigel Love and taking her time. She had already noted a sign that indicated it was a penny for a cup of tea, and so as she handed over the cup, she looked Mr Love straight in the eyes and requested payment.

"One pence, please."

"I shan't pay a penny for a cold cup of tea. You took too long," Mr Love snorted.

He took the saucer and was going to depart with his ill-gotten cuppa, except Clara deftly whisked the cup from the saucer and held it to her chest.

"Hey!" Love croaked.

"It is a penny and be glad I don't charge you more for being obnoxious."

"You can't treat me this way!" Love declared. "Don't you know who I am?"

Clara met his fierce gaze square on.

"Actually, I don't," she informed him, which had the expected effect of shaking his arrogance. "I do know I do not like people who make life hard for others and who attempt to get out of paying for things. If you want the cup of tea, I suggest you give me a penny."

Love's face began to flush red.

"I'll leave!" he said. "There will be no show without Brutus!"

"There are other dogs," Clara shrugged at him nonchalantly. "No doubt many of your fellow competitors would be glad to see you withdraw."

"It would not be a withdrawal!" Love snorted.

"It will be by the time I finish telling people about it," Clara smiled at him sweetly.

Love was trying to bluster when he had nothing to bargain with. Clara could care less who he was and if he stayed or not, and in the face of that he did not know what to do. He was so used to getting his way and people being too afraid to upset him, that he had not experienced such defiance.

"Cup of tea or not?" Clara asked him. "You are holding up my queue."

"I am not paying a penny for that!" Love barked.

"Fine," Clara poured the tea on the ground and looked beyond him. "Next."

"You can't do that to me!" Love cried as he was shoved out of the way by Mrs Monroe who happened to be next in the queue.

"Hello Clara, can I have a tea and a scone please," Mrs Monroe asked.

"This is unthinkable!" Love yelled as everyone ignored

him. "I shall tell Mr Jessop!"

Clara made Mrs Monroe her tea and picked out a nice scone for her.

"Good luck for today," she said as Mrs Monroe handed over her pennies.

"Thank you, Clara," Mrs Monroe smiled. "But I really do not need luck. My little Ling-Ling is the finest Pekingese here."

She headed off happy in her mind that she had already won the show. The next customer approached Clara while Love stood to one side looking gobsmacked. He had never been treated with such disregard and no amount of shouting and bawling seemed to be making a difference. He had discovered someone more stubborn than he was, and he did not know what to do.

As the last person at the tea table took their cup and saucer and left, Clara turned her attention back to Mr Love.

"Would you like that cup of tea, now?"

Love glared at her.

"Of course I would!"

"That will be a penny please, upfront," Clara held out a hand towards him.

He stared at it, his fat cheeks turning an entertaining shade of mauve. Then he dug in his pocket and produced a penny. Clara took it and prepared him a cup of tea which she handed over with a smile. She did not expect to be thanked, nor did she receive any sign of gratitude from Mr Love, who instead scuttled away before this cup of tea could be poured on the ground.

O'Harris had watched all this with amusement, knowing better than to interfere when Clara was taking a bully down by a peg or two.

"That showed him," he said.

The woman who had been running the tea table returned, with only a mild red patch on her hand to indicate the trouble she had been having.

"Thank you so much," she said to Clara. "I was getting

in such a pickle."

"It was no bother," Clara replied. "I saw Mr Love was making life difficult."

The woman shook her head and sighed.

"Who would have thought people who showed dogs would be so disagreeable? Though, to be fair, so far, I have only had issues with Mr Love," the woman was relaxing. "Elizabeth Trelawney. Everyone calls me Liz."

She introduced herself and Clara followed suit.

"Clara Fitzgerald and this is Captain O'Harris. I take it you are Mr Trelawney's wife?"

"I am," Elizabeth smiled. "Most people around here are not aware he has a wife. I tend to spend a lot of time in London where my mother is and where we have our townhouse. Bartholomew comes down here to work on the house. Once it is all sorted, we plan to move mother here and become permanent residents of Brighton."

"What a delightful plan," Clara said.

Mrs Trelawney clearly meant to say more, but there was a new queue forming for tea and she had to get back to work. O'Harris and Clara left her in peace and joined Tommy.

"Pip isn't in the ring until midday," Tommy told them as soon as they found him. "Fancy going for a stroll to pass the time?"

Chapter Four

"I am beginning to find dog shows a tad boring," Tommy said after they had circled the perimeter of the Mulberry Hall grounds and returned to find that the classes were running late, and Pip would not be in the ring until after lunch.

"Not inclined to make this a new permanent hobby then?" O'Harris asked, amused.

"Only if Pip displays champion quality straight off," Tommy said, attempting to emulate some of the other dog handlers' way of speaking with their noses in the air. They seemed to be sneering at everyone, even the judges. "And even then, I can find something better to do with my time. The Brighton amateur cricket team has reformed, you know. I participate every Sunday that I can, though my sprinting speed is not what it was."

"You are still a fast bowler and a damn good batsman," Clara said loyally.

Tommy grinned.

"I'll never be a professional, but I still enjoy it."

They were distracted by Mrs Monroe marching past at such a brisk pace that her poor dogs were doing their utmost to waddle speedily to keep up.

"Hello again, Mrs Monroe," Clara said casually, not realising the storm she was about to unleash.

"Miss Fitzgerald, you are just the person to deal with my situation," Mrs Monroe said sharply.

Clara was worried.

"Your situation?"

"Ling-Ling was not only denied his final champion ticket, but he did not even place!" Mrs Monroe declared in the sort of voice people usually reserved for telling you they had caught the vicar with his hand in the church donations box. "If you had seen his competition, you would have been outraged as well! Ling-Ling has been robbed! My poor precious deserved so much better. He strutted so beautifully around the ring too. The Peke that won had nothing on my Ling-Ling. It was an ill-bred, shabby sort of thing. I wouldn't dare call it a Peke if I had bred it!"

Mrs Monroe glanced down at her assortment of pedigree mop-heads and sniffed. Clara realised with some horror that her fearsome neighbour was on the brink of tears.

"Now, Mrs Monroe, don't take this all to heart. As terrible as it is, you must remain calm, for the sake of Ling-Ling," Clara said, somewhat desperately.

Mrs Monroe's eyes strayed to the aforementioned dog which gave her a boggle-eyed stare in return.

"You are perfectly correct," Mrs Monroe rallied. "I cannot change a fix, though I feel something ought to be done. It brings the whole hobby into disrepute."

"Perhaps mention it to Mr Jessop," O'Harris suggested, as he had just noticed the show organiser wandering past.

His distraction worked and Mrs Monroe pottered off to let her thoughts on the matter of the competition being rigged be known.

"That was a narrow miss," Tommy chuckled.

It was then a scream ripped through the air and Mrs Trelawney came racing out of the house and nearly fell down the stairs of the terrace. Her cries had ceased all conversation on the lawn and all eyes were directed her way. Her husband hastened towards her and clutched her arm.

"Oh dear, perhaps she has run out of cucumber sandwiches," Tommy said, his opinion on Mrs Trelawney being that she was somewhat flighty, impractical, and prone to dramatic outbursts.

Clara was watching her face and how the colour was draining from her husband's as she spoke. She did not think the conversation was about sandwiches. She suspected something bad had occurred.

The Trelawneys headed back into the hall and for the time being there was no more commotion. Tommy was getting bored again, not helped by Pip becoming restless and attacking his trouser legs. Usually at this time of the day she was curled up in her basket in deep sleep.

"We do not have to stay," Clara remarked to her brother.

"I shan't be deterred yet," Tommy said stoutly. "I have seen the competition and they don't have anything on Pip."

Clara admired his confidence and determination, but she would have quite liked to have gone home. She was tired of the savagery that seemed inherent among the ardent dog showing enthusiasts and the way they looked down on any mutt that was not theirs. She had seen the looks Bramble was getting from the poodle fraternity. There was only one word for them – disparaging.

"The judges are going to lunch," O'Harris noted. "I dare say we have a good hour to waste, and I had the forethought to bring a picnic."

Clara brightened up.

"That is good of you."

"I had a feeling it was going to be a long day," O'Harris said. "And what better way to pass the time then by eating pork pie and cheese seftons?"

They wandered around the house, back to the car, relieved to get away from the crowds. O'Harris was opening the boot of his car to produce the picnic hamper when they heard a scamper of feet across the gravel.

"Miss Fitzgerald, you are not going, are you?"

It was Mrs Trelawney. She had regained a good deal of her composure, but there was no missing the fraught look on her face.

"We were just retrieving our picnic," Clara explained. "Has something happened?"

Mrs Trelawney pulled a face that told them all.

"A dreadful thing has happened. Could you come inside, please?"

She led them into the house. It was the first time any of them had been inside Mulberry Hall and the first thing that struck them was the smell of new wood and paint. A lot of repairs had been undertaken to make the house suitable to live in. Clara could still see the workmen's tools heaped in a corner ready for when they began work again on Monday.

Mrs Trelawney led them deeper into the house, down a dark corridor and paused before a panelled door.

"We have had two bathrooms installed since acquiring the house. My husband's late uncle was somewhat old-fashioned in his plumbing arrangements and it would simply not do. I insisted on having a downstairs bathroom for the sake of my mother, who is unable to manage stairs. It was finished last week, and we have allowed it to be used by the visitors to the house, to save them watering the roses instead. If you understand my meaning?"

Clara did understand. When no toilet was available, the garden fauna tended to become an alternative.

"I suppose from that explanation, that this is the downstairs bathroom?" Clara said, motioning to the door they had stopped by.

Mrs Trelawney nodded miserably.

"That is where a dreadful thing has occurred. We have locked the door to prevent anyone else from entering."

She removed a key from her pocket and inserted it in the door. She seemed to move very slowly as she turned it in the lock and pushed the door open. It swung back to reveal Nigel Love sprawled on the recently laid blue and white floor tiles. He was face down and the back of his head had been caved in by something heavy.

"About half an hour ago he came into the kitchen and asked where the bathroom was. I gave him directions and I saw him heading down this corridor. When several minutes elapsed and he did not reappear, I went to see if perhaps he had become lost. I noticed the bathroom door was open and when I walked past, I saw him," Mrs Trelawney sighed to herself. "I rather lost my head and ran outdoors and screamed. But you saw that."

"Have the police been informed?" Clara asked.

"Oh no, not yet," Mrs Trelawney looked shocked by the suggestion. "We don't want to disrupt the dog show and alarm everyone. My husband and I rather hoped you could look into this discreetly for us. You see, the killer must surely still be here?"

"How do you come to that conclusion?" O'Harris asked.

"Well, I saw no one around other than the dog show participants," Mrs Trelawney said. "And Mr Love was not local to the area, so who would wish to harm him other than his fellow competitors?"

"There could be another explanation," Clara said. "Perhaps a burglar was prowling around the house while everyone was distracted by the dog show and Mr Love stumbled upon him."

"I doubt that," Mrs Trelawney said firmly. "I have locked the front door. The only way to enter the house is through the back doors leading to the terrace. A burglar would have been noticed."

Clara was not as convinced about that. She stared at the unfortunate Mr Love.

"Where is Brutus?" she said suddenly.

Mrs Trelawney placed a hand over her mouth.

"He had the dog with him," she said. "I wanted to protest. I was concerned the dog might cock its leg against the wood panelling, but Mr Love rather blasted past me before I could say anything."

She didn't add that she had been too anxious around

him to speak her mind.

"The killer must have taken Brutus. Curious," Tommy said thoughtfully.

"Please, Miss Fitzgerald, look into this affair for us. As soon as the show ends, we shall summon the police, I swear, but if we had to stop now it would be terrible. No one would ever come again, and my husband has put such a lot of work into making this a good day."

Clara did not like keeping secrets from Inspector Park-Coombs. She also understood Mrs Trelawney's distress. If the police arrived and started questioning everyone about a murder, the gossip would run through the town and the dog show would be spoken of in hushed tones forever more. Mr Trelawney would struggle to host another event of any description in his grounds, let alone another dog show and that could impact his plans to save the hall.

Reluctantly, for Clara appreciated police procedure, she agreed to the arrangement.

"You must keep the bathroom locked at all times," she told Mrs Trelawney.

The woman bobbed her head up and down in agreement. Clara took a step into the bathroom to take a closer look at Mr Love. A good-sized room had been converted into the downstairs bathroom, and it was one of the most spacious rooms of its type Clara had ever been in. The floor had been freshly tiled, a solid enamel bath with brass fittings installed, and a very modern looking toilet and sink fitted in the corner. Mr Love had rather made a mess of the floor when he fell. The one saving grace was the killer had not attacked him while he was in the process of using the facilities and thus, he was fully dressed.

Clara crouched by the body and felt for a pulse for thoroughness' sake. There was not a flicker, as she had anticipated. The wound looked deep and circular. A hefty blow had been levelled at Love's skull, crushing bone, and killing him swiftly. He had fallen forward, and blood had pooled down his neck and onto the floor. In one of those strange asides Clara sometimes had when she was contemplating a murder scene, she reflected that it was going to take a lot of effort to remove all the blood from the tiles completely. It had run down the spaces between the tiles and stained the grouting. The chances were it would never be removed completely.

There was no sign that Love had tried to ward off the killer. Clara guessed he had been taken by surprise and never knew what hit him.

"There is no murder weapon," Clara observed for the benefit of O'Harris and Tommy. "Unless it is underneath him."

O'Harris came into the room and helped to lift Mr Love to look beneath him, but there was nothing there. The murder weapon had gone with the killer.

Clara retreated from the room and motioned that Mrs Trelawney should lock it up.

"Who else was in the house at the time Mr Love went to the bathroom?" she asked.

"I don't recall anyone in particular," Mrs Trelawney said. "I was in the kitchen, getting more scones from the pantry. No one entered the house after Mr Love, that I remember distinctly because I was stood by the sink drinking a glass of water and I can see the back door from there."

"And you saw no one leaving before you found Mr Love?"

Mrs Trelawney shook her head.

"Who used the bathroom before Mr Love?" Clara persisted.

Mrs Trelawney frowned.

"I don't quite remember. Everything seems a little blurred. I do recall a gentleman with whippets popping into the house at some point to use the bathroom, but I am not sure when that was. It could have been first thing. In any case, he seemed very nice and not the sort to harm someone."

Mrs Trelawney said this in a hopeful way, as if she were trying to reassure herself that such a man could not have hurt Mr Love.

"Did you see him leave the house again?" Clara asked.

Mrs Trelawney hesitated, the realisation dawning that she had not seen him leave.

"No," she admitted. "I was very busy on the terrace. But I am sure he must have left."

"Then it is possible he stayed inside, or that someone else slipped in when your attention was occupied?" Clara said with care, not wanting to make the woman feel bad, after all, she had not expected a crime to be committed.

"Well, I suppose…" Mrs Trelawney looked bleak. "But I can honestly say that no one came out before I went looking for Mr Love."

"Could you point out the man with the whippets to me?" Clara asked, thinking it was a particularly flimsy lead and one she would only pursue if she became desperate.

Mrs Trelawney escorted them back to the kitchen, which was long and wide with several windows facing onto the back lawn. Mrs Trelawney looked out the nearest window to the many guests outside. After surveying them for a minute or so, her attention fell on an older gentleman walking four lithe dogs through the crowd.

"That is him," she said, pointing and then remembering herself and dropping her arm. "I was asking him about perhaps having a puppy. I rather fancy a dog in the house, what with all this space to walk it. He was very kind and told me all about the breed."

Mrs Trelawney fell silent a moment.

"I really hope it was not him who killed Mr Love. He seemed so nice."

What she did not add, but which they were all thinking was that Mr Love was not a nice person and it was difficult to feel sorry for him. He had been obnoxious and belligerent, but that was not a reason to kill someone.

"I shall do my best," Clara promised Mrs Trelawney.

"Thank you, Miss Fitzgerald. I cannot believe this has happened. We cannot afford such bad luck."

Clara had nothing to say to that, what could she say?

Chapter Five

"Where do we begin?" Tommy asked Clara.

They were all stood outside the bathroom, the door now securely locked. Anyone coming in to use the facilities would be directed upstairs instead.

"Well, for a start I would like to find the murder weapon," Clara said. "My instinct is that someone who was attending this dog show murdered Mr Love. I am not ruling out other possibilities, but our attention ought to be focused on those here who knew the gentleman and might have a grudge towards him."

"The champions circle," O'Harris said.

"The what?" Tommy glanced his way.

"When we were walking on the pier earlier, we saw Oliver Bankes taking a picture of a group of five people with dogs. We were told they were the crème de la crème of the dog world. Among them was Nigel Love," O'Harris explained.

"And none of them looked as if they cared for each other," Clara added. "I suggest we split up. O'Harris and I shall search the house for the murder weapon and any potential clues. Tommy, I suggest you go back to the dog show and scope out Love's rivals."

"Espionage," Tommy said with satisfaction.

"You shall be the spy in their midst," O'Harris chuckled.

"Much more interesting than this current affair of hanging around waiting for someone to tell you if your dog is ugly or not," Tommy agreed with a grin. "I shall see what I can find out."

He sauntered off, Pip in tow.

"Where shall we begin?" O'Harris asked Clara.

"That blow to his head looked like it was the work of something very heavy and solid. I was thinking a hammer."

"And there are a lot of workmen's tools about this place due to the renovations."

"I very much doubt the killer had time to thoroughly clean the weapon before Mrs Trelawney came to investigate. They have either taken it with them or disposed of it nearby," Clara said. "We may get lucky and find it."

They headed back to the main hall where they had seen the workmen's tools carefully stacked aside.

"What I keep thinking is that the killer must have been splattered with blood," O'Harris said. "But no one has noted a bloody individual walking around."

"Perhaps they were wearing dark clothing which masks the stains," Clara suggested. "They could wash their hands and face. It looked to me like a single blow to the head. There was perhaps not too much splatter."

"What a grisly discussion," Mr Trelawny had appeared from another room. He was nursing a cup of tea and looked very pale. "I thought it best my wife fetched you when she told me about the body. I have heard good things concerning your abilities Miss Fitzgerald."

"That is reassuring," Clara said. "How are you faring?"

Trelawney gave a weak laugh.

"I feel like I am going a little mad. A dead body in my downstairs bathroom!"

He swayed suddenly on his feet and O'Harris dived forward and caught his arm before he collapsed backwards.

"I think you best sit down," O'Harris said. "You are in

shock."

They helped Trelawney back into the room he had just come from, which proved to be a partly furnished sitting room. The furniture was very modern and rather stark to Clara's mind. They settled the poor man onto a very square sofa.

"Thank you," he whispered weakly. "I have been overdoing things lately and this incident has knocked me for six. I so desperately want to save this house, but there is so much to do. Every day a new problem seems to surface, and it is always expensive. I have been planning so many fundraising events to try to mitigate some of the costs. This was to be the first of a season of special events."

Trelawney pressed a hand to his forehead and gave a slight sniff that sounded perilously close to a sob.

"I fear this incident will ruin everything. People will avoid my home, fearing there is a killer loose. I shall not be able to hold events, for no one shall come and I shall have to give up this house," there was a definite wail to his words now.

"Let us not jump to conclusions," Clara said gently. "As someone involved with the Brighton Pavilion, I can tell you that the odd murder has never affected our visitor numbers. Quite the contrary."

Trelawney was not sure whether to laugh or be shocked at her matter-of-fact tone. That had been Clara's intention. He was now suitably distracted from his festering worries.

"Mr Trelawney, I shall discreetly look into this matter, but I feel it only proper we call in Inspector Park-Coombs," she continued.

"Oh, no!" Trelawney groaned.

"Hear me out," Clara said. "I shall speak to the Inspector and ask him to come alone and in civilian clothes so no one shall suspect he is here on business. It will be better that way, for I fear we could lose the murderer at the first hint of the police arriving. For the time being, I am hoping they are hanging around."

"No one will believe the police inspector just turned up

by chance," Trelawney said miserably.

"I have an idea for that too," Clara said. "Please, I think we must do this."

Trelawney cradled his head in his hand a moment longer, then gave a weary nod.

"I suppose we must," a thought then struck him. "Did you say you think the killer is still here?"

"If they are one of the other contestants, it seems logical," Clara explained. "I think we need to act swiftly to resolve this matter before the dog show is over. Otherwise, I am concerned the killer will simply depart on the next train and we shall never know who killed Mr Love."

Trelawney's mouth fell open at this news. Words failed him, but he managed a sort of choked grunt which Clara took as agreement to her suggestion they call the inspector.

"Do you have a telephone?"

"It was connected last week," Trelawney explained. "Let me show you."

He took two attempts to thrust himself out of the chair and looked very shaky on his legs still.

"When is the last time you had something to eat?" Clara asked, thinking if they were not careful, they would need an ambulance as well as the inspector.

"I suppose…" Trelawney frowned. "I had a light supper last night."

"You are tired and in shock," Clara tutted at him. "You need some rest and some good food inside you. If only Annie was here, I am sure she would have you fighting fit in moments. She does a special omelette she claims is a cure-all."

Trelawney did not know what to say, he just stood and swayed.

"Show me the telephone and then we must get some food and hot tea inside you," Clara added.

Trelawney managed to wobble his way out of the sitting room and showed Clara to a rather smart telephone booth installed beneath the staircase. Clara had read about such arrangements in fancy country houses. The booth not only masked the telephone, for some people found it a rather disagreeable intrusion to their decor but provided privacy to those using it. There had been a lot of concern about people being overheard on the telephone. Somehow the thing seemed less secure than say a face-to-face conversation. Smart, household telephone booths were the solution.

Trelawney opened the door and started to needlessly explain how to operate the telephone.

"Clara is perfectly able to use a telephone," O'Harris told him gently. "Let's get some cucumber sandwiches into you, old man."

He hustled away the poor gentleman, who seemed barely able to comprehend what was going on. Clara had thought Mrs Trelawney had seemed a little flaky, but next to her husband she looked quite competent.

"Oh dear," Clara sighed as she rang the police station and asked to speak to Inspector Park-Coombs.

"Clara," the inspector answered. "I hope all is well?"

"I am perfectly fine," Clara assured him. "Unfortunately, there has been a spot of bother at Mulberry Hall."

"That old ruin?" Park-Coombs snorted. "Don't tell me the roof has caved in and crushed someone?"

"You are ill informed, Inspector. The house has been substantially renovated by Mr Trelawney and today they are hosting a pedigree dog show."

"And there is some bother with the dogs? Neighbours annoyed about the noise?"

"Inspector, would I ring you for something so mundane?" Clara said, becoming frustrated by his interruptions. If he let her speak freely, he would soon know what the cause of her concern was. "There has been a murder, Inspector. One of the contestants has been clobbered over the head in the bathroom."

"Poor dog. Who would do that to a dumb animal?" Park-Coombs puttered. "It makes a man despair of humanity."

"It is not a dog that is dead, Inspector," Clara continued patiently. "It is the person handling the dog. Mr Nigel Love to be precise. He came into the house to use the bathroom and was found a short time later dead. I am of the opinion he was murdered by one of his fellow contestants."

"I shall come around with my lads at once," Park-Coombs said and was perilously close to hanging up the telephone receiver.

"Wait!" Clara said urgently. "For the time being the murderer is unaware that Mr Love's body has been found. We are not making a hue and cry and I think that best. At this moment all our potential suspects are gathered on the lawn. If the police appear then our killer is liable to slip away and with the number of people here, I think it very likely they will succeed. I was hoping you would be amenable to going about this discreetly."

"What are you suggesting?" Park-Coombs asked suspiciously.

"I think you should come under the guise of being off-duty. We shall make careful enquiries and with luck we shall bag the killer before the dog show is finished. I think we need to be subtle about this, Inspector."

Park-Coombs listened intently but was not certain he liked what he was hearing.

"You mean, pretend I am just a civilian for the day?"

"Yes, Inspector."

"It doesn't sound very... professional."

"Inspector, the second our killer spies a police uniform they will disappear. It is not very professional to jeopardise a case like that, is it?"

"But won't people be suspicious if the police inspector just happens to turn up?" Park-Coombs said. "You would have to be a very stupid murderer not to consider that suspect."

"That is why, Inspector, you shall come along with a

dog."

There was a pause on the line.

"Sorry?" Inspector Park-Coombs said.

"You shall bring along a dog. It ought to be a pedigree of some description. Just bear with me a moment," Clara put down the receiver and fumbled in her handbag, finally producing a piece of paper that was a programme of events at the show, detailing when each class was to be judged. "Ah, yes. The sighthound class is to be held towards three o'clock. Therefore, if you equip yourself with such a dog it shall seem perfectly natural for you to be attending. I shall make sure your entries are ready and you must dress in civilian clothes."

"Clara, are you quite mad?"

"Inspector, this is subterfuge at its finest," Clara reassured him.

"I am not convinced about this," Park-Coombs said.

In her mind's eye, Clara could see him twitching his moustache.

"Inspector, you have to trust me, and you really need to hurry. Once this show ends our prime suspects will be on the next train home and tracking them down again will be extremely difficult. I believe one of Mr Love's rivals murdered him. Quite what sparked the sudden attack I am not sure, but you will see the results for yourself when you arrive. But we must be subtle and not alert our killer that we are on to them."

"How is it you are there?" Park-Coombs said suspiciously. He knew as well as she did that quite often people summoned Clara first before the police. Sometimes they tried to avoid summoning the police at all.

"Tommy has entered Pip in the gundog class," she explained. "I happen to be here by chance."

"You always are," Park-Coombs muttered. "Fine, I shall do things your way, though I am not sure about the matter at all."

"It will be wisest," Clara said, though in the back of her mind she was thinking that if the killer did prove to be some random burglar Love had stumbled upon, then all this charade was pointless. She opted to ignore that nagging doubt. "Now, find yourself a dog."

"A sighthound?" Park-Coombs queried.

"Yes," Clara paused. "You do know what a sighthound is, Inspector?"

There was a hush on the line, as if the inspector were mulling over his options for responding.

"It's a type of dog," he said at last.

"Sighthounds are the sort that chase game," Clara elaborated. "Think whippets and greyhounds."

"Oh, like a poacher would have?" Park-Coombs agreed, finally understanding. "My neighbour has a nice lurcher, his name is Digger."

"Lurchers are not a pedigree breed Inspector, you cannot bring one of those," Clara was starting to see a flaw in her plan. "Please ensure whatever dog you bring has papers."

"This is a lot of trouble for investigating a murder," Park-Coombs grumbled, not pleased he had proven himself lacking in knowledge.

"It shall be worth it," Clara promised him.

"Very well," Park-Coombs sighed. "I shall get on with it. See you shortly."

"Thank you, Inspector," Clara said.

The telephone line went dead, and she headed to the kitchen to see how Mr Trelawney was doing. A cup of tea and several sandwiches, along with a thick slice of cake had restored some colour to his face. He looked at Clara with vague hopefulness.

"Well?"

"It is all arranged," Clara promised him. "The inspector is going to turn up with a dog, just like a regular contestant at the show. He shall need some entries to complete the disguise."

"I can sort that," Mr Trelawney said. "This is most appreciated Miss Fitzgerald."

Clara was not listening. She had glanced out of the

window and was looking at the crowd of people on the lawn, flanked by various dogs. Among them she spied an overgroomed poodle and was reminded of the 'champions' circle' as O'Harris had referred to it. She had also noticed Arnold Jessop wandering about. It seemed to her if anyone were to know about rivalries between the show contestants, it would be Jessop. He seemed to know who nearly everyone was, he certainly knew the main contenders very well.

"I must depart for a while, Mr Trelawney," Clara said, forgetting all about her intention to search for the murder weapon. "I need to talk to a man about a dog."

Chapter Six

Arnold Jessop had found himself in the heady world of dog showing quite by accident. He had started out as a paper bag salesman. It was surprising how many people needed paper bags and of all sorts and sizes. It was far more complicated a business than people appreciated, or so Arnold told anyone who had the misfortune to get him onto the subject. He was underappreciated in the paper bag business, no one took him seriously. No one understood the intricacies of finding the right quality, shape, and size for a customer's needs.

Arnold had ended up quite despondent when one day he was sent to deliver some extra paper bags to an event being held at Alexandria Palace. He would not normally do such a menial task, he was a salesman, after all, but there was no one else available and the customer was very important, or so he was informed. Hence, he headed off with a box of paper bags (assorted sizes) and it proved the most momentous occasion of his life.

He found himself arriving at a prestigious dog show. You could tell it was prestigious because most people were not talking to one another and had sour looks painting their faces. He walked among the pampered pooches, gazing at various coat clips and grooming styles, and realised he had stumbled into a world far outside his own personal experience.

He found the show organiser – a man of considerable age who looked on the precipice of a sizeable heart attack – and offered him the box of paper bags. You might have supposed he was presenting a gift to the gods of some ancient religion. The man near enough went down on his knees as he saw the extra bags.

"Thank goodness! I feared there would be a riot soon enough!"

"People like their paper bags here?" Arnold asked, conversationally. No one had, in his experience, ever rioted over a shortage of paper bags.

"It is all to do with excrement," the older man explained, waving his hands about. "Dogs produce a lot of it, all over the floor and people are expected to pick up after themselves. But they insist we must provide suitable waste receptacles," he indicated the paper bags, "and we were on the cusp of running out. I don't know what they feed them to result in such an amount of waste!"

The poor man started to breathe hard, and that heart attack really looked to be brewing. Since there was no one assisting the fellow and Arnold had nothing better to do, he offered to give him a hand. The show organiser accepted gladly, and Arnold felt quite sure he had saved his life that day. The decision had certainly transformed his.

All day and late into the evening he followed the old man about, listening to the woes of organising dog shows and learning about the various breeds on display. Despite the old man's complaints, Arnold sensed he really rather enjoyed his occupation which was why he had not done the sensible thing and retired. By the time Arnold was heading home, he had already agreed to return the next day and help some more. By the end of the weekend, as the show was being wrapped up, Arnold found himself being offered a job as the show organiser's assistant, and so it began.

He had never looked back. Oh, there had been difficult

years during the war, but he had always known the shows would begin again and he had not done so badly scouting out dogs for the army. He had found his niche, the place where he was content, and he had no intention of changing his life's work.

His old mentor had passed away last Christmas. It had been sad, as he had been anticipating the show at Mulberry Hall, thinking how once more there would be dogs strutting their stuff. On his death bed, he had wished Arnold well and bequeathed him his full collection of dog breed books, show catalogues and stud directories.

Arnold was in a nostalgic mood as he watched the show taking place, wandering around and checking all was well and people were happy – well, certain people. He wasn't fussed if the locals were enjoying themselves, that was not the point, as long as the top people were having a good day he was satisfied. He kept thinking about his old mentor, and a wealth of emotion would well up in him. Sometimes he would have to surreptitiously wipe a tear from his eye. He would have been proud, so proud.

Clara caught up with Arnold on the terrace steps. He was just about to have his first cup of tea of the day. He had been so busy earlier it had not been possible to stop and have a drink. He was thirsty and hungry, but he had opted only for tea. He rarely ate while overseeing a show, there was not the time and people seemed to think it unbecoming to see the man in charge covered in cake crumbs. It was perfectly fine to see him slurping tea, but to witness him making the time to eat was unthinkable.

"Mr Jessop?" Clara said as she approached.

Arnold glanced up. He had been intently watching a parade of corgis, all seemingly perfect specimens of their breed, as they were walked around the marquee.

"Oh, hello," Arnold said, barely taking his eyes off the dogs.

"We met on the pier," Clara reminded him. "When five of your top show people were being photographed with their dogs."

Arnold's eyes glazed over for a moment in memory, then he smiled at Clara.

"Oh yes."

"Could I have a quiet word?" Clara asked.

"I am somewhat busy," Arnold said. "If it is about the entry process, I am afraid you must take that up with someone else."

"It is rather more serious than that," Clara explained. "I really need to talk with you."

Arnold was reluctant to take his gaze off the corgis for more than a moment. You never knew what might happen the second your attention was distracted.

"It concerns Nigel Love," Clara added. "And it is quite serious."

Arnold was beginning to pay attention; the mention of Nigel's name had that effect on him. Of all the individuals Arnold mingled with in the dog show circles, Nigel was one you could never miss, yet who you desperately hoped to avoid. He brought some good sponsorship to the shows through his connection to Master's dog food, but he expected a great deal in return.

"I can give you five minutes," Arnold decided.

He walked with Clara to the edge of the lawn where an ancient beech tree provided a shady spot out of the sun.

"What is Nigel complaining about now?" Arnold asked.

"He has had an accident," Clara said carefully. "He shall not be able to participate in the rest of the show."

"Brutus bite him again?" Arnold snorted, then he seemed to register Clara's serious tone. "What sort of accident?"

"The fatal sort," Clara elaborated.

The colour drained from Arnold's face. Clara had opted to confide in him as she was going to need someone to assist her in finding the people most likely to have a grudge against Nigel. She was also confident that Arnold would want this handled discreetly and would be reliable about keeping quiet.

"You need to explain further," he said.

"Nigel Love was attacked while using the bathroom. He was hit on the head and the blow killed him. Also, Brutus is missing."

Arnold sucked air through his teeth. Just when you thought you had this whole malarky figured out and nothing could upset you something new came along.

"When did this happen?" he asked.

"A short while ago. The Trelawneys are aware and wish for me to handle this discreetly. I should add that I am a private detective."

"Well," Arnold said, trying to formulate a reply that suited the occasion and failing. "Well."

"I have informed the police inspector and he is going to come along in civilian garb and pretend he is just here for the show while we try to work out who did this."

Understanding dawned on Arnold.

"You think this was the work of one of the other contestants?"

"I think that a very strong possibility. Arnold was not known in the area, so we have to suppose it was someone here at the show who took a chance and dispatched him."

Arnold fell silent.

"You do not seem surprised," Clara said.

"I knew Nigel," Arnold sighed. "It does not surprise me someone had a grudge against him. It does shock me that they went so far as to murder him. And why steal Brutus?"

Arnold found that the most preposterous thing out of the whole affair. Brutus was an unpleasant sort of dog, the kind that would lick your hand one minute and bite off a finger the next. Aside from Nigel, he could not think of anyone who would care for the beast.

"I need to make quiet enquiries to try to find the culprit. I cannot afford to let this show come to a conclusion without a fair idea of who is responsible. I need your help."

Arnold had been lost in thought, then his mind flicked back to what she was saying.

"Help?"

"You know the people who were unhappy with Nigel.

You can point me in the right direction."

Arnold made that sucking noise again.

"That isn't a short list," he said.

"Nigel upset a lot of people?"

"He certainly did. You couldn't find a more disagreeable person. He seemed to prefer to make enemies rather than friends."

"I had an encounter with him earlier," Clara nodded. "He struck me as a bully."

"He was certainly that. Trouble was, he bred good bulldogs and has been very successful with them. It reached a stage where he expected to win and when he did not, he was unbearable. Another person we might have banned from shows, but Nigel had connections."

"Master's dog food?"

"And others. If he was attending a show you knew you would instantly have extra revenue as his sponsors would appear as well. Brutus becoming the face of Master's Dog Biscuits has brought the showing world a lot of attention and we desperately needed it after the hiatus the war forced on us."

"Master's are not here, though?" Clara pointed out.

"I did think that surprising," Arnold replied. "I fully expected them to attend. They usually sell a lot of dog biscuits at these things, but as you can see, they are not here. Nigel has not said a word about it."

"He shall not be saying a word now," Clara remarked.

Arnold paused.

"I am starting to wonder if there has been a falling out between him and Master's."

"Tell me more about the people who had a prime reason to dislike him," Clara asked.

Arnold glanced around the show, a little unsure where to start. His eyes fell on the judge assessing the corgis.

"That is Dominic Wood," he said. "A very good judge. Fair and honest. He fell out with Nigel a few weeks ago when he was judging a best in show class and failed to pick Brutus."

"When you say fell out?"

"Nigel threatened to knock his block off and called him blind and incompetent. I had to intervene," Arnold sighed. "I wanted to ban him. I should have banned him. Damn my material concerns."

Arnold was quite ashamed of himself. Clara did not know what she could say to help.

"There are others Nigel has upset?" she asked instead.

"Yes, ah, let me see," Arnold pointed to a young woman with a bulldog on a chain lead. "Melissa Painter. She and Nigel have had a long-standing rivalry due to showing the same breed. I think there might have been something more to it, as well, but I never got to the bottom of it.

"Over there is Nancy Kirkpatrick, she breeds pointers. She had a set-to with Nigel because Brutus attacked and badly mauled her champion stud. She has never forgiven him.

"Alan Kennedy is the man walking a pack of pugs. He and Nigel fell out when his black pug beat Brutus to win in a handsomest hound competition in one of the daily newspapers. I hear tell he wrote some rather nasty letters to him.

"Ah, and there is William Ryder whose Labrador, Skipper, was rumoured to have been the next face of Master's, but something occurred, and Brutus succeeded him. There has been gossip about something nasty happening in the background, but William has been very closed about it all."

"That is quite a list," Clara said, suddenly feeling her work was going to be more complicated than she had expected.

"Nigel was that sort of person," Arnold sighed. "But I cannot imagine any of those I just mentioned actually killing him."

"They may have lashed out impulsively," Clara said. "The result being his smashed skull."

"Then it was probably unintentional?" Arnold felt better hearing this. "This is very worrying though. It could bring the dog showing world into disrepute."

"Which is why I intend to investigate in a subtle fashion," Clara reassured him. "This will not be a heavy-handed affair. Quite on the contrary, we shall take our time."

"I wish I knew where Brutus was," Arnold said, glancing over his shoulder as if he expected the dog to suddenly appear.

"It is worrying that he has been snatched. Anything could have happened to him," Clara replied.

"I am more concerned what could occur if he gets loose," Arnold said. "Brutus is not a dog you want without a lead around his neck. I cannot imagine why anyone would want to take him. Certainly not out of affection."

"That is something I hope to discover," Clara answered him. "Finding Brutus ought to lead us to his killer."

"Or so you would hope," Arnold added, once more glancing behind him. He could almost hear the bulldog's deep, sinister growl. "Look, I shall do whatever you need me to."

"Thank you," Clara said. "For the time being, just keep your eyes open and if anything odd occurs, let me know."

"Nothing else is going to happen, is it?" Arnold said uneasily.

"You can never tell," Clara replied. "But I like to hope this is just about Mr Love and no one else shall be at risk."

Arnold grimaced.

"I do hope you are right," it was then that his attention was distracted by Dominic Wood finally picking a corgi from the line-up before him. "I have to go. I like to make sure the rosettes and trophies are correctly handed out!"

Arnold hurried away. Clara scanned her eyes over the people Arnold had pointed out to her, wondering where to begin her enquiries. As it happened, Melissa Painter had walked away from the main crowd to exercise one of her dogs. There seemed no better place to start than with Nigel's biggest rival.

Chapter Seven

While Clara was interviewing suspects, O'Harris had resumed the search of Mulberry Hall for a potential murder weapon. He found himself accompanied by Mr Trelawney, who had been revived by the sweet tea and sandwiches he had consumed. He was also feeling expansive about his home renovations.

"The staircase was alarming. Not a single piece of the bannister was sound. The moment you put your hand on it, it swayed awfully and more than one of the steps was rotten. The builder was amazed no one had put a foot through one or fallen down the whole set."

Mr Trelawney waved a hand at the rising staircase, the sort of grand affair all such houses were meant to have.

"I had it replaced with oak as much as possible, to compliment the style of the house. Though some of the steps we agreed to replace with pine. It is cheaper and once covered by a carpet no one shall know."

O'Harris, who had had his own issues with the old staircase at his hall, nodded sympathetically. Mr Trelawney seemed to have forgotten about the dead man in his bathroom, or at least he was doing a good job of not remembering him.

"The hall tiles were largely intact and just needed a good clean and polish. We had some issues with that odd little window over the porch," Trelawney indicated a narrow turret that stuck out from the wall above the door; it served, as far as O'Harris could tell, no useful purpose other than to provide housemaids with work. It was three-sided, with slim lead pane windows inset in each face. "Apparently they were all the rage about a century ago. Utterly pointless, of course, and we discovered whoever had installed it had not been fussed about its quality. The panes all leaked and beneath the external plaster, the bricks of the turret were fast coming away from the wall. Give it another few years, or a good storm, and it probably would have fallen off."

O'Harris was trying to politely listen while he went about the task of locating a potential murder weapon. He had paused by a stack of workman's tools. There was a wooden toolbox containing carpentry items. He lifted out a saw and then a small hammer. He studied the hammer carefully, but it did not look to have been involved in a murder.

"It's the done thing now to rig up the old chandeliers with electricity," Trelawney was saying behind him, staring upwards at the antique crystal chandelier above them. "But we rather felt that spoiled the feel of the thing. It is going to be a nuisance lighting it in the winter, probably we shall only do it on special occasions, but I do feel it will be much nicer."

The toolbox had been a dead end. O'Harris moved some tins of paint and wood varnish, and a cloth that was half covering a ladder, but he could not see anything useful.

"Are there tools anywhere else?" he asked Trelawney.

The man's attention drifted back to him from staring at the ceiling.

"Sorry?"

"Have the workmen left tools anywhere else?"

Trelawney glanced at the boxes.

"There are quite a few in the dining room. It is where they are working at the moment. Terrible damp around the skirting boards, they have had to strip the walls right back to the plaster," Trelawney paused. "Ahem, why are we examining the tools, again?"

O'Harris could have sworn he had already mentioned the point of his search, but it was possible he had forgotten or assumed Trelawney was aware of what they were up to. The man had just started to follow him, rather like one of those cats that suddenly take an inkling to pursue a person everywhere. In a way, O'Harris had been trying to shake him off without realising it, keeping up only a light pretence of interest in the man's conversation in the hopes he would wander off.

"I am looking for the object that was used to crush Nigel Love's skull," O'Harris said.

It was a rather blunt statement, and he felt a bit mean about it afterwards. Trelawney's face had taken on that grey hue again, the one that made him look like he was made of stone.

"Oh," Trelawney gulped slowly. "Why among the workmen's tools? They were not here?"

"Clara thinks it was a hammer or something similar that made the injury. It had to be heavy and with a relatively small end. One blow was sufficient to kill Love."

"Oh," Trelawney repeated, he had lost his enthusiasm. He stared about at his renovated staircase and the pointless porch turret with a strange expression of sadness on his face. The place he had been so devoted to had suddenly become tainted for him. How was he ever to live in this house with the knowledge a murder took place right under his nose? In his downstairs bathroom of all things!

O'Harris regretted his bluntness even more as he watched the man's face fall. He decided he had to make amends.

"I have had to do a lot of restoration work on my house too. It is probably about the same age as this place."

O'Harris gave him a smile, hoping it was enough to

bring Trelawny back around.

"Did you have damp in the skirting boards?" Trelawney asked quietly.

"Did I!" O'Harris answered him. "Thought we were going to lose the whole second floor to damp!"

Trelawney's colour returned and he made a good effort of putting murdered dog handlers out of his mind for the time being.

"The dining room is this way."

They headed through a room – this wing of the house being constructed in the old-fashioned style with no hallways – and went through a set of double doors without handles.

"These were like this when I moved in," Trelawney pointed out the missing door furniture. "I have never been able to determine whether my uncle sold them or if they were stolen. The house was not exactly difficult to get into back then."

"You have improved the security since?" O'Harris asked. He knew Clara had asked the same of Mrs Trelawney, but he was still curious to hear her husband's thoughts on the matter. If there was a possibility someone had entered the house through a window or unlocked door, then that raised the ugly spectre of an outsider being behind the murder. Clara's suggestion of a burglar being interrupted by Love could once more be on the cards.

"It was my first priority," Trelawney explained, pushing open the doors. "What is the point of fitting this place out with lovely things if they could simply be stolen in the night? I have had the doors and windows replaced where necessary and the local locksmith came and made sure they could all be secured. I dare say this house is one of the most secure in the district."

That put the blame for the murder back onto a fellow contestant, O'Harris concluded.

They entered the dining room which could not be described as anything other than a mess. The walls had been stripped of the paper that had once graced them. The skirting board had been ripped out and was stacked against a wall. The fireplace was swathed in a sheet and large tin cans sat on the covered mantel. The floorboards were covered in dust and scraps of paper and there was an overwhelming smell of disturbed damp.

"We have been trying to dry out the place for weeks now," Trelawney sighed. "Now the room is fully sealed and watertight, the damp should not progress. They are sealing the walls with this gluey substance to be sure."

He indicated a tin on the mantelpiece. O'Harris was more curious about the dust on the floor. It was thick enough that when he and Trelawney walked across it, they left footprints. But it was the third set of prints that intrigued him. They had smudged them when they came in and it was difficult to be sure of the size, but someone else had recently walked into this room.

O'Harris followed the prints with his eyes, noting that away from the door where they had not been over-trampled by himself and Trelawney, they became clearer, and he would have sworn they were made by a woman's shoe. One of the low-heeled sort he had seen a number of the practical lady dog handlers around the venue wearing. He had also noticed Mrs Trelawney wearing something similar, but she could hardly be under suspicion, could she?

"See those footprints?" he asked Trelawney.

"Yes, sorry about that. It is the plaster dust. My wife is dreadfully concerned that she will be sweeping it up for years and years, though my builder has assured me that shall not be the case."

"That was not my point," O'Harris grinned at him. "I was thinking that someone has walked into this room recently."

He headed to the spot the footprints ended and found himself looking at another of the wooden toolboxes he had seen dotted about.

"Is... is the murder weapon there?" Trelawney asked, finally catching up with what O'Harris was trying to imply.

O'Harris carefully emptied the toolbox, using a

handkerchief to slip out the tools. The murder weapon could have fingerprints on it, after all. He found a chisel, but decided the sharp point was the wrong shape. He removed rulers, a set square, pencils and pieces of chalk, pliers, pincers, various jars of nails and screws, but what drew his attention the most was the lack of a hammer. Surely if a man had nails he needed a hammer to bang them in? He found a set of screwdrivers which accompanied the screws and even a hand drill, but there was no sign of a hammer.

O'Harris took a moment to consider this. Was he jumping to conclusions? No, it seemed odd that a workman who carried all these things and a jar of nails would not have a hammer. Surely the humble hammer was one of the most fundamental items to have in a toolkit? He looked around just to be sure it had not been missed from the box, perhaps laid behind it, or beside it, but there was definitely no hammer and the footprints told their own story. They came here, to this box and then they went away again.

"I think someone has taken a hammer from this toolbox," O'Harris told Trelawney.

The man was fumbling with his fingers, his anxiety returned.

"Are you sure?"

"No," O'Harris admitted. "But I think there ought to be a hammer here and the footprints are another clue."

Trelawney looked at the footprints in the plaster dust and asked the most obvious of questions.

"Then where is it?"

O'Harris endeavoured not to sigh. Trelawney seemed to genuinely expect an answer.

"Well, probably our killer did not have time to bring the weapon back here. Think of the distance between this room and the bathroom. They were in a rush, not sure how soon the alarm might be raised. They either hid the hammer upon them and walked back outside, or they got rid of it somewhere closer to the bathroom."

O'Harris thought about this carefully.

"Let's retrace the killer's steps."

"Does that mean going back to the bathroom?"

"It does."

"Oh."

They returned to the downstairs bathroom and Trelawney unlocked the door. He grimaced at the sight of the body on the floor. Nigel Love had not been an attractive sight in life, death was doing nothing for him. The blood about his head was congealing and turning into a sticky stain on the tiles. His splayed body across the floor made it difficult to step inside, but O'Harris wanted to check something. It had occurred to him that when you dispatched someone your first thought was unlikely to be a rational one. You would act in shock and panic. What would be the first thing you would consider? Hiding the crime for as long as possible, of course.

Moving Love had been out of the question, so the murderer had to opt for the next best thing, getting rid of the murder weapon. If they did not clean it and return it to the toolbox – which would be a very calculated thing to do, but also would have taken time the killer was not sure they had, then they had to have either hidden it or cast it away in the hope no one would find it anytime soon. O'Harris was pretty confident the killer would not have left it in the bathroom where it would be found easily, but you could never be sure. He searched the cupboards in the bathroom and under the sink. Since the place was not yet in full use, it was an easy task, with most of the cupboards bare.

Trelawney watched him uneasily.

"Anything?"

"No," O'Harris said. "And I did not really expect there to be."

He then turned his attention to the bathroom window. It was a relatively large window and Trelawney had had rippled glass installed in it to give privacy. O'Harris also noted that it was slightly open, presumably to keep the room smelling fresh considering the amount of use it might get through the day.

O'Harris had to step over the body of Nigel Love to reach the window and he found himself imagining the killer doing the same. He took the latch of the window and pushed it wide open. Outside he saw the edge of the kitchen wall running at ninety degrees to the window and blocking the view of the terrace and lawn. Directly beneath the window was a large bush shrub. Not being a gardener himself, O'Harris could not identify the species, but what mattered to him was that the bush was very leafy and with large purple flowers.

He leaned as far out of the window as he could and looked down into the shrub in its pot. He was on his tiptoes, stretching his neck and he knew he must seem ridiculous to Trelawney. Just as he was about to admit he was looking in the wrong place he noticed a leaf bent down and a broken stalk. He stared closer and closer, and then he saw it. Hidden in the shrub, almost completely vanished among the leaves, was a hammer. The killer had done as he had surmised; in the panic after the murder, they simply wanted to be rid of the hammer and they had gone to the window, hoping to see a hiding place. They were in luck, with the big shrub a perfect hiding place. They tossed the hammer, washed themselves up and got out of the room as fast as they could.

"What is it?" Trelawney asked in a choked voice behind him.

O'Harris lowered himself back to the floor and turned around.

"I have found it."

Chapter Eight

"Miss Painter?"

The woman was tall, she had to be six foot, at least, and she was of a robust build, with substantial hips that on a shorter woman would have made her look dumpy and fat. Miss Painter's height did her a lot of favours in that department, making her curves merely voluptuous rather than worthy of a diet.

She was wearing a straight-waisted summer dress that was probably not advisable, especially with the pleats around the skirt which enhanced what were substantial thighs. The dress was pretty, however, and must have been specially made as Clara could not think of a clothing shop that sold off-the-peg dresses in that length. Perhaps Miss Painter was the talented sort who could make her own clothes, though she did not give that impression.

She looked fearsome. Wild, black hair had been diligently tamed into a bob, as was the fashion, but it was fighting its way free and reverting to what must be its natural state of dishevelment. Phrases like 'pulled through a hedge backwards' had no doubt been used about that hair on many an occasion and possibly explained the defensive way Miss Painter glowered at the world. She was a giant woman, with wild hair and features that could be best described as hard. Feminine charm had evaded her and left her exposed to the world as an oddity. In short, she was the sort of woman who was likely bullied for her looks and size as a girl, that is until the bullies discovered she had the sort of personality that enjoyed crushing her enemies.

The world had spurned Miss Painter and so she spurned it.

"Hello," Clara said, giving her most approachable smile. "I am Miss Clara Fitzgerald."

Miss Painter's unrelenting gaze turned down on Bramble, who was still at Clara's side. He was eyeing up Miss Painter's bulldog, trying to determine if it might try to eat him at some point.

"What is that?" Miss Painter asked, with the sort of sneer in her tone that you reserved for disgusting things found at the bottom of old buckets left out in the rain all winter.

Clara was offended on Bramble's behalf. She was also offended for herself and her pride got the better of her common sense for a moment.

"Have you never encountered a Bohemian Duck Tracking Hound before?" she enquired innocently.

Miss Painter did not look fooled.

"Appears to be a shabby poodle to me."

"That is a mistake people frequently make," Clara said lightly. "Do not feel bad about it. The breed is rare in its own country, virtually unheard of in Britain. I happen to have a cousin in Bohemia who breeds them."

Miss Painter gave Bramble another hard look.

"A duck tracking hound?"

"Yes. They can go for days tracking them through ice and snow," Clara continued in her fantastical elaboration. "Persistent little beggars."

Miss Painter was looking rather baffled, but she was not going to reveal her ignorance in this matter. As anyone in the dog world could tell you, there were new breeds being discovered in far flung places all the time and being introduced to the show world. Miss Painter went with the flow.

"Reminds me of a miniature Otterhound," she said. "Is that a working clip?"

"It is," Clara confirmed, not really sure what that meant.

"Suitable for protecting all the extremities as they work, I imagine?" Miss Painter carried on. "What does a show clip look like?"

"I am not sure the breed has had one devised for it yet."

"Ah, too novel?"

"Something like that. They haven't really entered the show world just yet. Mostly they are kept by peasants as working dogs. They nearly went extinct during the war, you know."

"Tragic," Miss Painter said, sympathetic to the plight of the humble Bohemian Duck Tracking Hound, now she was satisfied she was not being approached by someone with a ratty poodle on a lead.

"I wondered if I could trouble you for a moment? I wished to have a chat about bulldogs?" Clara had a feel for Miss Painter and the way to approach her now. A head-on assault was not an option, she needed to be subtle and to reach out to the woman in a way she would appreciate. That meant talking about dogs.

"I have a few moments," Miss Painter said, a new expression coming over her face. Talking about her beloved breed made her happy.

"You are most kind. I have already tried to speak to another gentleman about his dog and was treated as if I was a terrible nuisance."

Miss Painter raised an eyebrow.

"I can imagine who that was," she said.

"I was most put out, especially as I am sure I have seen his dog on a packet of dog food."

"Master's Dog Biscuits," Miss Painter sniffed.

"That's it!" Clara said, acting as if suddenly delighted Miss Painter understood. "I knew I recognised the dog. But the gentleman was rather unfriendly."

"You have had the misfortune to encounter Nigel Love," Miss Painter nodded.

"Quite frankly, he rather put me off speaking to anyone else. I quite wondered why I had bothered to come," Clara said, pretending to be hurt. "I have been considering a bulldog for some time and thought a dog show would be the best place to meet examples of the breed and talk to their breeders. Now I am not sure at all."

"You must not tar us all with the same brush as Nigel," Miss Painter said, completely ignoring the fact she had been quite dismissive of Clara ten minutes ago when she thought she owned an improperly groomed poodle. "He does not represent us all."

"I must say, I am glad I spoke to you," Clara said. "I feel a good deal better about everything and your dog is so much nicer than Mr Love's."

"Oh, Nigel's dog Brutus is a fiend. You know that bulldogs were originally bred for bullbaiting and dogfighting? Well, we breeders are endeavouring to salvage the breed's reputation and promote them as good all round family pets. Fearsome dogs worry people, they associate them with thugs and criminals. We want respectable families to take the breed to their heart and to appreciate their finer qualities," this sounded like a speech Miss Painter gave a lot. "Unfortunately, people like Nigel are not being as careful about their breeding as some of us. Nigel breeds for looks, not temperament. The result is Brutus and, as handsome as he might be, no one would want him as a family pet. He would savage the children, kill the cat, and bite the servants. The sort of dog, in short, who would-be best-off shot."

Miss Painter's abrupt statement quite took Clara by surprise, to the point she gave a slight gasp. Miss Painter nodded at her.

"It is a controversial statement, but if such examples of the breed are encouraged, we shall watch the temperament of the bulldog disintegrate into something nasty, and aggressive. We shall see their reputation destroyed and then who shall want to own one? Only the lower classes who are looking for a mean street dog, not a pet," Miss Painter sighed. "You try to make a difference, you really try, then someone like Nigel Love comes along and it destroys everything."

"I am so sorry," Clara said.

Miss Painter waved off the remark.

"We are far from finished yet. Our real problem is that so many judges are afraid of Nigel and the power he wields and are cowed into placing his dog ahead of others of better temperament."

"I do not understand," Clara frowned innocently. "Why would they be afraid of him?"

Miss Painter glanced around her to make sure no one was close enough to listen to them, then she motioned that she and Clara should walk over into the shade of a big beech tree.

"Rosa struggles in this heat," she indicated the dog. "Now, where was I? Oh yes, people fear Nigel because he has managed to secure a lot of useful contacts in the dog world. The Master's deal is just the tip of the iceberg. He has invested money in some of the bigger shows held about the country and is on several influential committees, including the one that confirms judges' licenses and decides which shows they are to be invited to."

"Isn't that rather self-serving?" Clara said.

"It is the way it is," Miss Painter shrugged. "Honestly, the committees mostly work fine, unless you get someone like Nigel on them. Technically he is not supposed to attend a show where he has assigned a judge for the bulldog ring."

"But let me guess, he does anyway?"

"Exactly," Miss Painter snorted. "And no one stops him. People are too worried to complain, in case he uses his influence to prevent them being able to show their dogs, or judges to get appointments."

"Oh dear," Clara said, seeing how bad this could be. "You must be very angry."

"I was," Miss Painter said. "But the war has changed things. The break away from showing meant people had time to reassess the situation. Some of the old names have opted not to return to the show world and new faces have emerged. Nigel's position, for the first time in years, is far from secure and he knows it. It is making him particularly bad tempered."

Miss Painter was pleased about this and the first smile Clara had seen grace her face now emerged on her lips. Here was a woman who knew she would soon see her enemy's comeuppance and was very happy about it. Clara had a hunch that Miss Painter was not a person to act rashly and murder her rival. She was far more interested in seeing him suffer. A quick death was not for her.

"I believe the bulldogs have been in the ring already?" she asked casually.

"They have done the Best Bitch and Best Dog classes," Miss Painter said. "The winning dogs from those now go forward to the Best in Breed. One shall be selected as the best example of a bulldog on that day. That shall be later this afternoon. Rosa has secured her place."

"How wonderful!" Clara said, feigning delight and rather feeling she overdid it. She was still struggling to get her head around all this. "Ah, so who is Rosa up against?"

"Who do you suppose?" Miss Painter groaned. "Mrs Doddington was the judge for Best Dog, and she is firmly in Nigel's pocket."

"Then you are against Brutus?" Clara suddenly saw an opening. Could Miss Painter have been so furious about Nigel's place once more being fixed in the Best in Breed ring that she argued with him, killed him, and stole his dog? It was motive, for sure, but she was still thinking how Miss Painter did not seem the impulsive sort.

"I was not worried," Miss Painter said with a smile. It was rather sinister. "Dominic Wood is the Best in Breed judge for bulldogs, and he shall show no favour to Nigel. I expect a fair competition, in fact, I expect the judging to go firmly in my direction."

"Surely Mr Wood would not allow his personal grievances to influence his judging decision?"

"You really do not appreciate how much he and Nigel hate one another," Miss Painter chuckled. "In any case, I am not concerned. I am rather looking forward to seeing Nigel's face when I am placed over him. There shall be nothing more satisfying than that."

Clara believed her. She did not think Miss Painter had harmed Nigel Love, nor stolen Brutus. She did not want her revenge to occur quietly in the background, she wanted to see Nigel humiliated publicly.

"Do you know, Nigel once asked me if I should allow Brutus to breed with one of my other dogs. That was a few years ago, before I was heavily into the world of showing and barely knew him. Back then I was naïve, and I thought Nigel Love was the expert in all things bulldog. I can appreciate how you felt earlier, you see, for I once thought the same. He was the face of Master's, and I really believed he knew his stuff," Miss Painter pulled a face, disappointed with herself and her poor judgement. "I soon changed my mind. When Brutus came for his little 'marriage' to my bulldog Cara, it was like some sort of nightmare! He attacked my poor Cara, and we could barely get him off her. Nigel still wanted to try for a pairing, despite the blood on the floor and Cara being terrified out of her mind! I sent him away with a flea in his ear. We have not exchanged a civil word since."

"Brutus has quite a reputation," Clara said, starting to worry again about where he had ended up. The last thing any of them needed was Brutus loose on a rampage.

"I am convinced that dog is quite peculiar," Miss Painter shook her head vigorously. "If rabies were not a fatal disease, you would argue he is a chronic case. Nigel has to dose him up with a sedative to get him into a ring with other dogs."

"That is surely against the rules?"

Miss Painter gave Clara a look that told her everything. Of course it was against the rules, but this was Nigel Love and he got away with anything.

"You must find this disheartening," Clara said to her.

"I am forever an optimist," Miss Painter replied. "And I am satisfied in the knowledge that one day Nigel shall have his comeuppance. I do hope it is in a show ring, however. Ideally Brutus would turn on him before everybody. Oh, I see you find that a terrible thing to say, but I stand by it. The real terror is the number of puppies Brutus has sired and who must carry an element of his madness. We shall be burdened by his impact on the breed for generations."

Miss Painter was unmoved by Clara's look of astonishment at her words.

"Best you avoid Nigel in future," she told Clara. "Now, about that puppy. I am planning on breeding Rosa this autumn. I expect a large, healthy litter. If you wish to put your name down, I shall consider you when the time is closer."

Clara found herself agreeing as she did not want to upset Miss Painter and potentially make it harder to speak to her later on. At least she had learned a lot without revealing that Nigel had been murdered, even if she was confident Miss Painter was off her suspect list. There seemed to be a lot more reasons for Nigel Love to be despised than just the ones Jessop had told her.

It seemed a good time to speak to Mr Wood and discover just how far a judge would go to silence his worst critic.

Chapter Nine

Tommy was not having a great deal of success as an undercover operative. He was starting to think, as the Americans would say, that he had been made. He had read that phrase in one of the many American detective handbooks he had accrued over the last few years. Of course, to be 'made' implied that everyone around him firstly knew Mr Love was dead and secondly that Clara was investigating the matter. Which did seem a touch improbable.

He was therefore left with the conclusion that he was just not very convincing as a dog handler and that people were avoiding him simply because he looked out of place and without a clue. If he was utterly honest with himself, it was a fair point. His version of being undercover involved loitering at the edge of a ring, trying to work out precisely what was going on, while also trying to keep his ears open for any hint that could lead to the murderer of Nigel Love.

"You look dreadfully lost."

Tommy glanced up at the statement and realised there was a young man of around his age stood next to him all of a sudden. The man was devilishly handsome and extremely well turned out in a smart grey suit with silver buttons.

"First dog show?" the man asked.

"Rather!" Tommy said, relieved that at last someone had taken pity on him.

"Your Labrador has nice form," the man continued. "I show Labradors too. What lines is she from?"

"Rosebriar, mainly," Tommy replied.

"Those are good dogs. Well bred, good in the field, sound temperament and very nice heads."

Pip glanced up at her admirer and grinned at him in that puppy way that spelt trouble and mischief.

"Did you buy her to show?"

"Not really," Tommy said. "She was a gift, from the kennel owners."

"What a gift!" the man's eyes widened. "My name is Alexander, by the way. Everyone calls me Alex."

"Tommy," Tommy replied, and they shook hands.

"So, what are your first impressions of the show world?" Alex asked him.

Tommy glanced across at the show ring before him where a collection of handlers were prancing around with Dachshunds. Tommy had lost track of whether these were the full size or miniature versions of the breed. Until that day he had not known there was a difference.

"I have found it rather confusing," he admitted to Alex. "And not everyone has been entirely welcoming."

"Don't take that to heart," Alex replied. "People get a little too serious at these things and wrap themselves up in their own little worlds. You will find that mostly everyone is friendly, when they are not worrying about where they left their best comb or whether Rex is striding out nicely."

"I suppose it was my misfortune to meet one of the few who is not terribly pleasant," Tommy said, throwing out the comment as an opening for further conversation.

"Who did you come across?" Alex asked, curious.

"I believe the gentleman's name is Nigel Love. He was making rather a fuss by the tea table."

Alex's affable expression suddenly darkened, and his

smile faded.

"Nigel is, how shall I put it?" he frowned. "The sort of person you would prefer not to be involved in the same hobby as yourself."

"Then he is disagreeable all the time?"

"All the time and to everybody," Alex sighed. "You understand a little bit of rivalry between handlers of the same breed, though generally we are quite close-knit and good-spirited, but Nigel is another thing altogether. He is nasty to anyone who crosses his path, no matter how innocently they might stumble upon him."

"That must make things difficult," Tommy observed.

"It makes things awkward, at times, but you get on with it," Alex shrugged. "At least he does not show Labradors."

"If everybody dislikes him, why does he keep coming to the shows?" Tommy said.

"Because Nigel does not care about people. That is why he is so miserable and unpleasant. He cares as much about people, as you and I would care about the average housefly. An irritation to be swatted out of the way and not something you worry about liking you or not."

"That is rather grim," Tommy meant what he said. The thought of someone despising other people so much he could care less how he treated them, did not suggest to him a person who was happy in their life. "Does he really hate everyone?"

"Maybe hate is too strong a word," Alex pondered. "Perhaps it would be better to say Nigel disdains everyone else. He is a very lonely man."

"It sounds like it," Tommy snorted. "I suppose he does well enough at the shows to keep coming?"

"He has produced a lot of champion bulldogs," Alex nodded. "Unfortunately, he has reached the stage where he considers his dogs the only ones of a standard to be worthy of winning, and he does not take it well when his dogs lose."

Tommy drew air in through his teeth, making a backwards hissing sound that implied his thoughts on

Nigel's attitude to the world.

"Exactly," Alex said.

"I cannot imagine anyone wanting to live that way."

"Then you have yet to fully appreciate Nigel Love," Alex shrugged. "Here, why don't you come with me and I shall give you some tips on showing your dog? There is a knack to it, you know."

Tommy had almost reached the point where he was considering withdrawing Pip from the competition, his nerves had started to jangle too much. Alex's offer was gratefully received.

"I would appreciate that."

Alex led him out of the tent and to a shady area under one of the many great trees in the grounds. There was a group of five Labradors resting in the shade, with another young man lying on the grass next to them, idly watching the world go by. At the sight of fellow Labradors Pip became excited and dragged Tommy towards them, greeting fellow members of her breed with puppy glee.

"A Rosebriar," Alex said to the man on the ground, indicating Pip. "This is Michael."

Michael gave Pip a look of approval.

"Good lines. Fetch is part Rosebriar," he pointed to a handsome black Labrador sitting at the back of the group who was doing a good job of stoically ignoring Pip's attentions.

"Tommy here is new to showing and has had the misfortune of starting his journey by encountering Nigel Love," Alex explained.

"What rotten luck!" Michael declared. "Sit down Tommy. We most certainly do not bite."

Tommy gladly sat down. Pip was calming now the novelty of meeting fellow Labradors was fading and she flopped down beside him, panting hard and struggling to keep her eyes open. She was soon sound asleep.

"You must not think Nigel represents us all," Michael insisted. "He is an oaf of the first class."

"I gathered that," Tommy said with a laugh.

"He ought to be banned from coming," Michael said stoutly. "The judges won't stand up against him, that is the problem. He has them scared, because of all the sponsorship he gets. They are worried if they say too much, they will upset the wrong people and get kicked off the judging circuit. That can happen, you know."

"But that is awful," Tommy replied. "It means that a man like Nigel is virtually running the show!"

"Tell us about it," Alex groaned. "It is a nightmare."

"Something will be done about it," Michael said promptly and with the sort of certainty that made Tommy think he was planning something.

"You must be able to group together and ban him?" Tommy said, hoping to get a little more.

"We are working on it," Alex confessed. "The whole system needs to be changed to prevent a person like Nigel Love from taking over. It just takes time. The old guard has to be politely retired, to allow the next generation to improve things."

"Still, that is not something to dwell on at your first show," Michael lightened the tone. "Are you looking for some tips, Tommy?"

Tommy agreed he was, and Michael was only too glad to oblige. They left Pip dozing and gave him Fetch to work. Tommy was soon learning how to walk at the right pace to get Fetch to stride out nicely and show off his form. Then he was being shown how to 'stack' his dog to get Fetch standing to his best advantage.

"Fortunately, there is not the grooming necessary for a Labrador as for other breeds," Alex explained. "A good brush or comb, and a sweep over with a soft cloth is enough to bring out a glorious shine."

Michael was observing Tommy closely, one finger pressed to his lip as he thought about something.

"You do not stride out so well with your left leg, as your right," he said. "I notice it when you are bringing Fetch around."

Tommy ducked his head. He hated when people noticed

his injury.

"I was shot, during the war," he explained.

"Michael! Do you have to be so brazen!" Alex scolded the other man.

"It was merely an observation," Michael replied defensively.

"It is perfectly all right," Tommy interjected before an argument began. "It was a reasonable observation."

"The war cost us too much," Alex sighed. "Not just in people either. The military took so many dogs, some of the best lines were decimated. They wanted Labradors for messenger dogs. The majority never returned."

This added a new bleakness to the conversation and Tommy was sorry to be the cause of it.

"That's a shame," he said, uncomfortably.

"I tell you one person who was in his element," Michael added, his voice dropping to a conspiratorial whisper. "Our friend Nigel volunteered a number of his dogs, started breeding them for the war effort, even. Some say it was to cover-up the fact the coward made sure to never go to the Front himself."

"We do not know that for sure," Alex added. "It was just a rumour at the time."

"He was young enough to serve, why was he never called up?" Michael said. "Because he made an arrangement, that is why. Provide the army with bulldogs and he was excused getting his hands dirty. Makes my blood boil."

"As you can tell, my friend here has rather taken against Nigel Love," Alex sighed.

"Just another nail in his coffin," Michael snorted. "You tell me that isn't why Dominic Wood alone out of so many judges will stand up to him? Wood was in the war, lost two brothers. I have heard him call Nigel a dirty coward and worse."

"Not to his face, surely?" Tommy said.

"There is a deep grievance there," Alex said quietly. "Wood has been rather vocal. When Nigel suggested he was playing favourites in the ring because he did not place Brutus, Wood lashed back with some rather unpleasant assertions."

"Those two have their own private feud going on," Michael agreed. "Not that you would know it from looking at Wood. He is professional in the ring, at least."

"The more you tell me about Nigel Love, the more I wonder the fellow has not ended up with a knife in his back already," Tommy said with a chuckle, only he knew his joke was a touch too close to reality.

The way Alex and Michael glanced at one another in silence caused a chill to run down Tommy's spine.

"Have I said too much?" he asked, uneasily.

"There was an attempt on Nigel's life not so long back," Alex said softly. "We were all in Liverpool for an Easter show. Nigel said someone followed him back to his hotel one night and threw a rope around his neck, tried to strangle him. Brutus bit them, and that was how he escaped. He never saw his attacker, but he was sure it was someone from the show world."

"Was not one of his fellow competitors sporting a limp the next day?" Tommy asked.

"No one," Michael shook his head. "The suggestion was it was one of the competitors who had already lost and was going home."

"Or Brutus did not bite as hard as Nigel thought."

"Did he report it to the police?" Tommy added, thinking that if Nigel was already a marked man before he came to Brighton, it made his death look less like an impulsive act and more like something carefully plotted.

"Nigel shrugged it off," Alex replied. "He suggested it was the work of a mugger, and there was no point reporting it to the police. They would never find the fellow."

"Some people even suggested Nigel made the whole thing up," Michael added. "Though I can't think why he would do such a thing."

"He had a fresh bruise around his neck," Alex said,

drawing a line with a finger around his own throat. "I believe it happened and I do not think it was the work of a mugger."

Tommy whistled to himself.

"That is serious."

"Made us all a little twitchy," Michael agreed. "You keep wondering if the same person might come for you."

"I think Nigel was a very specific target," Alex said solemnly. "I don't think this is some mad person who will strike out at random competitors."

"But nothing has happened since? I mean, that was some months ago," Tommy noted. "If someone had such a serious grudge, you might imagine they would try again."

"Nigel has not attended a dog show between that one and this one," Alex elaborated. "One of his bitches was in whelp and he stayed home. We did wonder if the incident had shaken him up more than he let on."

"I said to Alex before we came today, if Nigel is here, I wonder if someone will take a swing at him again!" Michael laughed at his own comment, not realising how close to the mark he had come.

"I told him that was poor taste," Alex countered.

"It was only a tease," Michael responded. "Look, Nigel is here and perfectly sound, isn't he?"

Tommy felt a terrible urge to say something, and he was sure it must be obvious to anyone looking that he knew more than he was letting on. He felt as if the secret within him was striving to get out. It was with extraordinary relief he spied Inspector Park-Coombs wandering across the lawn, looking both lost and annoyed at the same time.

"I have to abandon you, I am afraid. I see someone I need to speak to," Tommy smiled at them, extracting himself politely. "I am very grateful for your help."

"See you in the show ring, Tommy," Alex nodded to him. "You will do just fine."

Tommy had been touched by the kindness of the two men towards him.

"Thank you," he said. "I really do appreciate your help."

Then he darted off to catch up with Park-Coombs.

Chapter Ten

"Dominic Wood?"

The judge was taking a five-minute break from assessing dachshunds when Clara approached him. He had lit up a cigarette. He only smoked at shows, that was when his stress levels crept up. He enjoyed his chosen hobby and loved being a judge, but it was high pressure when you had so many good examples of a breed in the ring and their eagerly anticipating owners willing you to pick theirs.

Dominic had wanted a bit of time to himself, just to catch his breath, he was not delighted to see a woman with a scruffy poodle calling his name.

"I am taking a break," he said in a surly tone, wondering why people felt the need to disturb him when he was clearly relaxing and taking some time for himself.

"I wanted to talk to you about Nigel Love."

That short sentence was like a magic spell cast over Wood. He froze for just a moment, then he ditched the cigarette he had been smoking, crushing it under the toe of his shoe, before turning to Clara.

"Let's talk somewhere private."

They wandered over to the shelter of the beech trees which were proving quite a haven for the dogs and their handlers on this hot day. Dominic Wood was so intrigued about what Clara wished to say to him about Nigel Love, he was even prepared to ignore that she had brought a clearly non-show standard poodle to a pedigree dog show.

"Nigel Love," he said. "Why do you want to talk about him?"

"Aside from the fact he has been positively obnoxious today towards the Trelawneys, I wanted to discuss your association with him. I have been sent here to do a little, well, let us call it snooping, on behalf of interested parties."

Clara felt there was nothing less than truthful about what she was saying, she was just being somewhat vague on precisely which interested parties were employing her. She hoped Wood would mistakenly think she implied she was working for other dog handlers and judges annoyed by Love's behaviour.

It didn't take much prodding to send his mind in that direction.

"About time!" he spluttered. "Though they could have sent you with better cover."

He waved at Bramble, who gave him a sad look. The small dog was starting to get the impression he was not welcome around here and it was dimming his normally exuberant personality.

Clara ignored the observation.

"I have been making discreet enquiries and it has come to my attention that you are one of the few judges on the circuit not prepared to be bullied by Mr Love."

"That is quite right," Dominic said firmly. "I have always upheld my judging appointment to the highest of standards. I will not be swayed with bullying tactics or be threatened into allowing Love to win everything. If I think his dog is the best one in the ring that day, I shall place him. If not, then he just has to put up with the fact."

"Except Mr Love is not inclined to put up with anything," Clara pointed out.

"That is his problem, not mine," Dominic replied.

"I admire your principals," Clara said to him. "And your

determination. I fear you are somewhat alone in that stance, however."

Dominic Wood suddenly sighed and some of his determination faded.

"That is unfortunately true. Look, if you could gather evidence about Nigel's intimidation tactics, well, then the Kennel Club will have to take note."

"Easier said than done," Clara replied. "What with many people not wishing to put their head above the parapet, so to speak."

"Yes," Dominic agreed, looking downcast. "Starts to make you think only drastic action will pluck this thorn from our side."

"Drastic?"

Dominic opened his mouth, then reconsidered what he had been about to say.

"I do not wish the man ill," he said, which could not have been more blatant a lie.

"I hear some do," Clara observed slyly.

"There are those holding a grudge against him, but they would not do any harm. Not in that sense," Dominic shrugged. "We are all suffering in silence."

"It seems to me that is the worst way to suffer. Ultimately you cannot endure any longer and someone snaps."

Dominic did not quite know what to say, so he hedged his bets.

"Hence why we are trying to do things through official channels. I am most relieved to see that someone is at last taking an interest and has hired you to investigate. Exactly, what is it you do?"

"I am a private detective," Clara answered honestly.

"That would make sense," Dominic nodded.

"I have been trying to determine who might have the greatest grudge against Love," Clara continued. "I am developing quite a list. I would like to speak to anyone who has had serious dealings with him. If I am to gather evidence, I must speak to as many people as possible."

"Of course, well, you have quite a few to choose from around here," Dominic nodded. "Miss Painter, for instance."

"I have spoken to her," Clara told him. "She was very honest with me."

"She is concerned about the future of the breed with Nigel Love promoting Brutus as a champion stud."

"Yes, she told me about that. It seems to me that someone ought to have a quiet word with Master's Dog Biscuits about their spokesperson, or rather spokes-dog."

"They are not interested," Dominic snorted. "I have tried. You know, of course, who is one of the owners of the company?"

"I confess I do not," Clara said.

Dominic gave her a grin.

"Mr Love's own cousin. His uncle helped to found the business about forty years ago. That is how Love is connected to them and why they shall not have a word said against them."

"Oh," Clara said, because the information had come as a surprise. "Everyone has kept that rather quiet."

"Few know," Dominic explained. "I had to do a lot of digging to find out that titbit. I realised something was fishy when they dismissed the complaint I sent them out-of-hand. It struck me their rejection had more to it than met the eye. I decided to look into things deeper and that was when I discovered it. Love keeps the family connection hushed up. The uncle is on his mother's side, so of course the surname is different."

"Well, that explains that," Clara said. "Have you made this information known?"

"Not yet, I have been waiting for a suitably appropriate moment," Dominic's eyes glittered at his revelation. "In any case, it is not actually illegal or anything, but it will please a few people to know it was not down to pure merit that Brutus became the face of Master's."

"Indeed," Clara was trying to think if this incestuous scandal could be a reason for someone to murder Love, but she could not see it. In any case, it seemed Wood was the only one to know about it. "Do you suppose anyone would wish Love actual harm?"

"Plenty of people want to see his show career in tatters," Dominic answered.

"I was thinking more along the lines of physical harm."

Dominic gave her a curious look.

"That is an interesting thought," he said.

Clara hefted her shoulders.

"It strikes me he is a man gathering quite a few enemies around him, some might be tempted to take action against him. Especially if no one in authority is taking heed."

Dominic mulled on this for a while.

"I do not care to think about it and none of the folk here I could imagine being so... reckless."

"I hear Love has made it through to the Best of Breed class with Brutus," Clara gently changed tack.

"He has," Dominic sighed. "Damn shame. There were some nice dogs in that class, far nicer than him but my fellow judge, Mrs Diana Doddington is, shall we say, a little blinkered."

"She is afraid of Love?"

"Quite the opposite. She worships the ground the man walks on. She is a Shih Tzu breeder, herself, but I believe she received some advice from Nigel about producing a more compact head in her breeding lines. You ask me, it is all to the detriment of the dog, but then I am collie man myself, proper working dogs. I breed Roughs, Welsh and Border collies."

Clara realised a fraction too late that she was supposed to respond to this comment with approval and to ask about Dominic's dogs. She had become too absorbed with the fact that someone actually liked Love.

"Are you saying that Mrs Doddington is sweet on Nigel Love?"

"I thought that was quite plain," Dominic laughed. "I cannot think of another soul alive who would think of him with equal charity. I never had a doubt in my mind she would place Brutus when I saw which class she was judging."

"That's a shame for everyone else," Clara said. "It is hardly fair."

"Well, you learn to roll with the blows in this hobby," Dominic smiled. "I dare say we are all prone to a little unconscious favouritism."

It was then a thought struck him.

"Funny, I have not seen Nigel about for quite some time. He is usually shadowing my every move. He does it to try to intimidate me and put me off. Quite frankly I am so used to it I barely notice him now," Dominic looked around him again. "Still, it is strange he has suddenly chosen to give up his game."

"Maybe he realised it was not working," Clara suggested, not wanting Dominic to start to get suspicious about the man's disappearance.

"Nigel is not the sort of person who gives up that easily," Dominic shook his head. "He is like his bulldogs, doggedly persistent. Will hang onto something for all he is worth, even when it is pointless."

He started looking around him again, perturbed by the sudden disappearance of his archenemy. Dominic was one of those people who thrived on having someone pushing against him. He liked to lock horns with an opponent, as long as he was the one on the right side of the disagreement. He was rather enjoying his battle with Nigel Love; it gave things a little zing. It had been fun to ignore Love while he judged, knowing the man was wasting all his time watching him. It had been satisfying and had amused Dominic rather than upset him. He was rather annoyed Love had simply given up.

"Makes no sense," he muttered.

"I am sure he will turn up," Clara said casually. "Tell me more about his relationship with Mrs Doddington."

Dominic was scowling around the show, looking for his rival. He remembered himself eventually and spoke to Clara.

"Mrs Doddington is a scatter brain. She flutters about in this muddle of her own making. The only reason she has not been offended by Love is that she hasn't the sense to see when he is being rude to her," Dominic paused. "Now I think about it, Nigel has never been quite as rude to her as to everyone else. You know, I do recall once seeing him buy her a cup of tea, which was so shocking it made me blink. That man gives nothing to anyone."

"You almost make it sound like they are friends," Clara suggested.

"That would be a step too far," Dominic said, but he was now thinking hard about what Clara had said and he was beginning to wonder himself. "Except, now you mention it…"

He went a little pale as the full idea that had been drifting into his mind came to fruition.

"What a terrible thing to imagine," he gasped to himself. "It would beggar belief and put a man off his dinner!"

Clara, who was already two steps ahead of him in that thought pattern, offered her own interpretation.

"Could Mr Love and Mrs Doddington have been romantically involved?"

Dominic reached out for the trunk of the beech, feeling quite overcome for a moment.

"A man should not have to contemplate such things."

"But if he did contemplate them?" Clara pressed.

"Well, then I would say it is very possible, now you have brought the matter to my attention," Dominic was thinking over things he had seen and heard that had not really meant anything to him before and yet now seemed very significant. "They sometimes stayed in the same hotel or bed and breakfast," he gulped. "We used to say how brave Mrs Doddington was being under the same roof as him. No one else would do the same. No one. If you found out the room you had booked was in the same building as Love, well, you found a new room if you could. But it was almost as if Mrs Doddington did it deliberately."

Clara reached out a hand to steady the poor man who was clearly overcome by the shock of it all. There were some things a person ought not to be forced to think about and one of them was Nigel Love being romantically involved with anyone, let alone Mrs Doddington.

"Would you care for another cigarette?" Clara asked Mr Wood gently. She had noticed his cigarette case in his jacket pocket. "You look like you could do with it."

With shaking fingers Dominic produced his cigarette case and removed one. The first inhale of the tobacco calmed some of his horror.

"How am I supposed to judge the bulldog Best of Breed now with that thought in my mind?" he said to Clara, a grimace on his face.

"Oh, I wouldn't worry about it," Clara said darkly, fortunately Dominic was too shaken to pay heed to her tone.

He sucked deeply on his cigarette.

"A man shouldn't have to think about these sorts of things," he repeated to himself.

"Never mind," Clara remarked, but she was already moving away, for she had spied that Inspector Park-Coombs was present and she needed to speak to him at once.

"Thank you for your time, Mr Wood," she said swiftly to the judge, who was still rather faint from the horror, before heading over to the inspector.

As she was reaching him, she noticed Captain O'Harris appearing from the door of the hall with a strange look on his face.

"Inspector," she said. "How lovely you chose to come, and you have brought…?"

She cast her eyes towards a large white dog stood by his side. It had a hard-done-by expression on its face, and a bullet shaped head.

"His name is Angel," Park-Coombs sighed. "He is a

pedigree greyhound."

Inspector Park-Coombs gave Clara an unhappy look.

"Turns out my desk sergeant is a dog enthusiast. Angel is his. He has been borrowed, for the duration."

Angel did not look best pleased with this arrangement. It was at that point Bramble opted to bounce at his nose. Angel snarled and barred his teeth.

"Oh yes, he does that," Park-Coombs shrugged.

Chapter Eleven

The inspector was escorted discreetly towards the hall, on the pretence of sorting out his entry papers. Mr Trelawney, who looked on the verge of a fit, welcomed him warmly and endeavoured not to blow his cover as he led them all indoors. His smile was rather fixed on his face and he was twitching dreadfully. O'Harris was worried he might not last the day at this rate.

Park-Coombs was shown to the bathroom, which was duly unlocked to allow him to view the dead man. Nigel Love was lying on the tiled floor as Clara remembered. He had gone rigid, and his skin had lost the blush of life that for a short while after death can make it appear that a person still lives. Clara made space for the inspector to walk in and nose around.

Mr Trelawney had given a whimper at the sight of the dead man, the shock of seeing the corpse a third time worse than the first or the second. Love looked really dead this time. Really, really dead, and Trelawney was having trouble keeping all those sandwiches down. He was not a man with iron nerves, and he was amazed that Clara and the others were being so calm about the whole thing. Did they not realise there was a dead man on his bathroom floor and blood all over the tiles? He was never going to be able to enter that room again. Thank goodness it was for the use of his mother-in-law, who he had a less than amiable relationship with. He could get used to the idea of her using the bathroom where a dead man had lain, he rather felt she would not care, anyway.

"Bludgeoned. Single blow by the looks," Park-Coombs confirmed Clara's assessment of the situation.

"I would say this is the weapon," O'Harris had left the hammer in the sink after he had discovered it. It had not seemed appropriate to carry it about the house. "I found it in that bush outside the window. Hastily disposed of."

Park-Coombs took a look at the hammer without touching it.

"Any idea where it came from?" he asked.

"There are workmen's tools in the hall and dining room," O'Harris added. "And footprints in the dust suggesting someone walked in and picked out a hammer from the box in there. It is not really possible to say if any tools are missing."

"Footprints?" Park-Coombs said with interest.

"Faint, rather scuffed up as the person walked back over them on the way out. If they are the footprints of the killer, then I should say we are looking for a woman or a man with very small feet."

"Does that narrow things down?" Park-Coombs glanced at Clara, knowing she had already had time to investigate things.

"It leaves me with quite a few suspects still," Clara replied. "At this stage it seems an awful lot of people disliked Love. Well, hated him to be precise."

"Someone made an attempt on his life earlier in the year," Tommy added, repeating the information he had had from Alex and Michael. "It was at Easter. He was walking back to his hotel after a dog show, and someone came up behind him and tried to throttle him with a rope."

"Oh dear," Mr Trelawney whimpered just before his legs gave way and he slumped into a heap on the floor. It was quite elegantly done.

Park-Coombs stared at the crumpled man.

"No stamina," he sniffed. "People these days. All weak in the stomach."

"Perhaps we should find him somewhere to rest," O'Harris suggested, nodding to Tommy, who got the hint and helped the captain haul up Trelawney and carry him away to somewhere quiet.

Clara remained with the inspector.

"I get the impression Clara that this is a man who was due to be murdered at some point," he said in a wry tone.

"I think that is a fair assessment," Clara agreed. "But rather sad, nonetheless."

"It takes a certain sort of person to become a murderer," the inspector pondered. "The majority of people would never consider lashing out in such a way against a person, excluding instances of self-defence, of course."

"Naturally," Clara concurred.

"How do you think it happened?" Park-Coombs asked.

"Well, I have a few ideas. By the looks of it, Love never saw the blow coming, so either he knew his killer and turned his back on them, or he never even realised they were there."

Park-Coombs rubbed at his moustache. It was a bristle brush sort of moustache, that he kept neat but not over-fancy. His moustache told you a lot about the inspector's mood. Stroking it was a sign of thoughtfulness.

"Everything happened in a very tight window of time," Clara added. "We are not entirely sure how the killer came to be here, either. Mrs Trelawney is sure no one entered the house after Mr Love came in to use the bathroom."

"So, she is either wrong, or the killer was already inside."

"And seized an opportunity," Clara said, but she was frowning. "They had a stroke of luck, that is all I can say. The moment came around and they went for it."

"I agree it seems a crime of opportunity," Park-Coombs was looking at the hammer again. "If they had planned this, you would suppose they would have brought a weapon with them."

"And picked a better time. They could have been easily disturbed by someone else coming to use the bathroom, or Mrs Trelawney coming to see why her guest was taking so long. Which was what happened in the end and how she discovered the body."

"Someone must really have had a grudge against the man to have just lashed out and risked everything," Park-Coombs took a good long look around the bathroom. Nothing jumped out at him as important.

"There is also Brutus to consider," Clara distracted him.

"Brutus?"

"Mr Love's bulldog. He has vanished and apparently he was with Mr Love when he came to the bathroom."

It was the inspector's turn to frown.

"The dog simply might have run off. With all these dogs around, no one would notice one extra."

"You fail to appreciate Brutus' character. He is not a dog who would run loose among others quietly and calmly. If he were loose in the grounds, you would expect a blood bath."

"Oh," Park-Coombs said, glancing over at Angel who had been left in the corridor outside and was casting him the sort of look that can make a man feel very guilty. "I see. A bit like that one."

"Far worse," Clara said, giving Angel a reassuring pat on the head. "Brutus is mean, Inspector. I did not pick my choice of words lightly. When I said he would cause a blood bath, I truly meant it."

Park-Coombs hissed through his teeth.

"So we have to assume the murderer has him too?"

"I can only come to that conclusion. Perhaps they have hidden him somewhere?"

"But why?"

Clara had thought about this.

"Brutus loose would alert people to the fact his master was missing. Brutus would make enough ruckus in a short span of time that everyone would be searching for Love to give him a piece of their mind. Perhaps the killer realised this and decided it was best to keep Brutus out of the way."

"No one has been spotted with him?"

"No. And Brutus is pretty recognisable. His face is on Master's Dog Biscuits."

This meant nothing to the inspector who was more interested in his fishpond than dogs.

"I really ought to get Dr Death down here to take a look."

"Will he offer us anything more than we already know?" Clara asked.

Park-Coombs made a huffing noise that indicated he would likely not.

"He might be able to get fingerprints off the hammer," he said, still not happy about failing to follow procedure.

"Fingerprints are no use to us without a suspect and the second we begin to make a fuss we are likely to lose the killer."

Park-Coombs grumbled to himself, but he did see Clara's point. Currently they had the advantage in that no one aside from the killer knew about the murder. As far as the killer was concerned, the body had yet to be discovered and they could carry on as if nothing had happened.

"Let's look at these footprints," Park-Coombs said.

They locked the bathroom as they left and headed towards the hall. O'Harris and Tommy emerged from the sitting room as they appeared.

"Mr Trelawney is resting," O'Harris said. "I did suggest a doctor, but he has refused. He pointed out that might alert people to something being amiss."

"Just keep an eye on him," Park-Coombs said with a growl in his voice. "He is a suspect just like everyone else."

"I cannot see why Mr Trelawney would wish a man he had barely met harm," Clara countered. "Besides which, the incident has put all his plans for raising funds to save this house in jeopardy. I honestly don't think he is that foolish."

Park-Coombs' expression said that he was never

amazed by how foolish people could be and he was not about to consider Trelawney innocent, but he let the matter drop.

O'Harris showed them to the footprints in the dining room.

"They are badly scuffed," Clara said in disappointment.

Park-Coombs crouched down and studied them.

"I agree about the size. Too small to be an average man's foot," he got up. "And they lead to that toolbox."

He followed the trail.

"It doesn't offer us much, does it?"

"I have been all over the downstairs and aside from these tracks and the hammer, I have not found anything else," O'Harris explained.

"And the Trelawneys are positive no one could have entered the house other than through the terrace door?" Park-Coombs said.

"I checked the doors and windows myself. They are all locked," O'Harris responded. "Mr Trelawney is rather security-conscious."

"No signs of a bulldog?"

O'Harris shook his head.

"Right," Park-Coombs sighed. "Let's take a look upstairs."

They traipsed to the upper floor. It was noticeable where the refurbishments ended and the old hull of the house became visible, with its scratched woodwork, damp wallpaper and worryingly soft floorboards underfoot. The upstairs had barely been touched, aside from repairs to the roof to make it watertight. It was like stepping into a different house and Clara found herself wrinkling her nose at the overpowering smell of mould and rot.

"You can barely believe the downstairs looked like this too," Tommy said. "If I had inherited a place that looked like this, I think I would have called in someone to demolish it."

"Trelawney has vision to see the potential of this house, but he is right about it being a costly venture," O'Harris had lifted a wilting piece of wallpaper away from the wall to reveal a spread of black mould that stretched across the whole panel. "He is going to need every penny he can get."

Park-Coombs stood on a floorboard that gave way beneath him a little bit more than he liked, and he hopped back sharply. He was half inclined to call off the search of the upstairs, on safety grounds, but it was not the way a policeman ought to handle such matters, so he swallowed his unease and kept on.

They explored the upper floor as best they could, discovering that a number of rooms were locked and there was no sign of a key. Every window they found was also secure and they came to the final conclusion that no one had left or entered the house that way. Nor were there any signs of Brutus.

"My hunch is that the killer left when Mrs Trelawney was distracted by the body," Park-Coombs said with an air of authority as they headed back downstairs. "They would have had to be patient, but that seems the logical solution."

Clara agreed with him, she could see no other way the killer could have left, unless Mrs Trelawney had been less alert to those entering and leaving the house than she had indicated.

"Do you have any suspects?" Park-Coombs asked Clara.

"A few too many," Clara sighed. "I have barely had a chance to interview any of them."

She was going to start listing names when they all heard a familiar voice wailing blue murder in the kitchen. Fearing another tragedy had occurred they hastened through and found Mrs Monroe berating a hapless Mrs Trelawney.

"It is beastly, that is what it is!" Mrs Monroe cried.

"I am so sorry," Mrs Trelawney responded. "But all we can do now is take a good look around."

"What has happened?" Clara asked her neighbour, who looked close to tears.

"Princess Ping-Pong is missing!" Mrs Monroe said pitifully holding up the remains of a lead. "I left her in the shade of a tree with the others while I went to get a cup of tea. They were all secured to the leg of a bench beneath the tree. When I came back, someone had cut Ping-Pong's lead and made off with her!"

Clara took the fine cord lead from her hand. It was a dusky pink in colour and made from very soft leather. Clara examined the section of lead Mrs Monroe claimed had been cut.

"It rather looks to me as if this lead has been chewed through," she said.

"Don't be absurd!" Mrs Monroe declared. "What sort of dog thief chews through a lead?"

"I actually meant that maybe Princess Ping-Pong chewed through it herself."

"Heavens no!" Mrs Monroe looked appalled. "Ping-Pong is a very good girl and would never do such a thing."

"I have explained to Mrs Monroe that we shall gather everyone who is available and conduct a search for Ping-Pong," Mrs Trelawney said, sounding slightly desperate. "I shall not let the poor dog be snatched away on my watch."

"You shall help, shall you not Clara," Mrs Monroe said with the sort of deadly conviction that informs you bluntly you really do not have a choice, at least if you want to stay on reasonable terms with your next-door neighbour."

Clara wanted to groan, instead she smiled at Mrs Monroe.

"We shall all gladly help," she said. "Bramble is quite an expert at sniffing out missing animals."

Mrs Monroe gave the poodle a suspicious glance.

"That thing?"

"He found a tortoise," Tommy said proudly.

Bramble was paying very close attention to Mrs Monroe, which Clara found a tad worrying. He seemed fascinated by Ping-Pong's chewed lead.

"Oh, very well then!" Mrs Monroe declared as if she were doing them a favour. "I just want my poor Ping-Pong back and if he can find her, so be it!"

Chapter Twelve

Inspector Park-Coombs was not impressed at being roped into a hunt for a missing dog when there was a murder to solve, but as Clara explained, if he went off asking questions alone, he would arouse suspicion. Besides, Mrs Monroe was not going to just let them slip away, she had the whole show in virtual uproar over Princess Ping-Pong. With the sort of self-absorption usually only mastered by dictators, she strode out to the show rings and insisted everything be brought to a halt while her dog was located. Amazingly, the judges seemed so swept up by Mrs Monroe's demeanour and sheer gall that they did not resist.

Before long there was quite a search party ready, especially as Mrs Monroe's insistence that her dog had been snatched by a thief had caused a good deal of panic among the other show participants. Everyone wanted to find this dastardly criminal before more precious pooches vanished.

Only Clara and her party were quietly confident that no dog thief was involved in the affair. That was until Park-Coombs came up with an idea.

"There is one thing we have not fully considered," he

said, with an air of gravitas that worried Clara. "Princess Ping-Pong is not the only missing dog. Brutus the bulldog is absent too. Supposing the death of Mr Love was due to someone trying to steal his dog?"

"I am certain Ping-Pong gnawed through her lead and wandered off," Clara said hastily, concerned this was going to take them off at a tangent.

"Think about it," Park-Coombs insisted. "Someone with criminal inclinations realises that there is a small fortune to be made in ransoming stolen pedigree dogs. Brutus would be an obvious target as he is the face of Master's Dog Food. Ping-Pong was taken because the opportunity arose."

"Why not take all of Mrs Monroe's Pekingese dogs?" Tommy said.

"Ah, that would draw too much attention," Park-Coombs had worked out that argument already. "One small dog could be hidden in a coat and snatched away, but not a whole pack."

"You know, he has a point," O'Harris said. "It would explain why Brutus has vanished."

Clara held up a hand to halt them before they had completely strayed from the case at hand.

"Let us be rational. Firstly, if a thief was going to snatch Brutus, why do so when Love was present to stop him?" she said.

"Only opportunity he had," Tommy replied. "Love took the dog with him at all times. The bathroom break was the only time he might be distracted enough for the thief to work."

"Second," Clara persisted, "why go from simple theft to murder? Your theory would indicate Love was coshed to enable the thief to take the dog."

"Someone went too far, meant to knock him out, not kill him," Tommy suggested.

"You would have to be pretty stupid not to realise hitting someone with a hammer was likely to kill them,"

O'Harris said.

"Thirdly, Brutus was not the sort of dog to wander off with a stranger quietly. He was known to be protective of his owner. He bit the person who tried to strangle him, after all," Clara added.

"The thief did not know that," Park-Coombs said.

"He would have soon found out when Brutus turned on him. That bothers me the most about this all. Brutus would have protected his master savagely, so why are there no signs of our murderer being injured?" Clara looked between them all for an answer.

There was none offered.

"Still, we cannot ignore the possibility," Park-Coombs said. "Especially with a second dog missing."

Clara was far from convinced but bit her tongue. Mrs Monroe had finally gathered together enough people to satisfy her desire for a competent search party and was now approaching Clara and her party with a look of determination on her face that was rather worrying.

"I hope this poodle is as good as you claim," she said haughtily.

Poor Bramble had been maligned on all fronts that day and Clara was starting to tire of the judgemental nature of these people. Could they not see beyond appearances?

"Bramble is an expert at finding lost animals," Clara declared confidently. "There is more to a dog than its looks, you know."

Mrs Monroe did not seem to get her point. Behind her, Dominic Wood was looking on curiously.

"Precisely what is the dog going to do?" he asked.

"Bramble has a very good nose," Tommy explained. "Given a scent, he shall follow it to its conclusion. Regular bloodhound."

Wood folded his arms across his chest.

"This I have to see," he said, with a smug expression.

Mrs Monroe handed Clara Princess Ping-Pong's lead and a comb that still held some of her hair. Clara crouched down and offered these both to Bramble.

"Time to prove yourself, boy," she whispered to him. "Let's show these snobs what a real dog is made of."

Bramble gave the lead a tentative sniff, then turned his attention to the comb. It had been a long morning for the little dog, and he was beginning to long for his cosy basket next to the fireplace. He wasn't enjoying the attention everyone was giving him either. It was the wrong sort of attention and even a dog can work out when it is not appreciated.

He sniffed the comb a while, then sneezed.

"All right Bramble!" Tommy declared. "Let us go find a dog!"

Bramble did not look impressed. He glared at Mrs Monroe and the rest of the search party. If a dog could look resentful, he did.

"Come on Bramble," Tommy cajoled him. "Track the scent."

Bramble lifted one foot and trembled in the fashion very small dogs tend to do. Then something of his inner gundog emerged. The very first poodles had been used to retrieve game from water and though over time they had been developed into smaller varieties, deep down remained that ancestral memory — a memory of icy weather, cold water and plunging into rivers and ponds to fetch downed ducks and geese.

Another tremble ran through Bramble, but now the raised paw made him look like the tiniest pointer ever to be imagined. He turned his head from the crowd and gazed off into the distance. His tail seemed to bush up. Instincts took over, instincts you would not suppose remained in something so small and dainty.

Bramble charged forward, nearly dragging Tommy off his feet in the process. The dog's nose was on the ground and he was following a trail only he could locate, his whole body pulsing with excitement as the hunt began.

Had anyone happened to pass by the gardens of Mulberry Hall that afternoon, they would have seen a strange sight. A very small dog straining on a lead firmly clutched by a young man, was heading a party of well-dressed people walking across the lawn. The dog sometimes changed direction, walking right, then left, then straight on. Each turn was diligently followed by the party of people behind him. It was the most bizarre scene to observe. Like some strange dance only the participants understood.

Clara was just praying Bramble actually had the correct scent and was not merely following the trail of a rat. Bramble liked rats. They made interesting burrows and were fierce little things when cornered. You felt a master of the hunt after confronting a rat that was bigger than your head and besting it, at least when you were a dog.

The track Bramble took roamed across the lawn with no obvious purpose. Once or twice, he appeared to lose the scent and had to trot back and forth before discovering it again.

"This is ridiculous," Mrs Monroe declared. "He does not know what he is doing!"

"He knows exactly what he is doing," Clara replied, with equal authority, though she was starting to lose hope herself. Bramble was starting to amble around in a very uncertain fashion, as if he were not sure what he was about any longer.

"Let him have another scent of that comb," Tommy suggested.

Mrs Monroe presented the item to Bramble, who took a deep inhale. This appeared to refresh his tired mind and he was soon off again, charging forth with a newfound speed.

They had crossed a large section of the lawn; the house and show rings were far behind them and they were heading to a small patch of woodland that ran along the edge of the estate. It did not look promising to Clara, until they were nearly in the trees and Tommy gave a cry.

"I see a sort of hut."

"That is the old gardener's hut," Mrs Trelawney

explained. "He used it for storing things and he had a little stove for making tea in there. He retired years ago, while my husband's uncle was still alive and was never replaced. We had to look in the hut once for some ant poison. The place is nearly collapsing in on itself."

The hut had turned green due to the impact of the weather. Stains running down its faded and worn wooden boards. The roof had a nasty sag that suggested extreme rot and the tiny window in the end wall was impossible to see through due to an elaborate overlay of spiders' webs.

"No one comes here," Mrs Trelawney added. "There is no reason to."

"And yet, there are footprints in that soft soil by the door," Clara replied to her.

Before the door, the ground was damp, never receiving enough sun to dry out fully. There was a faint imprint of a shoe in the mud.

Bramble had reached the door and was now scratching on it with a paw and whining. From within came the most fearsome of barks, more of a declaration of war than a mere woof. Bramble was stunned by this response, jumping out of his skin at the sound. But never one to be defeated, he gave his best bark back, trying to sound as if he was considerably larger than his handful of inches.

From the hut came a cacophony of barks and growls to answer him and it looked as though matters were going to swiftly descend into a canine slanging match, so Tommy grabbed up Bramble and took him to one side.

"Well, we know there is a dog in that hut," Wood said, unhelpfully.

"It is not my Ping-Pong," Mrs Monroe said with a sniff. "She has a far more dainty bark."

Clara was rather worried about precisely who was in the hut, considering who they knew to be missing. She had not liked the sound of that barking and she was reluctant to open the door and unleash who she feared was within.

"Well, are we just all going to stand here?" Mrs Monroe snapped at them, marching forward to pull open the door of the hut.

"I am concerned…" Clara began, but her imprecations that an unfriendly bulldog might be behind the door went unheard, for Mrs Monroe had already opened it.

Clara cringed, expecting a blood bath inside. Brutus' reputation with other dogs was far from good. If Princess Ping-Pong had crossed his path it seemed likely it had been a fatal mistake. More to the point, Clara was fully ready for an irate Brutus to come flying out of the hut and savage Mrs Monroe, lashing out at her for his incarceration.

None of this, thankfully, occurred. Though the look on Mrs Monroe's face as she peered inside did not initially give Clara hope and when she gave a short scream, Clara pictured the worst.

"What is it?" gasped Mrs Trelawney.

"My Princess Ping-Pong!" Mrs Monroe said. "Come here, sweetie!"

Mrs Monroe bent down and there was an ominous growl from the hut. Dominic Wood had the presence of mind to grab the woman and pull her back. Clara decided it was time to brave whatever scene of horror was in the hut and moved around to look through the door.

What she saw was an ugly bulldog chained to the back wall of the hut, not that the chain gave much hope as the walls were so flimsy. Curled up beside him, quite content and happy was a small Pekingese. Princess Ping-Pong was neither dead nor maimed, there was no blood or sign of violence. She looked, indeed, very settled with Brutus, and made no attempt to move.

Bramble had started to frantically squirm in Tommy's arms at the opening of the door. It was quite a wrestling match to prevent him leaping to the ground and going inside to give Brutus a piece of his mind. Brutus gave another low grumble and moved protectively in front of Ping-Pong.

"This is a turn up for the books," Wood said, a grin forming on his face. "It looks to me, Mrs Monroe, that your dear Ping-Pong has sought herself a husband."

"What?" Mrs Monroe said in alarm. "No, no! That cannot be! She was all lined up to pair with Ling-Ling after this show."

"Seems she took matters into her own hands," Wood said, his smile growing. "And she chose Brutus."

"That ugly thing? How can I have puppies sired by him!" Mrs Monroe put her hands to her face and looked beside herself.

It was then that Wood realised what he was seeing, and his smile faded.

"Wait a minute, Brutus is never out of Love's sight," the judge stepped forward, receiving a growl from Brutus, and peered into the hut. "No sign of him."

He moved back and looked around him.

"Where is Nigel?"

People started to talk and mutter among themselves, trying to recall when they had last seen the man. Clara kept very quiet, not wanting to admit to anything.

"This can only mean that Nigel Love is missing," Wood said, his eyes now turning to Clara as if he could read her mind and knew she was keeping a secret.

"It makes no sense," Melissa Painter was among the search party and spoke up. "Why would he put Brutus in there and then disappear? Love never went anywhere without his dog."

Clara was relieved they were not asking more ominous questions. Wood was looking angry now, or maybe he was scared.

"We have to find Nigel, for a start he is the only one who can handle Brutus," he said. "Who saw him last?"

There was silence from the search party, people slowly realising that none of them had seen Nigel Love in quite some time and the implications of that. Mrs Trelawny had gone very pale and was sucking in her bottom lip to prevent her from saying anything. Clara was not sure they could keep the secret of Nigel's death to themselves for much longer, but she kept her mouth shut.

The silence was at last broken by Mrs Monroe, who was

still staring at her dog.

"Princess Ping-Pong! You harlot!"

Chapter Thirteen

Consternation arose over how to remove Brutus from the hut, or more precisely, who should remove him. Princess Ping-Pong had been cajoled out of the hut with the promise of cheese and chicken, but Brutus was another matter. While he was chained to the back wall of the hut, he was at least harmless, any attempt to draw near him caused him to growl in a manner that suggested he would eat a person's leg off. No one wanted to discover just how far Brutus would go.

"Well, someone put him in there," Tommy said quietly to Clara in an aside. "Heaven knows how they managed."

That was bothering Clara too. Either the dog-napper had worn extra thick clothing, something along the lines of chainmail would have been most suitable, or they had somehow won over Brutus.

"Could still be the work of a dog thief," Park-Coombs puttered.

"Princess Ping-Pong is in season and took herself for a walk to find a husband," Clara corrected him. "She chewed through her lead and managed to get into that hut through one of the many holes around its base. Look, there is a hole there with long strands of fur trapped in the edge of the wood."

"But someone took Brutus, and that is stealing and thus we have a dog thief around," Park-Coombs said in a huff, determined to be right.

"My point is, I do not think Mr Love was murdered as a consequence of dog theft. I think the removal of Brutus was an afterthought."

Park-Coombs twitched his moustache which was a clear sign he was not impressed.

The debate over what to do with Brutus was only halted when people started to talk about Nigel Love once more and his peculiar absence. If he was not in the hut with his dog, precisely, where was he?

Clara was keeping quiet as she feared alerting people to the death of Love would cause panic and enable the killer to slip away. They were still severely short of evidence as to who might be behind the murder and could not risk any suspects disappearing before they had had the chance to question them.

"We need to get Brutus out of that hut and take a look inside," Clara said quietly. "It is possible our killer has left some clue behind in there."

Park-Coombs leaned to the side and peered into the hut again. Brutus gave him a belligerent look.

"My suggestion is we shoot the animal. It is clearly a danger to people."

"For goodness' sake, no!" cried a feminine voice behind him.

They turned to see Diana Doddington stood just a pace from them looking horrified by Park-Coombs' idea. Mrs Doddington was a woman in her late fifties who was endeavouring to appear in her late forties. She was plump in a comfortable way but dressed in a style that hid most of her extra curves. She had greying hair swept up into a bun for the sake of the show and wore a very smart sun hat that had probably cost more than the rest of her ensemble.

In her youth, Clara guessed that Mrs Doddington had been attractive, perhaps not beautiful, but certainly pretty in a humble sort of way. She still had quite a youthful face and there was an old-world charm about her that made you think of a pleasant aunt who indulged her nieces and nephews. Her wide eyes were damp with tears at the shock of hearing what the inspector had proposed.

"You must not hurt Brutus," Mrs Doddington insisted. "What will Nigel think?"

"We cannot find Nigel," Dominic Wood called out to her. He had overheard most of the conversation. His personal opinion of the situation came down in favour of Park-Coombs' plan, unless they could find Nigel Love swiftly. "He is missing and that is odd in itself."

Mrs Doddington gave him a worried look.

"Missing?"

"Well, Brutus is here, and he is not," Dominic motioned to the hut. "That, in itself, is peculiar."

Mrs Doddington wandered towards the open door of the hut. She had an unhurried, short-stepping walk that made her seem to bumble along.

"I don't think you ought to go too close," Clara said to her quickly.

Mrs Doddington gave her a knowing look.

"Brutus would not do me any harm."

She wandered without concern into the hut and more than one person gritted their teeth and expected the worst. But instead of a growl and Mrs Doddington screaming as Brutus munched into her flesh, all was calm. Clara took a pace to the side and dared to peep into the hut. Mrs Doddington was gently stroking Brutus' head and cooing to him, like he was not a vicious thug of a beast capable of doing considerably harm to anyone who came near him.

"There, there poor Bru-bru. All will be well now. I shall not let them hurt you."

"It wasn't the dog I was worried about being hurt," Park-Coombs whispered in Clara's ear.

Clara was watching the scene with some amazement. Brutus was as soft as a kitten with Mrs Doddington and nestled up against her legs, seeming to seek comfort.

"I ought to take him out of this awful hut," Mrs Doddington declared.

"Where do you intend to put him?" Dominic Wood asked her with a hint of sarcasm. "He will attack almost anything on sight. He is best off in there, until we can find Nigel."

Mrs Doddington's face fell again as she was reminded of the missing dog handler.

"Perhaps he could be put in a room in the house which is more suitable," she said, glancing towards Mrs Trelawney.

Mrs Trelawney looked as if that was the worst idea she had ever heard of, but she was being asked it by one of the judges at her dog show and she did not want to cause more problems than had already occurred.

"Ah, well, I suppose we could," she said uneasily. "There is, ah, there is an old pantry where Brutus could go. The door is quite secure, it is nice and cool in there and we could give him a bone and some water."

"And a bed," Mrs Doddington insisted. "I cannot see him shut in this hut, all alone. Nigel will be so upset when he discovers what has happened."

On that front, Clara was not concerned. Nigel Love was not going to be upset about anything ever again.

Mrs Doddington was unhitching the chain from the wall. It had been looped around an old nail and looking at it again, it was alarming how insecurely Brutus had been restrained. Had he really wanted to go for the people observing him, one swift tug would have had him flying out the door, the nail a useless restraint.

Everyone moved back as Brutus was led out of the hut, though he seemed quite mellow now and happy to trot beside Mrs Doddington.

"What is being done to find Nigel?" the judge asked as she stood before them.

A perimeter of several feet had been unconsciously formed by everyone around her. Just about the length of Brutus' chain.

"We shall check around for him," Dominic suggested, not looking sure himself what was best to do.

"He has not come into the house," Mrs Trelawney fluttered in a fashion that made Clara want to cringe. No one else seemed to notice how suspicious she sounded.

"Maybe he has felt unwell," Mrs Doddington said.

"We shall search for him," Dominic said, one eye on Brutus. "But first we ought to get back to the dog show. We have a lot of judging to do as yet, and we are already running late."

There were murmurs of agreement all around him. Funny how a missing dog had aroused a desire to help at once in most of the exhibitors, but a missing person could take care of themselves. It might have been different if the person was not Nigel Love, of course.

"He is bound to turn up," Dominic persisted. "He won't miss best of breed."

Mrs Doddington did not look impressed, but she opted not to argue. She probably knew she was not going to win. Outside of herself, no one had the slightest interest in Nigel Love and certainly did not feel charitable towards him. She bit her tongue and headed off with Mrs Trelawney to arrange a safe place for Brutus to spend the day.

"Thank goodness for that," O'Harris said, relaxing. "I thought we were going to have to reveal all."

Clara had stepped to the doorway of the hut and was taking a good look inside before she stepped over the threshold.

"The killer of Mr Love is going to be on high alert now," Park-Coombs said in his usual cynical way. "I could call in my constables, search the place, detain everyone and interview the lot."

"You hardly have enough constables to do that," Clara reminded him. "There must be over a hundred people here, at a rough guess. How many constables do you have available to you?"

Park-Coombs looked glum as he reluctantly replied.
"Ten."

"Then I think it would be impossible for them to keep everyone here. We need to take this carefully."

Clara stepped inside the crumbling building and looked around for any clue left behind by the person who brought Brutus here. She touched the nail the dog had been secured to, if secured was the word to use.

They conducted a search of the hut that revealed nothing of great interest other than a few fat spiders and several old bottles of rat poison. In the process of the search, Park-Coombs managed to kick his foot through some of the wooden planks of one wall and nearly fell over.

"Bloody place ought to be condemned!" he yelled.

They agreed at this point that they would find nothing further in the hut.

"This gets more and more bizarre," Tommy said as they left the woods and stood in the glorious sunshine once more. "Love murdered and Brutus stolen."

"My hunch is that Brutus was removed from the scene to avoid raising the alarm about the corpse too soon," Clara said. "As it is, our killer is still under the impression we have no idea Nigel is dead and his body lying in the bathroom."

"Let's keep things that way," Park-Coombs grumbled.

They were heading back towards the show rings.

"What now?" O'Harris said.

"I still have people to talk to," Clara replied. "Tommy is due in the show ring shortly and the inspector ought to use his cover to poke around."

"And me?" O'Harris asked, amused at being left out.

"You were not forgotten," Clara smiled at him. "I rather hoped you would stick close to the Trelawneys. We cannot rule out their potential involvement, it was their bathroom after all, and Mrs Trelawney's own statement indicates that no one other than them was in the house at the time of Love's death. Besides which, I think they are both falling apart and if we want to keep Love's murder a secret for as long as possible, we need someone monitoring them."

"I am on it," O'Harris chuckled.

"We need to crack on," Park-Coombs spoke. "We have only a few hours left before all these people will be going home and our killer along with them. So far, we have no motive, no witnesses, and no clues to their identity aside from some dubious footprints."

"By dividing our efforts, we shall get more done," Clara concurred. "At least we no longer have the worry of where Brutus is on our minds."

Bramble gave a small snort beside her. Clara looked down to the poodle who was trotting diligently at her side looking wearisome.

"Someone deserves an egg sandwich," Clara said, picking up Bramble. "Brave man, seeking out Princess Ping-Pong with a vicious bulldog protecting her."

"I imagine his intentions were less than chivalrous," Tommy commented drily.

"Can you imagine fluffy miniature Brutus pups?" O'Harris said, a look of horror creeping over his face. "At least they shall not be big enough to do much more than savage your ankles."

"I think we should all be just glad that Brutus had reproduction on his mind and not anything else," Clara replied. "I had anticipated seeing a small fluffy, bloody mess in that hut."

They all fell quiet at this idea. Just then, Alex and Michael appeared alongside them.

"Are you ready for the ring Tommy?" they asked.

"As ready as I shall ever be," Tommy said, starting to think he was not cut out for the show world. He had butterflies in his stomach.

"Look at Pip's paws! Where have you taken her!" Michael declared.

"We were assisting in the search for Princess Ping-Pong," Tommy answered.

"We cannot have you entering a ring looking like that," Michael insisted. "Come this way at once and let's see if we cannot smarten you both up."

"Really, I am not sure about all this showing malarkey,"

Tommy said, wanting to beat a hasty retreat. "I think we are both not cut out for it."

"Nonsense!" Alex said. "Pip is a Rosebriar! Showing is in the blood! At least let Michael run a soft cloth over her coat to bring out the shine."

Tommy was ushered away by his new friends who were determined to get the best out of him in the show ring. O'Harris was barely containing his amusement.

"Do you suppose we ought to mention he is due to be married soon to his new companions?" he said to Clara. "Just so they know where he stands."

"Oh, I am finding this all far too amusing to spoil things just yet," Clara said, watching as Alex grabbed up a comb and started to neaten Tommy's hair. "They seem very helpful, anyway."

"That is one word for it," O'Harris grinned. "Well, time to divide and conquer."

O'Harris headed for the house to see to the Trelawneys. Park-Coombs, still looking miserable about the whole thing, trotted off with Angel to do some snooping, leaving Clara alone.

She glanced at Bramble.

"Egg sandwich first, then some detective work. A promise is a promise."

Chapter Fourteen

An idea had been niggling Clara ever since she had talked with Dominic Wood and, needing a break from the stifling heat and the commotion of the show, she headed back inside the house to resolve something that was on her mind.

She picked up the telephone and asked the operator to connect her with Master's Dog Food. She was not sure anyone would be about on a weekend, but she was in luck and found herself talking to one of the sales team.

"I wanted to ask about your sponsorship of Nigel Love and Brutus the bulldog," she explained.

"I shall stop you right there," the gentleman at the end of the line replied. "We no longer sponsor Mr Love."

"You do not?" Clara asked, surprised at this news.

"A professional disagreement," the salesman explained, he was rather bored in the office on a Saturday and a natural for gossip, so he was happy to enlighten her. "Mr Love had been taking liberties. We are on the lookout for a new representative for our brand. If you happen to know anyone…?"

"When did you drop Nigel Love?" Clara asked.

The salesman made a whistling noise, the sort that

implied he was having to think really hard.

"Just before Easter," he said at last. "We were through with his tantrums and demands. I thought everyone knew about this?"

"No one knows," Clara informed him. "Love is still telling people he is associated with Master's Dog Food."

"The slimy toad!" the salesman declared. "We shall have to put out an announcement or something. We were being tactful, what with his reaction to being dropped and all."

"I imagine he blew a gasket," Clara said sympathetically.

"It was worse than that," the salesman said darkly. "He tried to hang himself."

This information stunned Clara for a moment, as Nigel had not seemed to her someone who would do such a thing.

"Anyway, we made it plain we would not take him back, even after such dramatics," the salesman said merrily. "Can I help you with anything else?"

"No, thank you," Clara answered.

She put down the phone and considered this new information.

"Well, well."

The telephone conversation had given Clara back her spark and she now went in search of Nancy Kirkpatrick, the lady who showed pointers and had had an argument with Love over his dog attacking one of hers. She was standing near to the show rings watching the Labradors being put through their paces. Clara glanced over to see Tommy anxiously waiting to one side for the puppy category. Alex and Michael had truly taken him under their wing and were providing a necessary pep talk to keep his nerves contained.

"Nancy Kirkpatrick?" Clara asked the woman who had been pointed out to her.

She was a tall, elegant thing with a face that had sadly been sculpted by an inept hand. Nose too big and with a bump in the ridge, upper teeth rather prominent, ears a little too flared out and a forehead that just went on and on. When people described someone as looking horse-like, Nancy was the sort of person they had in mind.

What Nancy lacked in looks, however, she more than compensated for in having a warm, kindly personality. For instance, she was the first person at the whole show who looked at Bramble and smiled.

"What a dear little poodle! And not clipped in that outrageous fashion you see in the rings. Why, he could be a regular little gundog!"

Clara beamed with pride at this pronouncement. Nancy had even avoided mentioning the remains of egg sandwich on Bramble's muzzle.

"Thank you," Clara said. "He is obviously not here to be shown."

"A dog's worth is not defined by how it does in the show ring," Nancy said firmly. "When I am not here, for instance, my pack is doing what they were bred for, hunting and retrieving birds."

Clara found she very much liked Nancy. She was unpretentious and realised that the show ring was just about having a bit of fun. It was not to be taken so seriously as to impede your pleasure in your dogs.

"You show English pointers?" Clara asked, looking at the pair of dogs stood by Nancy.

They were long-legged creatures with turned up noses. One was mainly white with black spots, the other mainly white with brown spots. They rather suited their owner with their gentle and unassuming natures.

"I do indeed," Nancy smiled.

"My brother is showing his young Labrador," Clara indicated Tommy with Pip.

"Ah, I see that Alex and Michael have taken charge of him," Nancy chuckled. "They are quite the pair. They will look after him and help him get the best out of his dog."

Clara hesitated, a little unsure how to bring things around to the real topic she wished to discuss. She had told Dominic Wood she was quietly investigating Nigel Love's underhand dealings and it seemed sensible to continue with this ploy rather than to start inventing another and tie herself in knots. She had to bear in mind that Nancy might at some point talk to Dominic and if she had told them different cover stories they would be bound to find out.

"I wondered if I might have a quiet word with you about Nigel Love?" she began. "I have been tasked by some concerned parties to investigate his behaviour within the show world."

"That is interesting," Nancy said, her eyes lighting up. "Precisely what are you doing?"

"Gathering information and hopefully evidence to put together into an independent report that could then be submitted to the appropriate people."

"The Kennel Club," Nancy said, getting into the conspiracy. "Get him a lifetime ban from the show ring."

"I have no hand in the outcome. I am just looking to independently gather information and provide an unbiased report."

"Well, it is about time," Nancy agreed. "I suppose you are aware Nigel has gone missing?"

"I am," Clara agreed. "I was with the search party who found the lost Pekingese with Brutus."

"Oh dear, was the poor thing dead?"

"Quite the opposite! Princess Ping-Pong happens to be in season and took a shine to Brutus, who reciprocated likewise."

Nancy laughed, it was a very horsey laugh to match her appearance, but you could not hold that against her.

"I shouldn't laugh, of course, but when a bitch has one thing on her mind, she can be quite determined. I dare say her poor owner is mortified by the outcome."

"I think that is an understatement," Clara confessed.

Nancy was solemn a moment.

"Where was Brutus?"

"In a hut, chained to a wall. He has been removed to the house now and is secure in a pantry."

"Thank goodness for that," Nancy said. "Last year I had

a nasty encounter with Brutus. Nigel had left him chained up to a railing while he went to the bathroom. Brutus saw my dog Hugo and lunged at him, breaking his collar, and flying straight at him. It was terrible. Brutus grabbed Hugo's shoulder and latched on. Several people came to my aid, but we could not prise Brutus' jaws off. We were on the cusp of doing something drastic, like smacking the beast over the head with a rock. Someone had even produced a pocketknife and was going to slit his throat. Then Nigel ran over, screamed at us all to back off and grabbed his dog. Somehow, he got Brutus to relinquish his hold and yanked him away. Poor Hugo was screaming and wailing."

Nancy shook her head, her lips pressed together as she recalled the horror.

"I had to rush him to the vets and have his shoulder stitched up. He has never been right since and the scarring means he shall never be able to step into the show ring again. When it was all over with, I presented Nigel Love with the vet bill and informed him he needed to pay it. He tried to make out that the whole situation was my fault, that I had walked Hugo too close to Brutus, or Hugo had growled at his dog first! We were at least fifteen feet away from the beast and Hugo was concentrating on the cheese I had in my hand as we were about to enter the show ring.

"Next Nigel tries to tell me that Brutus had never done anything like that before and he could not have been expected to foresee such a thing occurring, therefore he was not responsible for the bill! I was livid but there was not a great deal I could do about it."

"I thought Brutus had a reputation for being aggressive to other dogs already?"

"But not snapping his collar to fly at them," Nancy explained. "That was Nigel's excuse. Anyway, ever since he has never allowed Brutus out of his sight. I am not sure if it is to make sure Brutus harms no one, or whether he fears someone might do away with Brutus if they have the opportunity."

Clara was startled by this information.

"Someone might really kill Brutus?" she said.

Nancy gave her a knowing look.

"More than one person has considered it, trust me."

"That must worry Nigel a great deal."

"As I say, that is why I am surprised he would leave Brutus somewhere unattended. It must have been for a very important reason he left him," Nancy frowned. "Though, thinking about it, a little hut was probably pretty secure. No one would have looked for him there had not that Pekingese sought him out."

"You must be pretty angry with Nigel," Clara said.

Nancy shrugged.

"I do not see the point, quite frankly. My anger will not change anything and ultimately the only person it hurts is myself. I like to go through life with a clear heart, it is much easier than holding burdens, such as grudges and grievances. I shall never be Nigel's friend, but I do not taste bile every time I see him."

"You would appreciate him being off the show circuit, though?"

"Of course, I would be lying if I said otherwise," Nancy raised her eyebrows in amusement. "However, I am somewhat cynical about it happening. Nigel seems to have all the right people in his pocket."

Clara was starting to think she had a point. Nigel had caused so much trouble yet had avoided any sort of action being taken against him. It was the sort of situation where people would start to lose their patience and do something drastic.

"I tell you who you ought to speak to," Nancy continued, she glanced around to look for the person she was referring to. "Where is he? Ah, I believe he is there at the tea stand."

She waved her hand at an older gentleman getting a cup of tea from Mrs Trelawney. Mrs Trelawney had reached a stage of shock over the death of Nigel that she was operating in the manner of an automaton with a strained smile on her face all the time. Clara guessed O'Harris was somewhere inside with her husband, Mr Trelawney needing his attention more.

"Eliot! Would you come over?" Nancy called to the gentleman getting tea.

He was the sort of man you could imagine belonged to a club and liked to go fishing. He had a good belly on him, barely masked by his well-tailored tweed suit and one of those fluffy moustaches that put Clara in mind of the walrus in Alice in Wonderland. He waddled over, rather than walked, his feet turning out either by nature or to balance his sizeable girth.

"Eliot, you must talk to this young lady," Nancy persisted as he drew closer. "She has been sent to make enquiries about Nigel Love's behaviour and underhand dealings."

Nancy dropped her voice as she said this.

"Well, it is about time," Eliot said to Clara. "Not that I expect much. Nigel Love could get away with murder."

Clara was glad she did not cringe at his words.

"I called Eliot over because he has had some quite serious dealings with Nigel in the past, haven't you Eliot?" Nancy added.

"The man threatened me with violence," Eliot said in the tone of voice one uses when you expect this information to shock someone, and you are actually quite delighted by that. Being threatened by Nigel Love seemed to be a badge of honour to Eliot.

"That is rather serious," Clara said. "What precisely occurred?"

"He wouldn't return the Darling Cup," Eliot said this as if Clara should understand exactly what he was talking about.

Clara did not, of course.

"The Darling Cup?" she asked, looking to Nancy for help.

"It is an award given annually to a person who has achieved great success in the show ring. You have to have made up at least two dogs into a champion to even be considered. The cup is given to the winner for a year, then taken back. Each winner of the award has their name engraved on it."

"That Nigel Love won it at all, shows the level of corruption in our hobby," Eliot said with a snarl. "Why, I remember a time when people did this for fun, now it is all about sponsorship and making your dogs so famous you can charge ridiculous sums for a puppy or in stud fees. The world has gone mad."

"Nigel won the Darling Cup in 1920 and ought to have given it back so it could be handed on to the next recipient the following year," Nancy explained. "He was sent letters about it."

"I was appointed to the Darling Cup committee in 1921," Eliot added. "It became my responsibility to retrieve the cup from Nigel. Honestly, it was a fool's errand and I rather fancy I was given the task because Nigel had some staunch allies on the committee, and they knew my feelings towards him. They thought if they could give me such a difficult task to begin with, I would wish to resign. How little they know me!"

Eliot chuckled at this.

"Anyway, after the letters failed, I began hunting down Nigel at shows. He made a good effort to avoid me."

"You mean, he was being this petty over an annual award?" Clara said, seeing a new facet of Nigel that did not portray him in a good light.

"You are starting to get an idea for the man," Eliot nodded. "That is his style. I think he truly believed if he avoided me long enough, I would give up and he could keep the cup permanently. Unfortunately for him, I am as dogged in my determination as the bloodhounds I breed!"

"Eliot has a very old line of bloodhounds," Nancy added as an aside. "His dogs are quite renowned, in the right circles."

"That is correct. I have even supplied them to the police as tracking dogs. I ask myself what has Nigel Love contributed to the dog world other than breeding a squash-faced mutt with the worst temperament known to man?" Eliot was proud of his dogs and his achievements.

They were going off topic and Clara sensed that Eliot was a man who given half a chance would talk for hours about his chosen breed. She wanted to get back to the point.

"Exactly what happened concerning the Darling Cup?" she asked.

"I eventually cornered Nigel," Eliot explained. "It was not easy, but he slipped up and I stood there with Brutus growling at me and I demanded he return the cup. He became irate and things got out of hand. He threatened to set Brutus on me and I told him he could do as he liked. I was not going to back down. The situation turned nasty pretty swiftly."

Eliot paused on this cliff-hanger and Clara wanted to groan in frustration.

"Then what happened?" she asked.

"We had come to a bit of a stalemate, so I let Nigel walk away," Eliot continued. "But I kept my eye on him and followed him to the train station afterwards. We argued again, on the station platform. I told him that cup better be back with the committee by the following week, or I was coming to his house to take it in person! You should have seen his face!"

"Tell her what he said to you, so she knows the sort of man Nigel is," Nancy nudged Eliot along.

"He started accusing me of being threatening, of using intimidation," Eliot said. "I was losing my rag by then. I told him, he had not seen the worst of me yet. So, he started to talk about unleashing Brutus on me. It was all getting rather heated, and the stationmaster was coming over to see what was wrong. I informed Nigel that if he did not start behaving like a gentleman, he was going to find himself in hot water. 'Why?' he said to me. 'What can you do, you old buffoon?' That was when I lost it completely."

Eliot laughed at them jovially.

"I turned to that man and told him I would throttle the

life out of him if he did not change his ways!"

Chapter Fifteen

Inspector Park-Coombs was not the sort of man comfortable in crowds, unless he happened to be among them on an official capacity. Then he was very happy, especially if he got to arrest someone for misbehaving. Park-Coombs was a policeman through and through, it was what made him, what pleased him, what gave him purpose and never, in a million years, would he have envisioned himself walking about a dog show with an anti-social greyhound at his side. Though, to be fair to Angel, he was helping Park-Coombs avoid having to talk to nearly everyone. He was content to prowl around and listen to what people were saying. Mostly it was very dull.

"Inspector Park-Coombs?"

The inspector turned to see a woman he vaguely recalled as someone to do with the parish council. He gave her a polite nod and tipped his hat.

"Good afternoon."

"I apologise for interrupting you off-duty," the woman said, making Park-Coombs silently satisfied that his cover was working. "But it is this business with dogs going missing."

"Ah, madam, rest assured both missing dogs have been

recovered," Park-Coombs reassured her in that politely confident manner a policeman masters over time.

"I am relieved about that," the woman said. "But I am troubled that the thief might still be about, just biding his time before stealing another dog."

Park-Coombs was rather enamoured with the idea that a dog thief was behind the whole thing. He had it all worked out in his mind. The thief had come to steal Brutus, thinking he could ransom this famous dog and make a quick few quid. The problem was that Nigel Love never let Brutus leave his side and so the thief followed him, tracked his every move and when Love went to the bathroom, he seized his opportunity and socked him over the head and stole Brutus. He did not mean to kill the man, for that limited his ability to ransom Brutus – a dead man could not pay up for his dog. But the thief had been rash and hasty, probably new to the whole idea of dog theft and a bit hazy on the best way to go about it.

Park-Coombs liked this idea, even if it overlooked quite a bit of the evidence they had collected. It seemed to wrap things up neatly in his mind.

"You are quite right, madam," Park-Coombs informed the woman stood before him. "This is a troubling matter."

"No one in authority seems to be taking it seriously," the woman said, slightly petulant. "A number of us humble exhibitors are concerned and want a police presence here."

"I am afraid that would be difficult to arrange," Park-Coombs explained to the woman, thinking that if Clara was right the last thing they wanted was a lot of constables wandering around. And if he was right, then the appearance of the police would have the dog thief running for cover and they would likely never get hold of him. "Such things have to be arranged well in advance, as it means removing bobbies from the beat."

The woman pursed her lips and frowned with such intensity that Park-Coombs half expected his moustache to catch on fire. He cleared his throat, feeling something more was expected from him.

"Of course, although I am off-duty, I am still technically a policeman and I can arrest someone, if the need arises."

The woman brightened.

"That sounds much more promising," she smiled. "Now, Inspector, I am pretty certain I saw a gentleman of suspicious appearance lurking around that greenhouse over towards the far side of the gardens."

The woman pointed out a very old greenhouse. Nearly every pane of glass was broken, and it was full of weeds that had taken advantage of the neglect and a sheltered place to grow. Ironically, there remained a sturdy padlock on the door. The greenhouse stood at an angle to the main lawn, next to a brick wall that formed the boundary of an old herb garden. It potentially provided a good view of the show while enabling the onlooker to stay shielded from sight. From a policeman's perspective, it held opportunities.

"When did you last see him, madam?" Park-Coombs asked the woman.

"Just before the search for the Pekingese began," she answered. "He was keeping low and obviously trying to avoid being seen. I pointed him out to my friend, but we were both too afraid to go over and investigate."

Park-Coombs straightened his shoulders, feeling empowered now he was back in his comfort zone. He might only be acting unofficially but doing a bit of detecting was exactly what made him feel worthwhile and it was much more entertaining than wandering around pretending to be interested in showing dogs.

"We shall go over now," Park-Coombs informed the woman. "I shall not let anything happen to you or your dogs."

The woman looked delighted.

"Mrs Cobb," she introduced herself. "Whippets."

Park-Coombs was thrown by this statement.

"Pardon me?"

"I breed and show whippets," Mrs Cobb added. "My

friend Beryl breeds rat terriers."

She motioned to a woman who had been standing a short distance away. Park-Coombs nodded, failing to see how this information concerning Beryl's breed choice was relevant, but happy to receive it.

"Well, let us, and Beryl, track down this thief. I shall need you to watch while I poke about and say if you see him again."

"I shall do that. We both shall do that, we are very keen to help," Mrs Cobb said stoutly then she raced off to fetch Beryl, calling out to her friend that she had known they would find help from Park-Coombs. The inspector was just glad she did not yell out his title. Of course, most of the local residents at the show knew who he was, but the outsiders attending the show did not, and Clara had been insistent they should keep it that way.

Mrs Cobb and Beryl returned. Beryl was the sort of robust individual who politely terrorised the milkman and postman when her delivery was late and did not look as though she needed a policeman to deal with a dog thief on her behalf. Possibly it was more for the sake of the thief that Park-Coombs had been summoned. There was no knowing what a person like Beryl might do to someone she felt threatened her rat terriers.

The trio headed off towards the decaying greenhouse where Mrs Cobb was convinced she had seen someone suspicious. They were soon wading through ankle deep nettles that had grown rampant about this untended section of the garden. It was decades since anyone had tended the herbs behind the wall, if they still existed, that is. The greenhouse, closer to, looked even more decayed than Park-Coombs had imagined. It slumped at an angle against the wall and was partly propped up by an enormous compost heap that had been stacked up behind it and now seemed to have developed a life of its own.

Angel was not impressed by the nettles and came to a sudden stop, refusing to go any further among this stinging mess of greenery.

"They have very sensitive skin," Mrs Cobb sympathised when Park-Coombs tugged on the lead, hoping to get the dog to shift. "Beryl, maybe you would just stand and hold the Inspector's dog?"

Beryl tutted. Rat terriers were as robust as their owner and didn't take nettles seriously. When you had been bred to be barely bigger than the thing you were supposed to hunt, and that thing was both vicious and intent on survival, you tended to have an attitude. You certainly did not take notice of things as innocuous as stinging plants.

Mrs Cobb patted Park-Coombs' arm and motioned for him to keep moving. They had survived the nettle swamp and were now upon the greenhouse, which was riddled with brambles, growing through every broken pane and starting to encase the framework. They were only rivalled by an enthusiastic ivy vine that was making a valiant attempt to secure the roof for itself.

At first glance, it would seem as if nobody had been near the greenhouse since the last gardener had locked the door, but getting closer, Park-Coombs started to see subtle signs that someone had been spending time here.

The struts at the back of the greenhouse had rusted through and created a gap that a person could crouch down and squeeze through, if they chose. Nestled behind a barrier of brambles, it was virtually invisible. One of the old tables that had served for years as a repository for plant pots and tools remained against one wall and was deep enough that feasibly a person could climb under it for shelter. The ground inside the greenhouse had definitely been compacted by someone walking about and weeds had been pulled up to clear space, bramble stems being broken to make room. If there was any doubt that a person had made this clearing and not some sort of large animal (Park-Coombs had a vague vision of a deer sheltering in the greenhouse for a moment) it was resolved by the sight of a cigarette stub on the well trampled ground.

"Someone has certainly been here," Park-Coombs

agreed with Mrs Cobb.

The woman beamed with pride that she had been proven right. Park-Coombs wandered around to the back of the greenhouse and spotted a track had been made through the undergrowth to reach the place. The traces were faint, but there were more crushed nettles and brambles had been pulled away.

"I knew it," Mrs Cobb said keenly. "As soon as I saw the fellow, I thought to myself 'there is a dog thief!'"

Park-Coombs was debating if it was necessary to attempt to make his way into the greenhouse following the route their dog thief appeared to have taken. It was the sort of thing you usually sent a constable to do.

"Describe the man you saw to me," he said to Mrs Cobb, buying himself time.

"He was lanky and old. Grizzled I think is the appropriate word. He had long hair and looked very disreputable."

This was not an entirely helpful description. People often described suspects to the police as looking 'disreputable' but rarely, if you asked them, could they explain what they truly meant by that. To a lord at his club, anyone who was not either in a service uniform or wearing the suit of a gentleman was 'disreputable'. To the average housewife, someone disreputable tended to be a person who they did not know and was not plainly working at that moment in time. When you got to some of the lower levels of society, the nuance of what made a person disreputable in appearance became very hazy.

"How was he dressed?" Park-Coombs asked.

"Brown trousers, and a shirt and waistcoat. The waistcoat might have been a dirty green, it was hard to say."

"He would stand out a mile among the dog show crowd then?"

"Oh yes! You could not mistake him!"

Park-Coombs softly sighed to himself, seeing his dog thief theory going up in a puff of smoke. If this man so obviously stood out and looked shifty, how could he mill around the crowds and steal a dog or two? How had he gotten past Mrs Trelawney without being noticed? No, it really did not seem logical. However, a lead was a lead and if there was a stranger lurking about then Park-Coombs was not going to cross them off his potential suspect list until he had a very good reason to do so.

After contemplating the track a while longer and debating how angry his wife would be if he snagged and tore his best suit on a bramble thorn, he caved to the inevitable. He followed the track, being very careful around the brambles. The moment he so much as feared he had snagged his clothes on a thorn he froze and checked himself all over.

"Oh, Inspector, your nice suit!" Mrs Cobb said, though she seemed quite glad he was making the effort.

Park-Coombs grumbled to himself but managed to reach the back of the greenhouse without taking any serious damage. He examined the rusted frame of the greenhouse, noting that the ground within glistened where pieces of glass had been crushed into the earth. He started to wonder what he was doing. This was the sort of place that schoolboys liked to use as a den, to sneak out from school and smoke where no parent could see them. He only had Mrs Cobb's word for there being a suspicious gentleman around this place. He looked in her direction.

"You are sure you saw someone here?"

"Inspector, my eyes are marvellous, do not doubt that."

Park-Coombs sighed and crouched down to edge himself through the hole and into the greenhouse. He could see where feet had scuffed up a depression from entering and leaving this place regularly. He attempted to follow them and soon discovered he must be taller than the person who had been in here before, as he banged his head on a rusty piece of the metal frame.

"Ow!"

"Inspector, are you all right?" Mrs Cobb asked anxiously.

"Fine, fine," Park-Coombs muttered, ducking even lower to squeeze into the hole.

He found himself in a cosy little secluded spot. The sun was nice and warm here and the brambles provided a barrier from the world. The ivy was making a good effort to replace the roof and you could quite enjoy sitting in this bower and feeling a little peace from the rest of the world.

Park-Coombs picked up the stub of the cigarette. It was a roll-up and did not tell him a lot, other than that his suspect smoked. He shuffled in a bit further and looked for anything else on the ground, but there was nothing. Whoever had been here had either not hung around long enough to leave clues behind or was very tidy. Satisfied he had gained all he could and annoyed he had risked his suit for so little, Park-Coombs began to edge himself back out of the space.

He was bent double and crouched down, an incredibly awkward posture but the only one sure to get him out of the greenhouse unscathed. It was as he was backing up that he felt a sharp twinge in the base of his spine, and he froze.

"Inspector, is everything well?" Mrs Cobb called.

Park-Coombs had one hand clinging on to the frame of the greenhouse, a grimace of horror on his face. He dared to move his foot a fraction and the sharp twinge burst up and down his spine again, telling him all he needed to know.

"Inspector?"

"My back's gone!" Park-Coombs called out, cursing himself for thinking he could do something like this. "I can't move!"

"Never fear, Inspector!" Mrs Cobb shouted back. "Beryl and I are on our way."

Park-Coombs groaned to himself. The only saving grace was that Clara could not see him.

Chapter Sixteen

Captain O'Harris had only briefly departed from the side of Mr Trelawney since he had found him again. The man appeared to be on the precipice of a nervous breakdown and was acting more and more erratic with each passing hour. O'Harris had been plying him with sweet tea and trying to get him to sit down for a while. Trelawney was restless and was constantly getting up and pacing about, wandering suddenly off into another room in a mindless way and becoming distracted by the renovations to the house, until O'Harris chased him down and brought him back to the sitting room. Either the man was suffering acute shock, or he was used to taking something for his nerves and was not coping without it. O'Harris had not ruled out the possibility the man was a drug user. His mood swings and random behaviour had all the hallmarks.

He would not have left him alone for a moment, except he had to use the bathroom himself – all that tea had come to pass. With the downstairs bathroom out of action, the only one available was a small one at the top of the stairs. You had to be incredibly careful where you walked, due to some of the rotting floorboards and Mrs Trelawney had taken to escorting visitors up to it. O'Harris battled his bladder for as long as was possible then conceded he would have to use the facilities and excused himself from Trelawney, hoping that little could occur while he was absent.

On the way back down the stairs, having avoided plummeting to his death through a rotten floor, O'Harris passed the kitchen and was briefly distracted by the sound of voices. Diana Doddington was asking Mrs Trelawney about the possibility of further refreshments for the judges as the increasing heat of the day was taking its toll. Tea was not enough, they were desperate for something cold, perhaps lemonade? Mrs Trelawney was running through her options rapidly in her head and not looking confident about what she could provide on the spur of the moment. She was already flustered by the day's events; a dead man in the bathroom and his savage dog in the pantry was not conducive to a relaxing afternoon and Mrs Doddington's enquiries were causing her more consternation than might otherwise have been the case.

O'Harris had been tasked to keep the Trelawneys calm, for fear they might reveal what had occurred, but it was quite the challenge when the pair seemed ready to fall apart at the slightest mishap. He decided to step in and assist Mrs Trelawney.

"Might I help?" he enquired.

"Oh, Captain O'Harris," Mrs Trelawney squeaked as if he had just stepped out of the shadows like a ghost. If her husband's nerves were virtually shot, her own were not far behind. "Mrs Doddington is asking about cold refreshments and I never thought about them. Isn't that dreadful? I remembered the tea and sandwiches, and I even baked cake, but I never thought about some lemonade or so forth."

Diana Doddington did not look impressed at this news and folded her arms across her chest.

"I have a class of twenty-five Yorkshire Terriers to get through shortly and I am ridiculously hot after all that aggravation with the missing Pekingese. I really need a cold drink to sustain me, and I think Mr Wood would benefit from the same. The heat is terrible and gives me a headache."

She had carefully avoiding mentioning that part of the 'aggravation' in the missing dog search had been due to the discovery of Brutus and the realisation that Nigel Love was absent. Brutus had gone to the pantry with his usual grace, which meant he had snarled and lunged at nearly every dog he went past. Mrs Doddington had remarked that he seemed more agitated than usual and must be worrying about his master.

"Let me look around, Mrs Trelawney, and maybe I can find something," O'Harris offered the woman, who looked at him with great relief.

"Oh yes, do!" she said. "Brutus is safely in the cellar pantry. You can look in any of the kitchen pantries without fear."

O'Harris went about his task, while Mrs Doddington continued to make a fuss.

"I have never known weather like it, so very hot and sticky. Not like the nice summers I knew as a girl. There was always a pleasant breeze to cool you then. I have agreed with Mr Wood that we shall delay the pug class until later, it is too hot for the little things in that ring. The tent makes it worse, holds all the hot air in."

"Oh dear," Mrs Trelawney said, on the verge of tears as all her arrangements for the dog show were ripped to shreds. "We thought it would be shady and… and better if it rained."

"Well, yes, that would be logical," Mrs Doddington graciously gave her that. "But it has not rained, has it? And I cannot help but think about Nigel. Where is he? In this heat he must be frantic about Brutus. Bulldogs are not dogs that cope with being hot."

Mrs Trelawney gave a strange little laugh; it was more like she was gagging on something. O'Harris knew when someone was on the verge of becoming hysterical and quickly emerged from the pantry.

"I found lemons," he said. "What we can do is fill a jug with water and slice some lemon into it for a little flavour. If we had some mint, it would be even better."

"I have a little pot of mint. I'll pick some leaves," Mrs Trelawney said, relieved to be able to get away for a moment.

"It is not ideal," Mrs Doddington remarked in a surly manner to O'Harris. "Fancy only being able to offer water to the judges other than tea."

"This is all very new to the Trelawneys," O'Harris said, finding the woman's tone tiresome. "I have no doubt they shall learn from this for future shows."

Diana Doddington gave him a look that suggested she was not considering coming back here for another show, or rather, she could not be dragged back by wild horses.

"Nigel will write a report about all this," she informed O'Harris. "He always does, and it shall be submitted to the Kennel Club and if he disapproves of a venue, or finds the organisation lacking, then they shall not be allowed to have another show under the Kennel Club's auspices."

"That is rather unkind," O'Harris countered. "The Trelawneys have really tried and only a few minor things are amiss."

He did not add, though it would have satisfied him to do so, that Nigel would not be writing any reports ever again and Mrs Doddington's smug attitude was utterly inappropriate.

"I am not happy that no one is searching for Nigel either," Diana added as Mrs Trelawney returned with mint leaves and a large glass jug she had filled with water from the tap. She took the lemons from O'Harris and started cutting them up.

"We are not sure he is missing," O'Harris countered casually.

He hoped he was the only one who noticed Mrs Trelawney flinch at his words.

"Well, it seems remarkable he is nowhere to be found," Mrs Doddington snorted. "However, I have faith he shall not miss the best of breed class with Brutus. He would be beside himself if that dreadful Miss Painter won with her ghastly dog simply because he was a no show."

O'Harris bit his tongue. It was time they got off this topic.

"There was also some cream and strawberries in the pantry," he said to Mrs Trelawney who had her back to him as she sliced lemons. Her hands were trembling so hard it was taking considerable enough to master the job.

"I bought the strawberries to decorate the cakes. I rather overestimated how many I needed," she said weakly, as if O'Harris was berating her.

"What I was thinking was if you whipped up the cream and served it with the strawberries it would be a very pleasurable and cooling refreshment for the judges," he added, hoping she would understand he was not getting at her.

Mrs Trelawney's shoulders sagged as she relaxed.

"What a splendid...d idea," she said. "I shall do that at once."

She had finally managed to slice up a lemon and pop pieces into the jug of water. This she handed to Mrs Doddington.

"Would you care for the strawberries at once? Why, I have some shortbread biscuits too to go with them. Wouldn't that be nice?" Mrs Trelawney's sudden enthusiasm and hyperactivity was on a par with that of her husband. O'Harris was desperate to get Diana Doddington out of the kitchen.

"Strawberries and cream," Mrs Doddington said, and she appeared to lick her lips. "Yes, that would be pleasant and would help restore my impression of this sorry affair."

She strode off with the jug of water, not so much as a word of thanks on offer to Mrs Trelawney who she had nearly harangued into a dead faint.

"I thought she would never go," Mrs Trelawney said weakly.

O'Harris helped her into a chair at the kitchen table,

acutely aware that he had left her husband alone for a lot longer than he had intended.

"Take a moment for yourself," he told her. "Then start on those strawberries. Have you had a cup of tea recently?"

"Please, please, do not fuss," Mrs Trelawney waved him away.

O'Harris backed off.

"Just give yourself a moment," he said, then he darted off to check on Mr Trelawney, worried that the man might have done something stupid while he was gone.

He was used to dealing with people with psychiatric disorders, but he generally had the back-up of a large party of staff and doctors. Also, he was not usually trying to keep a murder quiet at the same time.

Mr Trelawney was not in the sitting room where O'Harris had left him. This was far from surprising. O'Harris gave a soft sigh and then hurried across the hall to the dining room, which had been one of the places Trelawney had taken to wandering off to. O'Harris understood the need to remain active to cope with a difficult situation. Trelawney's coping strategy was to wander into the dining room, pick up a scraper and start to remove strips of wallpaper from the walls. O'Harris might have even left him to it, had it not seemed so out of place when he was meant to be running a dog show, and also the way he was attacking the walls was liable to result in an injury at some point. O'Harris did not want to deal with either people asking questions about their host's bizarre behaviour, or a severed thumb.

When Trelawney was not in the dining room, O'Harris was brought up short and looked around in confusion. Now where had he gone?

O'Harris retraced his steps back to the sitting room, scratching his head and desperately hoping Trelawney had not opted to go wandering outside. In his dazed and agitated state there was no knowing what might occur. O'Harris concluded he would just have to check all the rooms in the house and endeavour not to alert Mrs

Trelawney to the fact her husband was missing. That was the last thing he needed her to know. He was about to head through the double doors to the next room — an unfurnished secondary sitting room — when he heard a faint groan. It seemed to come from his right and he instinctively looked behind the nearest sofa in case Trelawney was slumped behind it. When he realised how foolish this was, he started to pay better attention. The groan came again, faintly.

O'Harris flicked his eyes up to one of the doors of the sitting room. This one led into the corridor closest to the bathroom. O'Harris had a sudden thought that Trelawney had, for some unknown reason, gone to look at the body of Mr Love.

He almost sprang over the sofa in his haste to get to the door and into the corridor. He jumped through it just as another groan issued from the lips of Mr Trelawney, who was lying propped up against a wall, one hand to his head.

"Did you faint?" O'Harris ran to him.

The corridor was an internal one and there was not a great deal of natural light to look at the downed man in. O'Harris hastily searched for a light switch and hoped the electrics had been connected in this part of the house. The corridor was sharply illuminated, and Mr Trelawney winced at the sudden brightness.

"What happened?" O'Harris asked again.

Mr Trelawney pulled his hand around from his head.

"Someone hit me," he said, struggling with disbelief at what had occurred.

There was blood on his fingers.

"Lean forward a fraction," O'Harris told him gently and the man obeyed.

There was a wet patch on the back of his head and a red stain now marred the new wallpaper of the corridor where Mr Trelawney had leaned against it. O'Harris opted not to mention that.

"What were you doing in this corridor?" he asked instead.

"I thought I heard something," Trelawney replied. "It was like someone very carefully depressing the handle of a door."

O'Harris glanced behind him. Opposite where Trelawney was sitting was the downstairs bathroom.

"What happened next?" O'Harris asked.

"I came out here and no one was around. I felt a little bit nervous if I am honest. The sound had been so eerie, and I am really all in pieces right now," Trelawney touched his head wound again and cringed. "I tried the bathroom door to see if it was still locked, which it was. I thought that maybe Nigel Love was actually not dead and needed help."

"That is not possible," O'Harris said quietly.

"But we had not summoned a doctor, had we?" Trelawney added plaintively. "Anyway, I thought I had the key for the bathroom. I forgot my wife had it. I felt in my pocket and pulled out another key, it was the one for the drinks cabinet I just bought. I keep it locked because of the workmen being in and out..."

Trelawney trailed off, a little sheepish that he had distrusted his workmen so.

"Keep going," O'Harris nudged him, ignoring the comment.

"Well, my hands were shaky, I was so agitated, and I fumbled the key as I took it out of my pocket and dropped it to the floor. I realised at once it was the wrong key and bent down to retrieve it. That was when there was this sharp pain at the back of my skull. I went right out and awoke a moment ago when you appeared."

Mr Trelawney stared at the blood on his fingers, a look of horror crossing his face.

"Captain O'Harris, did someone just try to kill me?"

Chapter Seventeen

"I mean, when he said the words it was just a turn of phrase," Clara explained to Tommy as they discussed her interview with Nancy Kirkpatrick and Eliot.

Tommy had survived the show ring and Pip had placed a respectable fourth in the puppy class. Alex and Michael had been elated and informed Tommy he was a natural for showing a dog off to its best potential. Tommy was just glad it was over and done with, he could not recall a time he had been so nervous about something so inconsequential. He was still sweating several minutes after leaving the ring. He drew out his handkerchief and mopped his brow.

His sister was frowning, starting to doubt her abilities over this case. She had so many motives for killing Nigel Love that she was feeling quite unable to untangle them all.

"You don't kill a man because he won't return an old trophy," Clara added.

"People can become petty over things. Get caught up in the moment," Tommy pointed out.

"But if that was Eliot, surely he would not have spoken so freely about threatening Nigel?" Clara felt very confused, whoever the killer was, they were playing a very cunning game and letting nothing slip. "I have yet to find someone who I truly believe capable of this crime. There is certainly plenty of hate towards Nigel, but actual intention to cause him harm is another matter."

Clara glanced around the show.

"And I seem to have lost track of Park-Coombs."

"Never mind," Tommy told her. "Something will come up."

"Well, we have Brutus, at least," Clara sighed. "Though I have yet to work out if that means anything or not."

"I need a cup of tea," Tommy said. "Have you anyone else to talk to?"

"Alan Kennedy," Clara replied. "He has pugs."

"That sounds like a disease. Like mumps."

Tommy was trying to cheer her up with bad humour, she appreciated the effort and smiled at him.

"The pug class has been postponed until later due to the heat," Tommy added. "We have time for a cup of tea before you track down your last potential suspect."

"I do not feel hopeful that Mr Kennedy will provide my solution, but I shall be diligent and interview him. But yes, tea first."

They headed over to the refreshment table, which was temporarily unmanned.

"The Trelawneys could have done with some help running this," Clara said, thinking that here were two very impractical people, attempting to do very practical things. Saving Mulberry Hall was their dream, but did they have the knowledge and skills to pull it off? She did not care to wonder.

"If Annie was here, she would have thrown herself into things," Tommy said, noting that someone had carelessly left the mesh fly screen off the cucumber sandwiches and they were now host to several insects. "I have half a mind to telephone her and beg her assistance. At least it would get her away from that damn wedding cake."

Tommy flicked his fingers at the flies, causing them to

137

dart in crazed circles around his hand, before promptly landing back on the sandwiches.

"I think she is best not disturbed," Clara said. She was fairly certain Annie would not consider attending a dog show a good distraction, rather she would resent being called away from her masterpiece and would become even more fraught.

Tommy was just in the process of helping himself to tea from the urn, when O'Harris appeared at the top of the terrace. He hurried down the steps to Clara, checking around him to see who was near. He caught her arm and moved her to one side.

"Mr Trelawney has been attacked."

Clara closed her eyes for a moment, wondering how events could get any more complicated that day.

"Is he all right?" she asked.

"Shaken up and got a nasty headache – they clobbered him on the head – but apart from that he seems sound. I thought I better fetch you."

Tommy appeared with his cup of tea. The urn had not been refreshed recently and the tea was brewed and full of leaves.

"What's the matter?" he asked.

"Best you come see," O'Harris said. "I was going to fetch Park-Coombs too, but I cannot seem to find him."

"He has quite disappeared," Clara remarked, feeling that was rather odd. The inspector was not one to abandon a case, even when he was not officially there to investigate it. "Perhaps he has a lead."

"We can only hope," Tommy said. "Well, O'Harris, let's see poor Trelawney."

O'Harris led them up the stairs and through the kitchen. He pressed a finger to his lips to indicate to them that he had not said a word to Mrs Trelawney, who was busy whipping cream for the strawberries. She was so intent in her work she did not notice them. When they were safely through the kitchen and in the corridor O'Harris spoke.

"I thought it best not to say anything to her yet. She is only just holding together."

"The Trelawneys are really having a bad day," Clara said with sympathy. "You would have thought a dog show would be pretty harmless, wouldn't you? But anything that involves people getting together has the potential for rifts and arguments."

"What you are saying is that people can't just enjoy a nice day out, they have to find something to complain about," Tommy grinned at her.

"Some people," Clara replied. "Mrs Monroe did not warn me this business was so cutthroat."

"All you have to do is think that Mrs Monroe involves herself in dog shows to get an idea of what it must be like!" Tommy replied.

Clara gave this some thought.

"True," she agreed reluctantly.

O'Harris was leading them into the sitting room, but via the door in the corridor, not through the main hall. They had to walk past the locked bathroom in the process and O'Harris caused them to stop just there.

"I found Trelawney sitting against that wall," O'Harris said, pointing out the bloodstain. "According to him he heard a sound, came to investigate and while attempting to locate the key for the bathroom, which he did not have, he was hit from behind."

"He saw no one?" Clara asked.

"Not that he can remember," O'Harris shrugged. "He thought he had the bathroom key in his pocket. Turned out it was the key for the drinks cabinet. As he pulled it out of his pocket, he dropped it and as he was bending to pick it up, someone hit him."

Clara surveyed the stain on the wall and then looked at the bathroom door.

"Why was he trying to get into the bathroom?"

"He had a notion that the noise had come from there," O'Harris answered. "Rather fancied that maybe Nigel Love was not as dead as we thought. He is rather desperate right now and not thinking straight. Discovering Nigel was alive would have solved a lot."

Clara understood that. Shock made people irrational and when a man was murdered in your bathroom, you were liable to wish for the evidence before your eyes to be wrong.

"He is through here," O'Harris added and led them into the sitting room.

Trelawney, for once, had not wandered off and was resting on a long sofa with a cushion behind his head. He looked very pale and was clasping a glass of water O'Harris had fetched for him.

"I have been trying to find him some aspirin," O'Harris said. "But Trelawney is not sure if there is any in the house."

Trelawney groaned weakly. Clara came around the sofa so she could see him better.

"How are you feeling Mr Trelawney?" she asked, lifting his hand to check his pulse. "I was a nurse in the war, so I know a lot about head injuries."

Trelawney gave her a grateful look.

"It throbs at the back and I feel rather sick. Also, nothing seems quite real at the moment, as if I am stuck in a terrible dream."

"That is the shock," Clara reassured him. "Can I look at your head?"

Trelawney winced as he leaned forward to let her look. The wound was wide and had bled well, as head wounds were prone to doing, however it was not deep, which was good. The size and shape of the blow suggested that someone had used a flat heavy object to hit Trelawney with, something like a cricket bat.

"I think someone was trying to kill me," Trelawney whimpered.

"I think someone wanted to get into the bathroom and you stumbled upon them," Clara corrected him.

"But I saw no one!" Trelawney said desperately. "Why would they hit me?"

Clara ran the scenario through her mind again, working out how it all occurred and then smiled to herself.

"Precisely what did you hear before you went to investigate, Mr Trelawney?"

Trelawney went to touch his head wound; Clara gently nudged his hand away.

"I thought I heard someone depressing the handle of a door. It was the rattling sound when someone goes to open a door that is locked. I know it was irrational, but at the time I started to think it was Love trying to get out of the bathroom."

Clara nodded her head.

"I see how this played out. Someone came to the bathroom, tried the door, and found it locked. They heard you approaching to investigate and slipped away, perhaps into another room. When they saw you reaching for a key for the bathroom and then drop it, they saw their chance. They wanted that key and so they struck you over the head. The key is missing, is it not?"

Trelawney looked at her in amazement.

"I don't know. I never had the chance to look for it," he searched his pockets just to be sure.

"I will check the corridor," O'Harris said, vanishing out the door. He was not gone long. "There is no key."

"Then, they took the key?" Trelawney gasped. "All they wanted was that? Thank heavens they were not intending to kill me!"

"Whoever took it, is going to be disappointed when they try it in the lock," Tommy said.

"The real question is why were they so desperate to get into the bathroom?" Clara glanced at Trelawney, remembering she had a patient. "You shall be fine, Mr Trelawney. It is a nasty blow, but not deep. You will have a headache for a while, but otherwise there should be no lasting damage."

Trelawny relaxed.

"Thank goodness!" he groaned.

Clara went over to Tommy and O'Harris. She spoke

softly to him.

"I think we have to assume the person who wanted to get into that bathroom was the killer. The way they attacked Trelawney in exactly the same way they attacked Love does not strike me as a coincidence."

"Which brings us back to your question about why they wanted to get in," Tommy nodded. "We have to assume it was not to check on the dead man."

"They were taking a big risk coming back to the crime scene," Clara said thoughtfully. "My hunch is that they were looking for something, something they had dropped perhaps, or something they suddenly thought could cause them to be identified as the person responsible."

"We did not notice anything," O'Harris said, his brow furrowing.

"Perhaps because we were not looking in the right place?" Clara suggested. "Or maybe because the killer is overly cautious, and they have not actually left a clue behind."

"They are being paranoid," Tommy snorted. "Wait, with the bathroom locked, surely that means they now know that we aware there has been a murder?"

They all paused at this thought.

"All they know is that the Trelawneys are aware of the murder and have locked the bathroom as a result," Clara said at last. "We need to act swiftly, however, for time is running out. Let's search the bathroom and see if there is something we have missed."

Clara had the key for the bathroom and was able to let them in. They carefully stepped around the corpse and surveyed the room.

"At least I can fetch some aspirin for Trelawney," O'Harris said, opening a medicine cabinet and noting there were some of the tablets in a box inside.

The bloody hammer was still sitting in the sink, it seemed to be accusing the universe by its bloodstained appearance.

"I was thinking," Tommy said aloud, "supposing the

killer never meant to kill Love, just to knock him out like they knocked out Trelawney. Maybe that is why they were much more careful about their attack on him?"

"I don't think we can speculate on that with the evidence we have," Clara answered him. "It could be they did want Love dead which is why they hit him so hard. It might not have been an accident."

The room was not revealing anything obvious. There were not a lot of places for something to become hidden in the room, no handy corners, or rugs to slip under.

Clara crouched down beside Love, taking a closer look at him. After a moment, she carefully opened his hands in case he was clasping something in them. They were empty.

"Could you help me lift the body?" Clara asked.

O'Harris joined her and gingerly they rolled the heavy-set man onto his side. He was starting to stiffen, and it was not a pleasant experience. Tommy, who was behind the corpse, helped to hold him up as Clara examined the space beneath him.

"What is this?" Clara picked up a small object from the floor.

It was a silver brooch with an additional clasp where something could be hung from it.

"Alex showed me one of those," Tommy said. "It is a special brooch for holding your ring number. People have them made in the shape of their chosen breed."

"This one is in the shape of a bulldog," Clara said. "Perhaps it is Love's?"

They lifted the jacket lapel of the corpse, which was hanging down and obscuring anything that might be pinned to it. There was a similar brooch on the lapel, still bearing the ring number Love had had in the ring.

"That solves it," Tommy concluded. "The killer realised they had dropped this brooch and came to retrieve it, knowing it would point directly at them."

"It belongs to someone who shows bulldogs," O'Harris mused. "There have to be about twenty such exhibitors here today. It barely narrows things down."

"But only one has a serious grudge against Love," Clara reminded him. "And she would know how to handle Brutus."

Clara stared at the brooch for a moment. It was a rather crude rendition of a bulldog; it made the dog uglier than it already was.

"It looks like Melissa Painter has some explaining to do."

Chapter Eighteen

Mrs Cobb and Beryl had sallied forth through the brambles and rescued the inspector from his predicament. This had been done under much protest, squeaks of pain as his back spasmed and general moaning and groaning about life, his ageing body and why he had ever thought to do something so foolish in the first place. It took some effort, but they managed to extract him from the greenhouse and lay him flat on his back on the ground outside. There were thorns sticking into Park-Coombs' flesh and a sensation of dampness, but it was a lot better than being stuck in a crouch. He sighed with relief as his back relaxed.

"Well, Inspector, what now?" Mrs Cobb asked him, her hands propped on her hips, looking like some elderly conquering Amazon ready for war. "We have to find the dog thief!"

Park-Coombs gave another groan at this information. He was quite prepared to spend the rest of the day lying here, if it meant his back didn't play up.

Beryl had been making her own survey of the area, while Park-Coombs was investigating the greenhouse, she now had an idea.

"What if we retreat to that walled garden and wait for

our thief to return? I reckon this is his hideout."

Beryl said this in a knowing way that suggested she had read one too many penny thrillers.

"Good idea, Beryl," Mrs Cobb agreed. "We shall be ready for him when he returns. Come on Inspector, no time to lie around."

Park-Coombs whimpered as each of the women grabbed one of his arms and levered him upright. He endeavoured to rise without bending his back at all, which was not really successful. Once upright, the pain eased to a dull ache and he pressed a hand into the sore spot right at the base of his spine.

"Walking will do you good," Mrs Cobb instructed him.

Had the inspector been less of a gentleman and with a reputation as a respectable police official, he would have said some choice words about her notions of what she thought good for him.

They ambled towards the overgrown entrance to the walled garden. Beryl had resorted to carrying Angel who had once again protested walking through thorns and briars. The dog lolled its head on her shoulder. They pushed through the undergrowth and found themselves in a secluded secret garden.

Someone had been here too, for though the brambles had been allowed to mask the gateway, once inside the weeds had been hacked back to open up the space. The old herb beds had been tenderly cared for and flourished with delicate leaves and flowers in multicoloured hues. A stone bench had been kept clear of encroaching plant life and was set in a perfect pool of sunlight.

Mrs Cobb assisted Park-Coombs to sit on the bench.

"Well," she said, because even she could see this was not the work of an hour or so in preparation to steal dogs.

Angel was now restored to the ground and wandered off to daintily sniff the herb garden. Park-Coombs gazed around the private space, trying to get a feel for the person who had been here. He noticed the remains of a cigarette butt on the ground near his foot. The only thing out of kilter in this wondrous place.

"This is the same as the one I spotted in the greenhouse," he said, bending over to pick up the stub and instantly regretting his actions. He gave a sharp intake of breath and pressed a hand hard into his spine.

Mrs Cobb took the stub from his hand and examined it in an authoritative way.

"A roll-up is the mark of a working-class man," she said with conviction. "A gentleman buys his cigarettes. Here is further evidence of our dog thief."

She passed the butt to Beryl.

"He must have discovered this little garden and realised it was the perfect spot to plot his terrible crimes from," Mrs Cobb continued. "Why, from the gateway you can see across the whole show. It makes my blood boil to think that man was here, deciding which dogs to steal."

Beryl crushed the cigarette stub between her fingers.

"He shall not get ours!" she said in a voice that spoke of terrible consequences for the thief if they even attempted it.

Park-Coombs was having mild pangs of doubt about his dog thief theory, now they had discovered this secret garden that was clearly being tenderly cared for by someone, but he was in too much pain to listen to his doubts. It was much easier to follow along with Mrs Cobb and Beryl's train of thought.

"The fiend cannot be far," Mrs Cobb declared. "We shall stick to our plan and ambush them when they return."

Beryl nodded her agreement. Park-Coombs just listened sombrely, worrying about his poor back and thinking that his wife was going to give him an earful when he got home for throwing it out in the first place.

"We should set a trap!" Beryl said with excitement.

Park-Coombs' attention was returned to them, despite himself.

"A trap?" he said unhappily.

"What would lure a thief out better than a lost dog that could be easily stolen!" Beryl announced and she gestured in the direction of Angel, who had found a cosy spot in the sun to lie down and bake in.

Park-Coombs grimaced; his desk sergeant would never forgive him if he used the greyhound as bait and then it was actually stolen.

"Now, now, let us consider this carefully…" he said, but the ladies were away and were not listening to him.

"We shall set Angel up outside this garden, as if he has just wandered over here. The thief will not be able to resist!" said Mrs Cobb.

"And we shall catch them red-handed!" Beryl clapped her hands in delight. "There you are, Inspector, we have wrapped up your case for you! We should be given a medal or something."

"We are quite the team," Mrs Cobb remarked to her friend. "Now, Inspector, there is no need for you to move. We shall prepare our trap while you rest your back."

Inspector Park-Coombs could not have this.

"I have to protest ladies. If anything were to happen to Angel…"

"Nothing will happen, we shall be watching the whole time," Beryl told him firmly.

"I really cannot allow…"

"Inspector, you are not thinking straight due to the pain," Mrs Cobb told him sternly. "We shall not be long."

With that she headed over to collect Angel and there was nothing the inspector could do but watch bleakly as the dog was retrieved and the ladies headed out of the garden to set their trap.

"Look, I am a police officer, you have to listen to me!" he said as the ladies marched off.

They didn't listen, of course.

"Wait a minute!" Park-Coombs yelled. "Oh, for crying out loud! Clara, where are you when I need you?"

The ladies squeezed back out through the briars and vanished from sight. Park-Coombs, utterly unable to move, whimpered to himself. There was no one he could summon for help and he was starting to realise what a fool he had made of himself. Clara would be most amused when she heard about this, though she would surely also be sympathetic.

He thought again about what his desk sergeant would say if Angel were stolen, and the whimper grew close to a wail. He had promised the man, hand on heart, no harm would come to that dog.

"Thank goodness they are gone."

The voice from behind him nearly gave Park-Coombs a heart attack. As it was, he startled and his back jarred painfully.

"Ow, ow ow!"

"Sorry about that," a man appeared beside him, he was wearing the well-worn corded trousers and waistcoat of a labourer, the fabric worn to a sheen in places from use. He was about sixty, though he had reached that stage of existence when it was hard to tell his precise age other than to know he was old. He was tanned brown like a nut from working outside all the time.

"Where did you come from?" Park-Coombs asked in alarm, thinking the man had apparently materialised out of thin air.

"From that gateway," the man pointed behind Park-Coombs and to the left.

The inspector cautiously swivelled around and saw a robust ivy bush that had claimed the corner of the walled garden with long tendrils of heart shaped leaves. There was no sign of a gateway. The older man could see Park-Coombs' confusion and so wandered over to the ivy and dragged back several tendrils, revealing an old archway leading through to a second walled garden. Park-Coombs relaxed now it was apparent he was not dealing with a ghost or someone who could walk through solid walls.

The old man nodded at him.

"My name is Fred Bottle," he introduced himself and came to sit beside Park-Coombs. "This is my garden."

"Your garden?" Park-Coombs asked him.

Fred nodded his head again.

"I was under the impression it was the Trelawneys' garden," the inspector persisted.

Fred Bottle took a folded wallet from his pocket and opened it to reveal spindly tobacco strands and papers for rolling cigarettes. He began the complex procedure of creating a roll-up to his precise and exacting standards. Park-Coombs waited. He knew men who rolled their own and the process was not one you should interrupt. It was rather like a ritual for them.

Fred ran his tongue along the edge of the thin cigarette paper and rolled it into a tight straw.

"The Trelawneys don't know this place exists," Fred shrugged when all this was done, and he was pulling matches from his pocket to light his cigarette. He offered the tobacco wallet to Park-Coombs, who politely refused. He had never been a man for roll-ups. "I have been tending this garden and all its herbs and little flowers since I was fifteen. I'm seventy-five now."

"Ah, you must have been the gardener who worked for Mr Trelawney's uncle," Park-Coombs realised.

"That's right," Fred agreed with that same gentle head nod. "Back when I started there were ten of us and we looked after the whole grounds. But the years moved on and things were not so good and gradually one after another the gardeners were let go until it was just me left. Still, I made a good job of things and kept the lawn up and the flowerbeds and this garden. It has been hard work, but I can't let the place go to ruin."

"Wait a minute," Park-Coombs interrupted him. "I thought I was told the last gardener here retired several years ago and was never replaced."

"Oh, I retired officially," Fred agreed. "But I never left. The place needed tending and, to be truthful, I did not want to leave."

Fred took a deep draw on his cigarette and then blew out smoke.

"I kept up the garden, just without the pay. The old squire could not afford to pay me. You have seen the state of the house inside?"

"I have. I am somewhat amazed it is still standing."

Fred smirked.

"Hangs on by a thread that place does. Still, the Trelawneys are making a good go of things."

"Then it was you who Mrs Cobb saw about the greenhouse?" Park-Coombs said.

"I go there for a little nap at dinnertime," Fred explained. "It is nice and warm and the butterflies dance about it. This dog show affair does not bother me. I just carry on with what I am doing."

"And no one has noticed that the garden never gets truly overgrown?"

"The old squire turned a blind eye," Fred chuckled. "He knew what I was about, but he opted not to notice. The new folks, well, I dare say they have not had the time to think about it too hard. They have been so busy."

"But you don't mind being here and working hard for nothing?"

"It isn't work, not really," Fred grinned. "I love this place. I love the trees, the flowers, the very air. It would be more of a burden to me to be expelled from this place."

Park-Coombs rather understood. He could not imagine stopping being a police detective and leaving the station, though one day in the future he would have to retire. He did not like to think about it, as he had no idea what he would do with himself without his work.

"Were you aware a bulldog had been hidden in your old shed?" Park-Coombs asked Fred.

"The one over in the woods?" Fred responded. "I don't use that anymore. The roof leaks. I built myself another shed in the walled garden beyond here. It is very private."

"I can see that," Park-Coombs replied. "I don't suppose you have seen anything suspicious around here lately?"

"What sort of suspicious thing?"

Park-Coombs hesitated. His dog thief notion was becoming less and less plausible.

"Perhaps someone lurking about?"

"Only you," Fred answered.

"And nothing at the house?"

Fred frowned and Park-Coombs was sure he knew something, but right at that moment Mrs Cobb and Beryl reappeared.

"There he is! Inspector arrest that man!" shouted Mrs Cobb.

Fred jumped to his feet more spryly than it would have been thought a man in his seventies would be able to and legged it back through his secret gateway. Beryl was in hot pursuit.

"Stop! Thief!"

"He is the gardener!" Park-Coombs yelled at her as she dashed past.

Beryl was scrabbling at the ivy, trying to find the gateway when his words hit her. She stopped.

"What?"

"He is the old gardener!" Park-Coombs informed her. "Not a dog thief!"

Beryl let go of the ivy and walked sheepishly back towards the inspector. Mrs Cobb drew nearer with Angel in tow.

"I don't believe it," she said.

"I do," Park-Coombs said plainly. "You saw him around dinnertime, yes?"

Mrs Cobb considered for a moment and then nodded.

"Yes."

"That was when the fellow was having his regular nap in the greenhouse. He tends the gardens just like in the old days and he does not steal dogs."

Park-Coombs' fierce tone impressed on the ladies the reality of his statement. They were both looking abashed now.

"Oh," said Mrs Cobb. "Well, that does explain why I thought I saw him carrying a spade."

Park-Coombs threw up his hands.

"Had you told me that sooner we might not have been in this pickle!" he cried. "I might not have hurt my back!"

"I did not know there was a gardener here," Mrs Cobb said stoutly. "In any case, he is gone now. No harm done."

Park-Coombs wanted to snap at her, say there was a lot of harm done where his back was concerned. More to the point, he was sure Fred Bottle had seen something that troubled him, and he was sure he had been about to say something when the ladies waltzed in. However, since Park-Coombs could not mention the murder, all he actually did was glare at her.

"Thank you very much ladies. Thank you very much!"

Chapter Nineteen

They had regrouped in the drawing room. Trelawney was still looking bewildered, clasping at his split skull, and almost alarmingly spaced out. Clara held the fallen brooch in her hand. Melissa Painter had a lot of explaining to do.

"I am going after Miss Painter. Perhaps one of you two could try to find Park-Coombs?" she said.

"I think I ought to stay with Trelawney," O'Harris said. "He really isn't coping well."

They all looked at the unfortunate owner of Mulberry Hall. He had his eyes shut and there was a grimace on his lips as if he were attempting to concentrate very hard on alleviating his own pain. Clara motioned for her brother and the captain to come towards her, and they huddled into a conspiratorial circle.

"We have not discussed the possibility of the Trelawneys' involvement in all this," she whispered to them.

O'Harris glanced at the injured man, frowning in consternation.

"He doesn't seem the sort."

"Few murderers do and if it was an accident, a spur of the moment thing, well, that makes a difference too. He might have thought he was attacking a burglar or something," Clara replied.

"He is a tad unstable," Tommy added thoughtfully. "The type of person to act without thinking."

O'Harris was not convinced. It was not so much that he thought the man innocent or even that he liked him too much to be able to consider him a killer. It was rather that he just seemed incapable of such violence.

"In any case, he didn't hit himself over the head and then lose the drinks cabinet key," he pointed out.

That was a fair comment.

"He might know more than he is letting on," Clara suggested. "But you are right, he could not have struck himself over the head like that."

"And Mrs Trelawney could not have done it as she was in the kitchen with Mrs Doddington," Tommy interjected. "I suppose that rules out the judge too."

"She was not really a suspect anyway," O'Harris shrugged. "Seeing as she is about the only person around here who liked Nigel Love."

"I best speak to Miss Painter," Clara said, not prepared yet to commit herself to who might or might not have been able to kill Nigel Love. "I really would like to know where the Inspector has got to."

"Presumably he is following his own leads," Tommy replied. "He cannot be far. I shall find him and point him in your direction."

Tommy paused for a second.

"Could I leave Bramble and Pip with you O'Harris? They are dog tired, excuse the pun."

Captain O'Harris was happy to have the company of the two dogs as he remained to tend to his patient. They would provide a welcome breath of sanity into what was rapidly turning into a madhouse.

Clara and Tommy headed outside, passing Mrs Trelawney on the way. She seemed to have developed a sudden obsession with cheese sandwiches and was making enough to feed an army.

"Cannot have people starving to death," she said as they walked past, with a strange, strangled laugh.

Clara exchanged a smile with her.

"When did you last have something to eat?" she said.

"Oh, I never have luncheon. On principle," Mrs Trelawney was buttering bread as if she were a clockwork machine someone had overwound.

"Perhaps today ought to be an exception?" Clara suggested. "At least have a cup of tea?"

"Tea!" Mrs Trelawney squawked, a look of panic on her face. "The urn must need refilling by now! It shall be terribly brewed. Excuse me."

She dashed outdoors to retrieve the copper urn.

"They suit each other," Tommy reflected. "Her and Mr Trelawney. They both have a screw loose."

"They are not experienced with coping with things like this," Clara defended the poor couple.

"Coping with a murder in your bathroom? Who is experienced with a thing like that, except maybe a habitual murderer."

"You know what I mean," Clara moaned at him. "She has never had to govern a big event like this alone before. That, in itself, is stressful enough. But then she has this nightmare of a matter with the unfortunate Nigel Love. Very few people would hold up under such circumstances."

Tommy snorted. His view was that people either rose to the occasion or crumbled, it was a matter of nature. You could have people who seemed fragile on the surface who could prove remarkably capable in a crisis, and then you could have the opposite. He had seen that plenty during the war.

They were outside by now and Clara was scouting around for Miss Painter.

"I think I should help Mrs Trelawney with that urn before she drops it on herself," Tommy said to his sister, drifting off to assist the unhappy hostess who was struggling with the giant urn.

Clara continued to scan the grounds for Miss Painter.

Her eyes alighted on her at the far end of the terrace, where she had found a section of shady paving where her dogs could rest and cool down. Clara wandered over.

"Bulldogs do not thrive in heat," Melissa said as she spied Clara. "Do you know, last century a prize-winning bulldog was taken to the States to participate in a show there and perished from the heat. He was a champion, quite the tragedy. His body was stuffed and placed in one of the big American museums."

Clara found that rather grim.

"I don't suppose I could ask you to fetch a jug of cold water for my dogs?" Melissa asked next. "I do not want to leave them, not with all this mischief going on today."

"You are not concerned about a dog thief as well?" Clara asked her.

Melissa shook her head.

"I do not know what to think. Love missing, Brutus discovered in an old shed, chained there by someone and, of course, the wandering Pekingese. I admit that seems to be an instance of an amorous bitch seeking a companion, but still, I am feeling a little more on edge than usual."

She looked around her, suddenly suspicious of her fellow contestants.

"I shall get your dogs some water," Clara assured her. "But first, I wonder if you could look at this?"

Clara held out the brooch she had found beneath Nigel Love. Her eyes were on Melissa's face, ready for her reaction. The bulldog fancier glanced at the pin innocently.

"What a crude little thing," she observed. "I would hardly recognise it for a bulldog."

"It is not yours, then?" Clara asked.

Melissa's expression now changed, she looked affronted.

"I have higher standards than this sort of cheap tat. I doubt it is even pure silver, more like silver plate with tin beneath. Here is my pin," she had discarded the jacket which completed her ensemble onto one of the terrace steps, it simply being too hot to wear it any longer. She lifted the jacket now and turned it so that Clara could see a shiny brooch on the lapel.

It was a very smart piece, the bulldog well-sculpted and standing in profile, its head slightly raised as if looking up at the wearer. There was no comparison between this accomplished piece of artistry and the brooch Clara had found.

"I shall not say how much I paid for this, but it will suffice for you to know it was considerably more expensive than that tawdry thing," Melissa flicked a finger at the brooch in Clara's hand. "I appreciate the thought, however. Had I lost my brooch I would have been most upset."

Clara was flummoxed. She had thought the pieces of the puzzle were coming together and yet now it seemed she had been mistaken and was back to square one.

"I don't suppose…" Melissa paused, a frown wrinkling her brow. "It looks the sort of thing Nigel would wear. He will never spend pennies when he does not need to. It might be his, in fact."

Clara almost blurted out that she knew for a fact it was not his but caught herself in time.

"Where did you find it?" Melissa asked.

"Just lying on the floor," Clara answered innocently and, as it happened, perfectly truthfully.

"Well," Melissa said thoughtfully. "I don't suppose that particularly assists us in the search for Nigel, if it is his brooch."

No, thought Clara, right at that moment it did not.

"Maybe one of the other bulldog exhibitors here has lost their brooch?" she said.

Melissa shook her head.

"You might have noticed a dearth of bulldogs at the show," she said sadly. "Nigel's monopoly on winning at these things has caused many people simply not to bother coming along. Aside from myself and an elderly lady who mainly turns up for the social side of things, there are no other bulldog exhibitors remaining here today. They all departed when Nigel's Brutus was clearly going to win everything."

Clara was disappointed with herself that she had failed to notice this.

"This elderly lady…"

"She wears a gold plate clasp pin with inlaid emeralds and pearls," Melissa interrupted her, knowing exactly what she was thinking. "It is quite a work of art. She would never wear a thing like that. She would rather walk into the ring with her number fastened to her lapel with a safety pin."

And that was that. What had seemed a promising clue now appeared to be another dead end. Yet, the brooch had come from somewhere, hadn't it? What if Nigel Love carried a spare and this was actually his? It had fallen from his pocket, perhaps, when he crashed to the tiles. If so, then what had the killer been trying to get back into the bathroom for?

"You look rather disheartened," Melissa Painter said, sympathetically.

"I was rather hoping to place this back into the hands of its rightful owner," Clara replied, though her motives for finding the brooch's wearer were somewhat different to what she was implying to Melissa. "Never mind, I am sure whoever it belongs to shall ask for it at some point."

She slipped the brooch into her pocket.

"Did Diana get Brutus into the cellar without losing any fingers?" Melissa asked, a hint of bitterness to her tone.

"She did, he appeared quite happy to go with her."

"We all know the story between her and Nigel," Melissa added snarkily. "The only one who appears oblivious to it all is her husband."

"It seems rather remarkable," Clara said. "What with Nigel's temperament."

"You mean he was downright horrid to everyone? There is no accounting for taste, is there?" Melissa had a cruel smile on her face. "Still, I did sometimes wonder just how much he was interested. The affair always seemed somewhat one-sided to me. Then again, that could have been because Nigel was trying to keep it a secret. Not that it worked. There are no secrets within the dog world."

There was one, Clara thought to herself, at least for the moment.

"I suppose that is why people have been happily talking about the assault on Nigel Love earlier in the year," Clara said casually. Tommy had told her what Alex and Michael had revealed to him. "No one seemed concerned about mentioning it."

"You mean that episode where someone tried to throttle him?" Melissa turned her head, glancing out at the show. "I dare say there is more than one soul here who would have taken such a chance to be rid of the man."

"That is a sinister thing to say," Clara announced, a little startled.

Melissa shrugged.

"People say it was a mugger after him. I think they do that to throw suspicion off themselves. Everyone really thinks one of us did it. Someone with a grudge, but no one has the nerve to admit to anything."

"Brutus bit the culprit, I was told," Clara added.

"Well then it was someone who was not going to be staying for the second day of the show, for certainly no one was wandering around the next day with a sore leg. I stand by my instincts on this, more to the point, Nigel never made a fuss about it, never went to the police. He is not the sort of man to let things drop quietly, in fact, it is odd he was so quiet about it all. That suggests to me he has a good idea who was responsible."

"If that were the case, a man such as Nigel Love would use the information to his advantage," Clara responded. "That he apparently didn't suggests to me he did not know who was responsible."

"Or he preferred to do nothing," Melissa answered. "Honestly, who knows what goes through that man's mind? He defies reason sometimes. Like this disappearance. I am half inclined to think he has done it on purpose to see how we all react."

"Really?" Clara said.

"Oh yes, see if it draws out the people against him. Know thy enemy," Melissa tapped the side of her nose.

Things were getting far too convoluted and unnecessarily confusing for Clara's mind. There was no sense to Melissa's theory, but then she knew that Nigel Love was very, very dead.

"If anyone happens to mention losing a bulldog brooch, will you let me know?" Clara said in conclusion.

"I would not want to lay claim to that thing," Melissa pulled a face. "But if someone mentions it, well, I shall point them in your direction. Now, about that water?"

At her feet, three squash faced dogs were panting hard, lying stretched out on their bellies to try and cool off. Clara felt sorry for them.

"I shall fetch you some water," she promised.

She was about to move away when Melissa threw out a comment that had her immediately come to a halt.

"Has anyone begun to consider that Nigel might be dead?"

Clara spun on her heel.

"Why would you say that?" she asked.

Melissa looked uneasy.

"I don't know, really," she admitted. "Nigel is not the sort of man to just abandon a dog show and the discovery of Brutus in the shed seems so very peculiar. It makes me think Nigel is not around anymore to take care of the dog."

Clara did not need rumours starting to spread about Nigel being deceased. She was doing her best to keep that firmly between herself, the Trelawneys and the killer. She fixed a smile on her face and spoke to Melissa as light-heartedly as she was able to.

"Oh, I really don't think that could be it. No, no, I mean, people do not just go around dying all the time," she gave a laugh, but it did not sound as easy-going as she had meant it to. "He shall turn up soon, I am sure."

Melissa stared at her for a moment, her expression serious, then a smile broke on her lips.

"Yes, yes, of course he will."

Chapter Twenty

Inspector Park-Coombs hobbled through the concealed gateway in the wall, moaning and groaning with each step.

"Honestly, man, you make more fuss than my old grandmother when she fell down the stairs!" Beryl harangued.

"Didn't your old grandmother die from the fall?" Mrs Cobb interjected.

"She did," Beryl said stoutly. "But she didn't moan about it."

Park-Coombs was not in the mood for all this, and he was heartily relieved to see Tommy hurrying in his direction.

"What have you done to yourself?" Tommy asked in horror at the sight of him. "Has someone attacked you?"

"I pulled my back," Park-Coombs grumbled. "While investigating these ladies' suspicions that a dog thief was lurking in the old greenhouse."

His tone had been suitably irksome, and Mrs Cobb took offence.

"We were not to know the fellow was the gardener, were we?" she protested.

"Look, take the dog, will you?" Beryl said to Tommy,

handing over Angel.

Tommy was not sure if he should be hurt that she seemed to think him incapable of relieving her of the load of the inspector, or whether he should be glad to get away so lightly. He took the greyhound without a word of protest.

"If we get him to the edge of the terrace, we can sit him down there," Mrs Cobb suggested to Beryl.

The terrace ran around the corner of the house on this side, providing ample shade on the steps nearest the old walled garden. It was also largely out of sight of the main lawn. Still groaning with each step, the inspector was edged towards the terrace and deposited. He sat on a middle step, so he could rest his back against the next one up and stretched his legs out. This alleviated a good deal of the pain.

"Are you a friend?" Beryl asked Tommy sharply.

He almost jumped at the way she addressed him; her voice full of unconcealed distrust.

"Tommy is a good friend," Park-Coombs said hastily. "I shall be quite fine with him."

The ladies gave Tommy a hard look, then finally seemed satisfied.

"We ought to get back to the dogs," Beryl declared.

"We left Mr Cobb in charge of them," Mrs Cobb added. "He gets fraught if we are gone too long. Farewell Inspector, thank you for your assistance."

With that the two ladies departed, satisfied their duty was done.

"Not even a word of apology for the trouble they put me through unnecessarily," Park-Coombs snorted. He pressed a hand into the small of his back and tried to stretch out his spine. Something clicked and he looked horrified for a moment, then relaxed. "That's better."

"I did not know the Trelawneys employed a gardener at this present time," Tommy observed, taking a seat beside the inspector. His own legs were starting to ache. They had never been quite the same after he was shot in the war and he was feeling a faint burning in his left calf that was liable to get worse before it got better.

"They don't," Park-Coombs replied to him. "He happens to be the former gardener, retired, supposedly, but he has no inclination to stop gardening here. He loves the place too much. So, he carries on without pay, keeping himself out of sight of the Trelawneys in that old walled garden."

Tommy pulled a face at how bizarre this sounded.

"I rather had the impression the fellow had information for me, but he was scared away by those damn women before I could find out what it was."

Tommy was thoughtful.

"I think I would be scared away by those women, too," he smirked.

Park-Coombs chuckled to himself, feeling a lot better already. He dared to stretch out his legs further and was satisfied that no pain followed the attempt. He breathed deeply.

"Someone hit Mr Trelawney over the head," Tommy said to him.

Park-Coombs was instantly back on the alert.

"To kill him?"

"No, we think it was to render him unconscious so they could steal what they thought was the key to the bathroom."

"Ah, but it was not the key?"

"No, it was actually the key to the drinks cabinet. Anyway, we have to assume that at some point the culprit will attempt to sneak into the house to use the key. Maybe we will catch them that way?"

Park-Coombs stroked his moustache, finding a wispy dried blade of grass caught in it. He removed the offending item with disgust.

"This is very interesting Tommy. I suppose you checked the bathroom to see if you could discover what the killer might be looking for?"

"We did," Tommy nodded. "Clara found a brooch and is asking someone about it as we speak. We may, at last, have our culprit."

"That is very promising!" Park-Coombs said, generous enough not to be annoyed that his own investigations had proved misguided. "I feel we should join Clara to be in on the final chapter of this sorry affair, don't you?"

The inspector marked his words by levering himself up from the steps with an outbreath of air. He pressed both hands into his back again and took a couple of paces before freezing in place.

"Not as resolved as you had hoped?" Tommy asked, coming up to take his arm and steady him.

"I think I have had another spasm. Maybe if I walk a little it will ease off."

He shuffled onto the grass with Tommy's assistance and then they began a slow procession across the reasonably flat lawn. The inspector did not dare attempt to turn, so they walked in a straight line. They had walked into the full blazing rays of the sun and Park-Coombs was swiftly sweating hard. Tommy was equally gasping at the heat and it was with some relief they made it into the shade of the side of the large tent the Trelawneys had arranged for the judging of the classes.

Here they paused, Park-Coombs taking a deep breath, though he was nervous even such a simple action might set off his back again.

"My wife is going to be livid with me," he said morosely. "She wants me to give up my fishpond because of my back, this will only add fuel to her cause."

He sniffed miserably to herself.

"She has never been fond of my fishpond, says it makes it difficult to hang out the washing what with it being in the middle of the garden. I offered to build her a bridge over it."

"Never mind Inspector," Tommy consoled him. "With any luck, we shall be able to get your back right before you have to go home."

Angel the greyhound, who had followed them in the moping way such dogs did when they were contemplating their bed and were quite heartily fed up with being conscious still, moved towards the inspector and lightly licked his hand. It was a tender moment of camaraderie. Park-Coombs stroked the dog's head.

"This has been a right fiasco, Tommy," Park-Coombs sighed. "I do not think we are any further forward."

"I am not so sure about that, Inspector," Tommy declared, trying to encourage him. "We have learned a few things."

"Such as?"

Tommy thought for a bit.

"Nearly everyone hated Nigel Love."

"That is not helpful."

"The person who attacked him had a way with Brutus."

Park-Coombs nodded his head.

"There is that."

"And the killer left something behind," Tommy added.

"And will surely come back for it," Park-Coombs agreed. "That is something. And then there is this gardener fellow, who seems to know something."

Park-Coombs dared to look over his shoulder towards the old greenhouse.

"You know what I am thinking Tommy, from that greenhouse you have a very good line of sight to the bathroom window."

Tommy took a pace to his right and considered what the inspector was saying.

"You are correct. Anyone at that bathroom window would be in plain sight of the greenhouse."

"While the person sitting within the greenhouse would be largely camouflaged by those brambles," Park-Coombs was smiling to himself. "I am starting to wonder if we have a witness to this drama after all! We need to find the gardener, come on, Tommy!"

Rejuvenated by this thought, Park-Coombs began a fast shuffle in the direction of the walled garden. Tommy easily kept up with him.

"The gardener could be the key to this. Just think, he

could have seen the killer disposing of the hammer!" Park-Coombs continued. "I knew he wanted to speak to me, I saw it in his face."

"But why, if he knew something important, did he run at the sight of Mrs Cobb and her friend?" Tommy argued. "Is that not more the behaviour of a man with a guilty conscience?"

"The ladies were accusing him of being a dog thief and he did not want trouble. Remember, the Trelawneys do not know he is here, and I suspect he is concerned about losing his chance to visit and work this garden."

Tommy was not so sure, it seemed slightly odd the gardener had bolted when he already had the police inspector on his side, but he did not argue with Park-Coombs. It was just good to see him more like his old self.

They reached the overgrown opening in the wall and Park-Coombs demonstrated how the thick weeds made perfect cover for the old gateway.

"Who would think someone was using this as their private space?" he said as they worked their way into the inner sanctum.

The walls of the garden were doing the exact job they were meant to and were pooling the heat of the sun making the place bake. Angel began to pant hard. Tommy noticed the signs that someone was taking care of this place – the neatly tended plants, the trimmed grass and raked fallen leaves.

"A secret garden," he said. "Well, all good homes should have one."

"There is another gateway on this wall. I saw the gardener go through it," Park-Coombs hobbled towards the wall and pushed back ivy strands to reveal a second archway. This one led into a garden turned over partly to vegetables, and partly to fruit trees. The walls collected enough warmth to allow an orange tree to tentatively bloom with small fruit on its boughs. There were apple and pear trees, and against the far wall another long greenhouse, this one well-maintained. Trays of seedlings sat on wooden shelves, there were bags of compost, lots of pots in various sizes, trowels, pruning shears, spades, buckets and even an old scythe. This was the heart of the gardener's little world. However, the man himself was not here.

"He must have slipped out," Tommy indicated a gate in the far wall that led back into the main gardens.

When they went over to investigate, they discovered it was padlocked from the far side, the lock being rather new and shiny, not some old, tarnished thing that had sat on the gate for years and years.

"He must lock this gate to prevent people getting in when he is away," Park-Coombs sighed. "This is the only obvious gateway into this area, so I suppose he feels safer keeping it locked."

"We could wait here for him?" Tommy suggested.

Park-Coombs was already limping over to a wooden bench set against the wall behind the fruit trees. He lowered himself onto it with a groan of relief.

"That sounds a very good idea, Tommy," he declared.

Tommy watched him for a moment, then wandered off to inspect the greenhouse for something to do. Park-Coombs allowed the sunlight to soak into him, heating up his muscles and bringing fresh relief to his aching body. He was quite content here, he decided. At least until his inner policeman woke up again and prodded him to get back to work.

"You know what I am wondering," Tommy said as he came back towards the inspector.

Park-Coombs had closed his eyes and leaned back his head to enjoy the sun, now he tipped his head forward and cautiously opened an eye.

"What are you wondering?" he asked.

"We have yet to determine how the killer slipped out of the hall without being seen. I wonder if they might have clambered out of the bathroom window."

"Someone would have noticed," Park-Coombs brushed

off the idea.

"Would they?" Tommy asked him. "Everyone was busy and there is a wall running at ninety degrees to where the window is, masking a lot of the view of it from the lawn."

Park-Coombs considered for a moment.

"But there is the bush. The person would have fallen into it and crushed it."

"Maybe," Tommy said, "then again, maybe not. If the person were careful and not too heavy, they could have slipped out without causing the shrub harm."

Park-Coombs was now starting to pay attention as this idea grabbed hold of him.

"We have debated the culprit being a woman, because of the shoe prints in the dining room. A woman might have been small and light enough to get out of that window without doing a lot of damage."

"And the gardener ran when he saw two women approaching," Tommy reminded him. "Perhaps, rather than being concerned about accusations of dog theft, he was troubled that one of them might be the person he saw climbing out of the bathroom window."

"But he couldn't know about the murder," Park-Coombs brought them both back down to earth. "All he saw was a person climbing out of a bathroom window."

"Even if he just considered them a burglar, he saw them," Tommy said. "We cannot ignore that fact."

"We are jumping to conclusions," Park-Coombs warned him. "We do not know for certain this man saw anything."

"But if he did," Tommy was not to be deterred, "then we shall be one step closer to discovering who murdered Nigel Love."

"When we find the gardener," Park-Coombs added. He took another look around the walled garden. "Let's hope he has not gone home for the day. He might have had enough of all this dog showing business."

"It is rather alarming," Tommy reflected sitting down beside the inspector. "Who would think it was so competitive? So cutthroat."

"That is a very good word for it," Park-Coombs agreed. "And we have proof enough of that with the corpse in the bathroom."

"Sometimes I despair at people," Tommy sighed. "They take something that was supposed to be a bit of fun and turn it into a miniature war. Sometimes I wonder where it will all end and can't help thinking humanity is not yet tired of conflict."

"Let's not be grim, not on a nice day like this," Park-Coombs said gently.

Angel sprawled out on the grass at their feet and gave a fluttering sigh of contentment. It was rather as if he understood all they had said and was making a point.

Chapter Twenty-One

Clara was feeling somewhat stumped. There seemed too many motives for wanting Nigel Love dead and not a single person who was an obvious prime suspect. It was troubling that one man could be so universally despised. Even during the last war, the Kaiser had had numerous cronies who liked him, or at least liked what he stood for. But, aside from Diana Doddington, Clara could not find a person who had a good word to say about Nigel Love. Even worse, the man seemed to have enjoyed making enemies.

Clara rather aimlessly headed across the lawn, vaguely recalling she was meant to be speaking to Alan Kennedy, but she had somehow lost her momentum for interviewing suspects. She felt there was something she was missing, something important. The brooch was a clue, she was sure of it, it had been the only thing in the bathroom that the killer could possibly have been searching for. Yet how did it fit into this puzzle?

She was wandering towards the tent again, thinking maybe a second discussion with Dominic Wood would reveal something useful, when she felt a sizeable thump against her leg. She looked to her side to see a young Labrador cheerfully grinning at her and wagging its tail furiously. It had apparently crashed into her leg to gain her attention.

"Terribly sorry!" cried a man who was rushing over to her.

"It is perfectly all right. We have a Labrador ourselves. Just a pup at the moment, but quite the character," replied Clara, calmly patting the dog's head.

The man frowned at her, some thought occurring to him.

"Would that be Pip?"

"That is her, you must have met her," Clara smiled.

"We did, we had a long chat with Tommy about dog showing. You must be his...?"

The question hovered in the air.

"His sister," Clara answered, and she was sure the man looked relieved at this answer.

"I am Michael," he introduced himself. "My friend Alex and I breed and show Labradors. It makes it a little easier working together."

He added the last rather hastily, as if he feared Clara would wonder why two men would share such a hobby. Clara was too busy wondering about the murder of Nigel Love to notice.

"I don't suppose you have seen my brother around?" she asked, thinking that now he had disappeared too, when he had meant to be looking for the inspector. "People keep vanishing on me today."

Clara placed her hands on her hips and took a good look around the lawn.

"No, sorry," Michael replied. "We haven't seen him since he came out of the show ring."

Alex had wandered over to join them.

"I think he found the experience rather trying," he said, catching the end of the conversation.

"Tommy can be quite sensitive about his dogs," Clara shrugged. "He thinks the world of them. Bramble really took him out of himself and helped him to overcome his war injuries."

"We noticed his limp," Michael said self-consciously, acutely aware he had made quite an error pointing it out. "Are you worried about him?"

"Not particularly," Clara answered lightly. "More frustrated that I seem to have lost track of all my friends."

The Labrador at her side chose that moment to vie for her attention and nudged her hand hard with its solid head. Clara had not been expecting the nudge and had only been lightly clasping the cheap bulldog brooch in her fingers. It tumbled out of her grasp and onto the lawn.

"Hedger show some manners," Alex scolded the dog.

Michael bent down and picked up the pin. He looked at it curiously and Clara could almost hear him wondering what she was doing with a bulldog brooch.

"I found it, inside the house," Clara said to him swiftly. "I have been trying to find its owner, but no one wants to claim it."

Michael showed the brooch to Alex.

"Looks like Nigel Love's," he said, he knotted his brows together as he considered this information. "It is very odd that he has vanished too. It is almost like something is happening to people at this dog show."

Clara could not tell him that she knew perfectly well where Nigel Love was and she did not think that the disappearance of Park-Coombs and Tommy was related in any sinister fashion to the crime - at least, she was hopeful that was not the case.

"Well, you know what I think," Alex said solemnly to his friend.

Clara was intrigued; it was always interesting hearing what people thought about a case, sometimes it revealed information she had not learned of before, and sometimes it was meaningless. You never could tell.

"What do you think?" she asked Alex.

Alex seemed reluctant to talk all of a sudden, fortunately Michael did not share his reticence.

"Have you heard that Nigel was attacked after a dog show in Liverpool?" he asked her.

"Tommy mentioned it," Clara confirmed, thinking she knew the truth about that scenario, but it was useful not to mention that as she continued her questioning. "Something along the lines of a disgruntled fellow contestant?"

"That is what everyone concluded," Alex agreed. "It seems to be the theory Nigel has been sticking to. He has been on edge ever since."

"He took several months away from the show circuit, claiming it was because one of his dogs was having puppies, but it rather seemed to us that he had been badly unsettled by the whole affair and was keeping a low profile."

"He was fearful something else might happen to him," Clara extrapolated. "He did not strike me, from the little I know of him, to be a person who scares easily."

"You mean because of the amount of people he has happily offended over the years?" Alex snorted. "I think Nigel is so arrogant that for a long time he supposed everyone would just put up with his antics. Typical bully, never expecting his victims to turn on him, but a coward deep down."

"Personally, I would probably stay close to home a while if I thought one of my fellow dog exhibitors had tried to strangle me," Michael reflected. "It is not very nice, is it? But tell her what you were thinking, Alex."

Alex still looked uneasy about revealing his thoughts, but Michael was physically nudging him now with his elbow. He gave a deep sigh and braced himself.

"I could not help but wonder if perhaps, after getting here, Nigel felt threatened and decided to make himself scarce. It would be hard to slip away with Brutus in tow, that dog rather makes his presence felt. So, he hid Brutus in a shed, planning to come back for him later and made his escape. He must have gone into town and is keeping out of the way until the show is over."

As theories went, this was not a bad one. Had Clara not known that Nigel was a stone-cold corpse in the bathroom, she would have considered it a very logical assumption considering the known facts.

"This is Nigel's first dog show since the incident," Michael added in a conspiratorial tone. "It makes you think, doesn't it? The man must be pretty spooked."

Clara realised there was a question she had failed to ask before, yet one that was quite important. She was annoyed it had not sprung to mind sooner.

"Are there many people here who were also at the Easter show?" she asked the two men.

Michael and Alex exchanged looks and then glanced around the show.

"A handful," Alex said after a moment, though he did not seem entirely sure. "The Liverpool show was a big championship affair. This is a smaller event, less prestigious. It has attracted mostly those local enough to travel here easily in a day."

"Can you point out these people to me?" Clara asked.

Alex gave her a strange look, but it was Michael who spoke.

"Why would that interest you?"

There was only so far Clara could push the idle curiosity card she had been playing. She opted instead to offer a half-truth.

"Mr and Mrs Trelawney are very upset about the disappearance of Nigel Love. They fear it shall turn into a scandal that shall ruin any future chances of having other dog shows here. They were so upset, I promised to try to help them. Mrs Trelawney is quite flustered and has taken to making cheese sandwiches in quantities fit to feed an army, while Mr Trelawney has had to go lie down."

This news drew the sympathies of the two men. They nodded their understanding.

"I can understand their anxiety. Nigel made a terrible fuss at the Easter show, acted as if it was the fault of the organisers he was assaulted walking back to his hotel. I dare say that news has spread and must worry the Trelawneys. Nigel Love is the sort of person you cannot afford to upset if you wish to hold further shows."

"I fear you are right," Clara sighed. She pointed out the pin Michael was still holding. "Hence why I am doing my best to restore order for them. We already have rumours of a dog thief at work, we hardly need to add to that the idea that someone is pinching people's things too."

Michael handed her back the brooch.

"Not that this is worth pinching," Clara remarked. "It is an ugly thing."

"Exactly Nigel's style though," Alex shrugged. "Cheap and nasty. I swear I have seen this on his lapel."

"Perhaps you could assist me with all this? If I can track down Nigel it will be very reassuring for the Trelawneys."

"Of course," Alex said, looking genuinely concerned. "And they have made a real effort with this show. I would gladly come here again. Right, you want to know who is here who was also at the Easter show."

He pressed a finger to his lip as he looked around the lawn.

"Melissa Painter," he said instantly.

Clara nodded, not saying that Melissa was already largely off her suspect list.

"Wasn't Dominic Wood the reserve judge at Liverpool?" Michael added. "I know he did not judge the Labradors."

Alex started to reel off names, far too many for Clara's liking and her heart sank further. Some of them were familiar, but others were people she had not come across in her investigations so far. When he finished, she realised she had a list of at least twenty people who had been at both shows. Clara felt despondent again.

"Does it sound evil to say this might all work out in our favour?" Michael remarked suddenly.

Clara glanced his way and Alex gave him a stern look.

"I think you ought to explain that," he said.

"I see it this way. If Nigel becomes too afraid to come to shows, because he fears someone is after him, well, it will serve us all well. Get him out of our hair and let the show world become a happier place again," Michael seemed unconcerned about his remarks, though they could be interpreted sinisterly.

"That is rather crass," Alex told him, not impressed.

"I doubt I am the only one thinking it," Michael shrugged. "Maybe that was the whole point of the thing? Someone trying to scare him into stopping showing. It would solve a lot of problems."

"It is a heavy-handed approach," Alex scoffed.

"Well, the other approaches were not exactly working," Michael reminded him.

There was nothing Alex could say about that, it was entirely true. Clara wondered how many people would breathe a sigh of relief when they learned Nigel Love was dead and would no longer be a thorn in their sides. It was not a comfortable thought.

"Nigel won't stop showing," Alex shook his head. "It is his livelihood. He couldn't afford to give it up."

Michael became glum at this news.

"Then he will no doubt reappear just after the show ends to retrieve Brutus," he said. "And we shall all go back to the way we were, with no one daring to stand up to him and tell him he is a disgrace to the show world."

There was venom in Michael's tone, but Clara did not take it as anything more sinister than anger over the way Nigel treated everyone. She did not have a reason to suspect either Michael or Alex of meaning harm towards Nigel, at least not compared to the half dozen people who had a very real motive to wish him ill. She imagined if she spoke to everybody here, she would soon discover that nearly all of them shared Michael's feelings and would be glad if Nigel Love disappeared altogether.

Of course, one of those people had taken steps to ensure that would happen.

"I wish we could do more for the Trelawneys," Alex said to Clara. "I really feel they are being hard done by, under the circumstances. They have tried really hard with this show and Nigel is just being his usual insensitive self and ruining it all."

"I don't suppose you recall the last time you saw him around?" Clara asked them.

The pair exchanged looks again.

"He was in the ring earlier," Alex said. "Brutus won best dog, but honestly we all knew he would with Diana Doddington judging."

"And there are hardly any other bulldogs here. People cannot be bothered to compete against him," Michael added.

"We were keeping our distance from him," Alex continued. "We always do. After the judging was done and he was parading his rosette we lost interest."

"I remarked to Alex something along the lines of it all being a foregone conclusion," Michael said. "Honestly, sometimes I wonder why we bother."

"Because we show Labradors," Alex reminded him. "In any case, Dominic Wood was judging the best bitch ring and we knew for sure he would have no time for Nigel. So that meant Melissa's dog Dahlia had to win it and lo and behold, she did."

Alex was smirking to himself. It seemed to Clara that the whole affair was rather a fix, when it came down to it. It was less about the dogs and more about who liked who. Perhaps she was being harsh, the situation with Nigel being somewhat extreme.

"We never saw Nigel after he was in the ring with Brutus," Michael confirmed to her, as if he were reading her thoughts. "We did not even know he was missing until much later and I cannot say it troubled us much."

"Michael is too callous," Alex said stoutly. "I, for one, hope Nigel is found very soon safe and well."

Michael snorted at him.

"Really," he said. "You are hopeless!"

Chapter Twenty-Two

Clara was thoughtful as she went in search of Alan Kennedy. She was mulling over her best course of action when Arnold Jessop intercepted her.

"Have you discovered who killed Nigel yet?" he asked her, looking very alarmed.

"No," Clara answered. "Were you aware of Nigel being hurt at a show in Liverpool?"

Arnold winced.

"You've heard about that?"

"I have."

"It was an unfortunate business," Arnold tried to shrug off the discussion. "A failed mugging."

Clara decided to play along for a bit.

"I rather fancy no one considers it a mugging gone badly, Mr Jessop. Least of all Nigel Love."

"Oh, but it was," Arnold insisted, though it was a little half-hearted. "Nigel didn't want any fuss made about it, so he never went to the police."

"And then he went into hiding for several months?" Clara queried.

"Hiding!" Arnold laughed. "That is preposterous!"

"Is it?" Clara demanded of him, feeling Arnold knew

more than he was letting slip. "What if I told you that Nigel was not attacked and that his injuries were actually caused by a failed suicide attempt?"

"That is… That is…"

"Preposterous?" Clara suggested for him.

Arnold held his breath for a moment, then let it all out.

"I cannot have people discussing such things at a dog show. It would make everyone depressed, and we are only just recovering from the war."

"I appreciate that," Clara sympathised with him, she really did understand the situation he was in. it was the same as the one the Trelawneys were facing. "I am not suggesting we announce to the whole show that Nigel Love tried to hang himself at Easter, but I am suggesting you talk to me. I am trying to solve this matter discreetly and it would be of great benefit to me if people were inclined to be more honest."

Arnold looked unhappy, she was sure he would much prefer it if they could somehow announce Nigel died of natural causes, such as a heart attack. In fact, had Clara not been there she could envision Arnold conspiring to make circumstances appear exactly like that – Nigel collapsing and hitting his head hard enough to kill himself. But she had intervened, and no cover-up was going to be possible. Sooner or later, the word would get out that Nigel had been murdered.

"I have just heard that the Brighton Gazette are sending a photographer and a journalist over to record the results of the show," Arnold explained, revealing why he was so agitated suddenly. "They want to write a big piece about it. I don't know what to do about Nigel. They will expect him to be here for best of breed, he is famous, after all. About the only person in the show world people know the name of, or rather, the name of his dog."

"We can arrange for Brutus to be present, if needs be," Clara reassured him. "And we shall say that Nigel is indisposed. Hardly a lie, after all."

Arnold shook his head.

"Today just gets worse and worse. People are complaining about the heat, as if I can somehow control the weather and Diana Doddington says she is feeling unwell and wishes to leave early. I am trying to locate my reserve judge, but they appear to have wandered off."

"We cannot let anyone leave early," Clara said, reflecting that Diana was one person who it would be useful to interview but she had yet to get the chance. The woman always seemed to be judging in a ring.

"You try explaining that to her," Arnold snapped. "This whole mystery with Nigel vanishing has quite upset her."

"I am surprised she wishes to leave while he is still missing, at least to her knowledge," Clara remarked. "I would have thought she would have been anxious to hang around until he turned up."

"She looked very peaky when I spoke to her last," Arnold said. "I do not need another person dropping down on me. People will start to think something is wrong with my shows!"

"Why don't I come with you to talk to her?" Clara suggested. "Perhaps she would feel better if she had a rest indoors?"

"She did mention something like that," Arnold nodded. "Said if she could have a rest for an hour or two somewhere quiet, she was sure she could carry on."

"She has probably just been overwhelmed by the heat and the worry concerning Nigel. As far as I can tell, she is about the only person to care about him."

Arnold's head nodding was becoming more vigorous, he rather looked as if he might nod his head completely off if he kept it up.

"Please do speak to her. She is over there, having a quick break while Dominic judges the Fox Terriers."

Arnold escorted her over to Diana Doddington, who was sitting on a picnic blanket in the shade of a tree. Clara had formed an impression of the woman earlier and it had not been terribly favourable. She seemed stubborn, dogmatic and opiniated. There was an arrogance to her bearing, which underlined a person who was actually quite lacking in self-confidence. That she sneered at Clara as she approached did not improve her opinion of the judge.

"Mrs Doddington, Miss Fitzgerald is assisting me today with the arrangements of the show," Arnold spoke to the judge, suddenly very obsequious and grovelling. Clara wanted to kick his ankle. "She is a friend of the Trelawneys. She has suggested you go into the house for a while and relax, she can find you somewhere quiet to rest."

Diana turned up her nose even further.

"That would be acceptable," she declared.

"I just have to find our reserve judge," Arnold looked around helplessly. "I might see if he has gone for a walk, he is prone to doing that. Can I leave you in the capable hands of Miss Fitzgerald?"

Mrs Doddington surveyed Clara through half-closed eyes, as if she were debating the quality of a dog in her ring.

"I think that will be acceptable," she said.

Arnold hurried off in search of the reserve judge and Clara settled herself politely down on the grass beside Diana.

"Mr Jessop explained to me you have been feeling under the weather?" Clara asked, as a means of opening a conversation. "I was a nurse in the war, I might be able to assist."

Diana did not look impressed.

"It is the heat. Any fool can tell you that. There have been no cooling refreshments and I have been expected to judge far more dogs than is reasonable under the circumstances," Diana cast her hand at the big tent where a ring packed with sturdy little dogs was being judged by Dominic Wood.

"The circumstances? You mean the concern about Nigel Love's disappearance?" Clara said, hoping she would knock loose some information by being blunt.

"I meant the heat," Diana snorted. "Though, I am rather upset about Nigel going missing like that and leaving poor Brutus tied up in a shed."

"You think Nigel left him there?"

"I don't know what to think," Diana corrected herself hastily. "All I know is Nigel never goes anywhere without that dog."

Diana looked forlorn, some of her arrogance slipping. She lifted her hand to her temple as if there was a throbbing pain hurting her.

"I understand you are a good friend to Nigel," Clara said aiming for a sympathetic tone. "It seems to me not everyone around here is so fond of him."

"People are jealous of success," Diana snapped, her fire returning. "I find it is a British condition. We fawn over valiant underdogs and those fighting against dreadful odds to try to succeed, but the moment that person triumphs we, as a nation, detest them. We consider their success shameful and no longer support them."

Clara felt that any dislike for Nigel had far more to do with his general personality and attitude towards others, than any inherent distaste for a person succeeding.

"Nigel must find that hard," Clara said conversationally.

"He is stoic, that is what I admire so much about him," Diana said stoutly. "He never lets these things get to him."

Clara allowed a slight pause to fall before she asked her next question. She wanted to see if Diana had heard about Nigel's suicide attempt.

"I have been hearing some odd rumours, people are saying that Nigel was attacked last Easter at a show, and it has left him very nervous. They are even suggesting he has disappeared today because he is afraid someone intends to harm him again."

"What rot!" Diana snorted and Clara could almost have believed she meant it. Almost.

"He was not attacked last Easter?"

"He was attacked," Diana conceded. "It was some petty criminal after the money in his pocket. He fought them off. Brutus gave them a good bite on the leg."

"We only have Nigel's word for that," Clara remarked in a way she hoped would draw Diana's ire.

It worked.

"Nigel would not lie. That would be ridiculous!" Diana was offended. "Brutus is quite a thug, you know. Bulldogs have very powerful jaws and when they take a dislike to you, you know about it."

"What of the reverse?" Clara asked. "When they take a shine to you?"

"Well, then they are your most devoted ally and will do you no harm. I admire the nature of the bulldog, quite simple, yet with a good degree of honour. Actually, it reminds me a lot of Nigel's personality."

Clara thought that was pushing things, as far as she had seen, honour was not something Nigel had ever come across.

"Then, Nigel did not take several months away from shows?" she asked.

"Yes, but Nigel is not a coward! Who has been saying these things? It is absurd! He had a bitch in whelp, and it took a while for his neck to heal from the assault. He could not talk or breath properly for a while," Diana was fiercely defensive of the man she was rumoured to be having an affair with. It was remarkable to hear someone defending Nigel instead of criticising him.

"Then he has not disappeared out of fear, in your opinion?"

"Far from it!" Diana declared. "He would rather stand up to any assailant and show them what he is made of."

Clara wondered if that was the reason Nigel was lying dead on a bathroom floor. Had he stood up to the person who wished him ill, and it had ended badly?

"How long have you known Nigel?" she asked, deciding to change the topic to be a little less contentious.

"Oh, years. Since he first joined the show circuit," Diana said swiftly. "Back then I was showing Shih Tzus, but I became enamoured with the bulldog breed."

"You show bulldogs now?"

"Oh, no," Diana said with a sniff. "I still show Shih Tzus, occasionally. I agreed with Nigel that it would be imprudent for our friendship if we were to be in the same show ring all the time. We should be against one another and it would be difficult."

Knowing Nigel's reputation, Clara could well imagine that being an issue.

"I own two of Nigel's bulldogs," Diana continued, now on a topic she was happy to discuss she was proving quite vocal. "Both daughters of Brutus. Nigel helped me to choose them. They are not quite show quality, but that is perfectly fine as I was never intending to put them into the ring."

Clara was not certain, but she thought she heard a twinge of hurt in Diana's voice as she said this, as if she had had other plans, but Nigel had scuppered them by giving her dogs that were not good enough to show. Perhaps the agreement that they did not both show bulldogs had not been entirely acceptable to Diana.

"And it is not awkward judging Nigel's dogs?" Clara asked. "As he is a friend."

"A judge is always impartial," Diana said snootily, lying through her teeth.

Clara would bet Melissa Painter would have something to say about Diana's 'impartiality'.

"So, why do you think Nigel has disappeared?" she asked, hoping Diana would be a bit more forthcoming now.

"I really do not know," Diana said, reaching to her pocket for a handkerchief. "I cannot envision a reason. I am really quite concerned something terrible has happened to him and no one is taking any heed. The police ought to be called, surely?"

"The police won't usually investigate the disappearance of an adult unless they have been absent a certain length of time," Clara countered. "I believe they have to have been gone a full day and night before the police will start to intercede."

Diana dabbed at her eyes, though they did not look very wet.

"Even if people are worried about a person?"

"Even so," Clara replied. "Nigel is a grown man, and he is entitled to go off without telling anyone where he is heading."

"I keep telling myself he shall most certainly return for best in breed. He can't possibly let that Painter woman take the class by default," Diana sniffed and then blew her nose loudly.

"I am sure he will," Clara lied, feeling it was necessary to mollify the judge. The last thing the Trelawneys needed was one of their judges in fits of tears and having a nervous breakdown in their drawing room. After all, Mr Trelawney was doing a good job of that all by himself.

Arnold Jessop reappeared at that moment. A man trailing behind him was presumably the reserve judge, he looked like a rather bemused schoolteacher.

"I have found the reserve," Arnold said with relief. "Feel free to go have a lie down now, Mrs Doddington."

Diana sniffed and nodded her head; the handkerchief being returned to her pocket.

"I will do that, today has been most trying."

Clara stood up and Diana followed her.

"I shall show you inside," Clara said with a smile. "And I shall make sure you have everything you need."

"I can hardly see how that is possible when our hosts seem ill prepared for having guests," Diana's arrogant disregard was back.

Arnold caught Clara's eye and gave her a sympathetic glance. Clara was not perturbed; she had dealt with the likes of Diana Doddington many times before.

"You need a good rest, that is all," she told the woman firmly.

"Don't we all," Diana sighed, mostly to herself. "Don't we all."

Chapter Twenty-Three

They had been sat a considerable time awaiting the gardener, and though the sunshine was very pleasant, and the possibility of sitting there all afternoon was appealing, their time was not their own and they had to get on with catching a killer.

Finally, they could sit around no longer, and they agreed to head back to the house and see what Clara was about. Persuading Angel to leave his sunny patch was a struggle, but once the dog was grudgingly on its feet they headed towards the hidden gateway and back out into the bramble-stricken mess that masked the walled garden.

Angel, who until this point had been quite sluggish and dragging his feet, suddenly pricked up his ears and became intently interested in the decaying greenhouse, or at least the area around it. He was so intrigued that he strained to the end of his lead and refused to move.

"Rats, I suspect," Park-Coombs said, sounding quite knowledgeable on the subject of dogs – greyhounds in particular – even if he had only been in the company of one for the space of a few hours.

He had handed over Angel's lead to Tommy, insisting that his back could not manage a dog that might abruptly pull. Tommy watched Angel's sudden change in demeanour with a frown.

"Our gardener friend did not seem the type to tolerate rats, even in his hidden refuge," Tommy said, still trying to glimpse what had caught the eye of the hound.

"Rats are pernicious little things," Park-Coombs said with an air of authority. "They have taken a shine to my pond. I suspect they are swimming into it and picking up any bits of fish food that gets left on the surface. Mind you, I wouldn't put it past them to start eating the fish too."

Tommy was only half listening. He had this strange feeling in his stomach. He could not quite describe it, but it was making him uneasy. He took a step towards Angel and the greyhound instantly exploited the slack in the lead to take several determined paces forward.

"Whatever that dog has spied must be good. He is not even fussing about the thorns anymore," Park-Coombs remarked.

Angel was in fact trying to pull his way through the brambles, Tommy in tow. That unsettling feeling was growing in Tommy's belly. He was starting to think it was an instinctive reaction to something being out of place that his rational senses could not pick up.

"Maybe we should look at the greenhouse?" he said to Park-Coombs. From where he was standing the remains of the greenhouse were so festooned with ivy it was impossible to see inside. "Perhaps the gardener has returned there?"

"It does seem to be his little cubby hole. Smokes there, eats there, I imagine he sleeps there too when he wants a nap," Park-Coombs twitched his moustache. "I am not climbing in again. It is more than my job's worth. My back and Mrs Park-Coombs shall never forgive me for this as it is."

"You hold Angel then," Tommy said to the inspector. "I am not pushing through all these brambles. I shall go around the front and come at the greenhouse from the other side."

The inspector made a little noise that suggested his agreement and took the lead.

"You better not pull," he informed the greyhound firmly.

Tommy headed away from the greenhouse, edging out of the briar patch and then following around its edge until he could see a narrow trackway through the weeds and thorns leading to the side of the greenhouse. The depression could have been mistaken, at a casual glance, for the track of a fox or even a small deer. In any case, he doubted the Trelawneys looked this way too hard, or would even think to wonder at such a thing.

Tommy followed the trackway, that anxious sensation gnawing at his stomach. Maybe he had spent too much time with Clara, or maybe it was some instinct left over from his time in the war but there was this growing sense of something being amiss, even though he could not put his finger on it. His trousers snagged in brambles, but he was not paying attention to them, his eyes fixed on the corner of the greenhouse. With each step he could see a little further into the building, over the tops of the weeds.

"Anything?" Park-Coombs called out.

Tommy had been so intent on walking towards the greenhouse, and feeling so agitated, that the cry made him jump. He cursed himself for being so stupid and responded.

"I cannot see anything as yet."

He walked nearer to the greenhouse, seeing the old workbench come into view, a few forlorn terracotta pots still standing on it. He crept around to where the brambles had been cleared from the glass to make a way inside. He could not explain why he acted so cautiously; it was almost as if he expected to disturb someone.

He was not, however, in any danger of disturbing the old gardener. As he stood peering into the greenhouse through the smashed panes of glass, he reflected that his anxiety had been spot on.

"You ought to come take a look, Inspector!"

Park-Coombs muttered to himself.

"The dog won't move!" he called back to Tommy. "How desperate is it?"

"Pretty desperate," Tommy sighed. "Let Angel go, I am confident he shall come straight here."

Park-Coombs battled briefly with his concern of losing the greyhound and having to explain himself to the desk sergeant, but his aching back and practicality won. He released the dog which immediately galloped through the brambles, springing over them in places and attempted a hairpin turn into the greenhouse, except Tommy deftly caught Angel's lead and prevented him.

"You'll cut yourself up on that framework," he told the dog, which gave him a mournful, hurt look. "Besides, you cannot go in there."

Inspector Park-Coombs, puttering to himself the whole time, made his way towards Tommy. He was not keen to be back at the greenhouse. His back twinged just at the sight of it, as if it were just the presence of the decaying structure itself that had magically caused his back to break.

"What is it?" he demanded of Tommy.

Tommy pointed into the greenhouse.

"I am not crawling in there again… oh," the inspector fell silent as he saw what had snared Angel's attention.

The old gardener had indeed headed for his greenhouse, presumably for a bit of peace and quiet. He was now enjoying eternal peace, for someone had picked up one of the shards of jagged glass from the frame of the greenhouse and had jammed it hard into the back of his neck. He was lying face down in a pool of blood.

"Oh," Inspector Park-Coombs repeated. "That is unexpected."

Tommy ducked and gingerly edged himself into the greenhouse. He did not suffer the same back problems as the inspector, but he did have trouble with his legs and his knees protested. He was glad to stand upright again as soon as he was within the greenhouse.

"Poor fellow," Park-Coombs said miserably. "But why kill him? And who did it, for that matter?"

His mind started to whirl.

"Might Beryl have done it? She seemed somewhat volatile!" he added.

Tommy crouched and dipped his finger in the edge of the pool of blood.

"It has not had time to dry," he said.

"Does the corpse feel warm?" Inspector Park-Coombs asked.

Tommy carefully touched the hand of the victim.

"He does, but we are under the sun here."

Park-Coombs pulled a face.

"Can't have happened that long ago," he said. "The sun would have dried the blood up swiftly. He must have been killed while we were sitting in the far garden waiting for him."

"That's an unhappy thought," Tommy sighed. "I assume this is the gardener you were referring to?"

"Oh, yes, it is him," Park-Coombs sniffed. "I recognise the clothes."

Tommy took a closer look at the shard of glass.

"I am no expert, but I think this would have severed his spinal cord when it was thrust in. If he wasn't already dead when he hit the ground, he certainly could have not done anything to help himself. The loss of blood would have made sure he was doomed."

"Killer got lucky," Park-Coombs frowned. "They lashed out and hit a very fatal blow straight off. Seems to me we are dealing with a person that when they lose their temper, they go completely off the rails and become extremely dangerous."

Tommy sat back on his haunches, thinking hard about what he was seeing. Death was not unusual to him, but it never stopped being sad when he saw a person slain viciously, their lives snuffed out.

"We have to report this, call in the rest of your forces," Tommy remarked over his shoulder. "No more hiding the matter."

"I disagree," Park-Coombs said, much to Tommy's surprise. "The killer is clearly worried and acting irrationally. We can see that by the assault on Mr Trelawney and now the gardener. I think if we act hastily, we shall set them to flight, but if we are cautious, we shall be able to trick them into revealing themselves."

"Surely that is too great a risk after all this?" Tommy replied. "Someone else may be hurt."

"We need to be careful, indeed," the inspector nodded. "But I have come around to Clara's thinking on the matter. If we call in the police, we shall lose the murderer. They will disappear and we shall not know where to look. We don't have many clues as it is and certainly nothing to point at a suspect."

Inspector Park-Coombs became melancholy.

"I really hoped the gardener was going to help us with that. I was sure he knew something."

Tommy was looking around the scene to see if he could spot anything useful. It looked as though the gardener had been in the process of rolling himself a cigarette when he was attacked from behind. He had probably never even seen the threat coming, which was a minor consolation.

"Our murderous friend is nervous," Park-Coombs continued, rubbing at his chin thoughtfully. "They are lashing out because they fear they shall be discovered. They are anxious that they left something behind in the bathroom, something that will point to them, and presumably they feared the gardener had seen them."

"We must at least warn the others. This is becoming serious," Tommy replied. "Everyone needs to be on their guard."

Park-Coombs was not listening, he was gazing over at the scene of the show. He could see the people on the lawn from here, as well as the show tent and the side of the house where the downstairs bathroom was.

"Sitting here, the gardener had a prime view of everything," he noted. "If only he had said something to me!"

"What do we do about him?" Tommy asked, very reluctant to leave the man here, but aware that they had already done something similar with the corpse of Nigel Love. Funnily, he had not felt the same guilt about that, and he supposed it was because Nigel had been a difficult person to like, whereas the gardener was more innocuous. Perhaps it came down to the idea that Nigel had laid the groundwork for his own death, and it was not entirely surprising such a man had incurred a person's wrath, whereas the gardener seemed utterly undeserving.

"We should cover him up," Park-Coombs said. "Keep the flies off him and allow him a sort of privacy."

Tommy looked around the greenhouse and discovered an old rectangle of oil cloth that had served many purposes over its lifetime but had never before been used to cover a dead man. He threw it over the gardener and then carefully weighed the corners down with a large pebble and three flowerpots.

"It is the best we can do, under the circumstances," Park-Coombs consoled him as Tommy edged his way out of the greenhouse. "You know what strikes me? How dangerous it was for the killer to act here. They must have been stood just outside the greenhouse as we are, for climbing inside is too difficult to do without making a sound or being noticed by the gardener. If anyone had been looking over at that moment, they would have been spotted. For that matter, if the blow had not been so instantly deadly, the gardener might have cried out. The murderer must have been pretty desperate to act so rashly and risk so much."

"Yet, it paid off," Tommy sighed. "The one person who might have been able to tell us something is dead, and we are not closer to knowing who the culprit might be."

"There has to be something!" Park-Coombs said in frustration. "Killers are never cautious enough. They always miss something."

He became distracted looking at Tommy's hand which

was crimson with blood.

"Have you cut yourself?"

Tommy glanced at his hand.

"No, that is blood off the shard of glass. I picked up the blood when I touched the shard to see how firmly in it went," he paused as he realised what he was saying. He looked at Park-Coombs sharply. "There is blood on the shard, why, that must be the killer's, mustn't it?"

"Cut their hand when attacking him," Park-Coombs' eyes had lit up. "Makes sense. Even if they wrapped a handkerchief around the shard, the edge is so sharp it could have sliced through into their hand with the force they thrust that jagged edge in. That means our killer has left us a clue!"

"We look for someone with a cut hand!" Tommy agreed eagerly. "Thank heavens for that!"

"Yes, now all we need to do is examine the multitude of people here to see who has a cut palm," Park-Coombs said wryly. "Without alerting them to what we are doing, that is."

Tommy turned his gaze towards the lawn and all the people milling about. He felt a little despondent again.

"It is better than nothing," Park-Coombs reassured him. "We must find Clara and inform her of all this. We are closing in at last. In their endeavours to silence the one person who may have witnessed their crime, our killer has left us even better evidence of their guilt."

Tommy took his own handkerchief out of his pocket and wiped his hand clean. He glanced sadly at the fallen gardener.

"He did not deserve that," he said solemnly.

"No," Park-Coombs agreed. "He did not."

Deep down, the inspector was thinking how the gardener would never have been known as a witness had he not stumbled upon him, and thus he would not now be dead. But such ways of thinking brought only trouble and he deliberately pushed the idea to the back of his mind.

Chapter Twenty-Four

Mrs Trelawney nearly fainted at the sight of Diana Doddington walking into her kitchen. She managed to grab the back of a chair before her knees completely gave way and managed to save herself.

"Mrs Doddington is not feeling quite herself and has come in for a rest," Clara informed her.

"It was the lack of cooling refreshments," Diana could not resist adding.

The colour further drained from Mrs Trelawney's already pale face and Clara would have liked to have thumped the judge, had it been possible to do so.

"I shall attend to Mrs Doddington," Clara promised Mrs Trelawney. "Perhaps you would benefit from a lie down yourself?"

Mrs Trelawney shook her head.

"I have to keep on top of things, man the trenches and so forth," her strained expression did rather remind Clara of a soldier going into war. The enemy was the heat, the secret of the corpse in the bathroom and the endless demands of those attending the show. Mrs Trelawney looked like it would take her weeks to recover from all this.

"If you are sure," Clara said to her, "but at least make

yourself a cup of tea."

She would have liked to have done more for the woman, but Mrs Doddington was starting to tap her toe on the floor, and it seemed prudent to get her away from Mrs Trelawney as swiftly as possible. Clara motioned for her to go out into the corridor.

"I could do with using the bathroom," Diana said, heading unerringly towards the downstairs bathroom.

"It is this way," Clara said calmly. "Upstairs."

Diana gave her an odd look, there was a moment when she seemed ready to argue, then she conceded.

"I could have sworn Mrs Trelawney said the bathroom was down that corridor," she grumbled. "Having to go all the way upstairs is quite inconvenient."

"I think it is rather a marvel this old house has indoor plumbing at all," Clara countered mildly. "The old owner was quite a stick in the mud, by all accounts and rather let the place go to ruin."

The bannister wobbled under Diana's hand and she winced.

"I see what you mean," she sniffed. "The Trelawneys have their work cut out for them."

"That is why this show is so important to them," Clara explained. "It is enabling them to keep up the restoration of the place. They are hoping to host many more events, not simply dog shows, but all sorts. I hope you will be kind when you are asked your thoughts about this show, under the circumstances."

Diana gave that haughty sniff of hers, the one that suggested everything was beneath her and she could do as she wished. A good or bad word from Diana about this show could be very influential. Though perhaps not so influential now Nigel Love was dead.

As Diana threaded her way to the upstairs bathroom, following a route hastily marked out with dining room chairs to avoid guests accidentally stepping onto rotten floorboards, Clara found herself thinking that the woman was a perfect match for Nigel Love. Nasty, arrogant, and utterly selfish. She would use her powers as a judge to benefit herself. There was not a charitable bone in Diana's body and certainly not an ounce of kindness or goodwill.

Clara waited for her outside the bathroom impatiently, feeling she was wasting time up here when there was still a murderer on the loose. Not that she had much idea of where to look next. There still remained too many questions she had no answer for.

How did the killer slip in and out of the house without being seen? Unless Mrs Trelawney was lying, it would appear the murderer evaded her attention if they came through the kitchen. Since the other doors to the house were locked, logic dictated the killer had come through that way.

What did they come back for in the bathroom? She was starting to doubt it was the bulldog pin since no one recognised it and Alex and Michael thought it looked like something Nigel would have.

And why did the killer want Nigel dead? Well, that was probably the easiest question to answer, there were plenty of motives to pick from.

Diana emerged from the bathroom. She seemed momentarily surprised to see Clara waiting for her, then regained her composure.

"I feel a little better now, but I would still like to have a rest," she said.

Clara nodded to her.

"There are not many rooms finished and furnished. I suggest we head down to the drawing room."

Diana did not protest, and they headed downstairs, past the door of the dining room where the killer had obtained the hammer and across to the doorway opposite. Mr Trelawney and Captain O'Harris were in the drawing room. The former was still nursing his head and sitting half-dozing in an armchair. O'Harris had found a book to read, as he could do little more than monitor his patient and keep an eye on the locked bathroom. He looked up curiously as Clara entered, though Mr Trelawney did not rouse himself.

"I cannot recall if you have been introduced to Diana Doddington," Clara said formally to O'Harris. "She is one of the judges."

"We have met," Diana said coldly, then her gaze flicked to Mr Trelawney. "What has happened to our host?"

Mr Trelawney now opened his eyes and gazed her way.

"My dear lady, terrible things are afoot…"

"He had an accident," O'Harris hastily interrupted. "I found him on the floor. He doesn't remember a thing about how it happened."

Mr Trelawney, by some miracle, cottoned on to what was being said and remembered that it was by his request that the murder of Nigel Love was being hushed up. Weakly, he spoke to Diana.

"I remember nothing," he confessed. "It is all a blur."

"I wondered if something like a lump of plaster fell from the ceiling down on him," O'Harris added. "Not that there was any sign of plaster. Maybe he tripped and hit his head."

"I don't remember a thing," Trelawney said meekly, a line he had clearly determined to stick to, much to Clara's relief.

"This place is falling to bits," Diana said sharply. "You would have been better off pulling the whole thing down and starting afresh."

"That would be sacrilege!" Trelawney hissed in alarm. "Some parts of this house date back to the sixteenth century!"

"Exactly, it is too old," Diana huffed.

Clara was beginning to regret bringing her in this direction. She seemed determined to offend whoever she could.

"Mrs Doddington was feeling a touch under the weather and she has come in for a rest," Clara said to O'Harris, wishing she could take him aside and explain properly why she had brought the woman indoors. It was to prevent her from leaving the show altogether. "Hopefully, after an hour or two, she will feel up to returning to her duties."

"I am still in half a mind to go home," Diana did her sniff again. "I have quite had enough for one day."

"Oh, but you could not abandon us in our hour of need," Trelawney said in a pleading voice. "When we arranged this show, we put such effort into finding reliable judges who were respected in the dog showing community. Your name was top of the list. It would be dreadful if you were not able to judge some of the best in breed classes."

Diana preened under the praise. Clara had to admit that Trelawney knew how to butter people up. He might be a useless, flighty sort of person when it came to everything else, but he could persuade a person to do what he wished.

"Tell me, Mrs Doddington, what can I do to persuade you to stay? I am at your disposal, whatever you wish, I shall fetch for you," Trelawney continued.

As much as Clara wanted Diana Doddington to remain where she was, she did not wish for Trelawney to start running around for the woman with his broken head. He needed to rest too.

"Mrs Doddington just needs some peace and quiet for a while," she interrupted firmly. "Why don't you settle on that sofa, Mrs Doddington? It is out of the sun and we can put plenty of cushions up one end for you to rest your head on."

Diana seemed to slowly recall why she was in the house.

"That will be fitting," she said in her tone of unrelenting disapproval. Nothing, it seemed, could please her.

She headed to the sofa and sat down. Clara wanted to give a sigh of relief that at last the woman was out of her hair, though she did feel bad that she had now become O'Harris' problem.

"Has Park-Coombs won the greyhound class yet?" Captain O'Harris asked, a subtle way of bringing the conversation around to the topic of the missing inspector.

"I have no idea," Clara replied. "I became side-tracked talking to Melissa Painter."

She had thrown out the name on purpose to see what

reaction it might elicit from Diana. She was not disappointed.

"That woman!" Mrs Doddington spat. "Parading around with her third-rate dogs. She is detestable!"

"I thought that at one time Mr Love was considering breeding Brutus to one of her dogs?" Clara said innocently.

"That was before he had the chance to examine them closely and see their true quality. I warned him about them, of course. But Nigel tends to do things his way," Diana patted the arm of the sofa as if she were expecting dust to cloud up from it. "I am so worried about Nigel. To be gone so long seems very odd."

"It is worrying about him that has made you feel unwell," Trelawney said sympathetically. "No doubt he will appear in time for the relevant best of breed class."

"I hope you are right," Diana said solemnly.

She was fumbling in her pocket and produced a small tube of mints; in the process she drew out her handkerchief that fluttered to the floor. She did not notice it immediately and O'Harris kindly went to retrieve it.

"You dropped this…" O'Harris paused as he lifted the handkerchief. "It appears to be covered in blood."

Diana looked at the handkerchief without alarm.

"It is my blood," she informed him. "I caught my hand on something at the shed when I was retrieving Brutus."

She revealed her left hand, which had a gash across the palm.

"That looks nasty," Trelawney winced.

"Oh, I have had worse," Diana shrugged. "I was once bitten by a big mastiff. That left quite the impression. Anyway, it has healed over now."

"No wonder you are feeling unwell after that," O'Harris said. "A rest is very much in order."

Diana studied her injured palm for a moment, then leaned back on the sofa. She looked tired and there was a grey tone to her face. Despite her unpleasant bluster, Clara felt a touch sorry for her.

"O'Harris will be here if you need anything," she told

her. "He is keeping an eye on Mr Trelawney because of his head injury."

"Head wounds can be nasty, I want to make sure Mr Trelawney does not suffer any ill effects," O'Harris elaborated.

Trelawney had shut his eyes and appeared to be dozing again. They had placed a towel beneath his head so he would not stain the cushions he leaned against. Clara wished Mrs Trelawney could be afforded the same sort of rest, she certainly needed it.

"I had hoped to be alone," Diana said coldly. "I do not much care for resting in a room with two gentlemen."

She did seem unsettled by the notion. Clara wondered why. It was not as though she was in danger of being molested – it would be a brave man indeed who would even consider such an option. Perhaps she snored and did not want others to know about it.

"There are no other rooms suitably furnished," O'Harris explained to her.

Diana did not look pleased.

"Is there not a bedroom?" she pressed him.

"Only the Trelawneys' own one and I rather think they would prefer their privacy maintained," O'Harris added. "Not that I question your integrity, but it is rather personal having a stranger in one's own bedroom."

"Wouldn't Mr Trelawney be better off in his own bed?" Diana continued.

"Cannot go too far. Got to keep an eye on things," Trelawney muttered from his daze.

"You shall be perfectly all right here," Clara encouraged Diana. "I shall come back for you in a couple of hours and see how you are."

Diana did not look convinced, but there was little else she could do. She settled back on the sofa, looking as though she had swallowed a wasp.

What a happy person, Clara thought to herself.

"I shall be on my way," Clara said, trying to signal her silent apologies to Captain O'Harris. "I really ought to work out where Park-Coombs went. And Tommy for that matter."

"More missing people?" Trelawney asked, proving he was still awake and alert to the situation.

"Not really missing," Clara reassured him. "Simply misplaced. They have wandered off."

"It is the day for it, apparently," Diana huffed. "If I must remain here, could I at least have a blanket? I feel a draught."

Considering the heat of the day, which was making the room warm, Clara thought this unlikely, but she left O'Harris in charge of locating a blanket, while she headed back to the kitchen. She was hopeful that Mrs Trelawney had followed her instructions to make herself a cup of tea and take a seat for a while. There were only so many cheese sandwiches and gallons of tea people could consume. She must be able to take a break.

The woman was indeed at the kitchen table, and there was a cup of tea, but instead of drinking it, she was just staring into its murky depths. Since she did actually appear to be resting, of a sort, Clara opted not to disturb her. She headed outside onto the terrace, trying to think what to do next. As she was looking across the lawn, she sensed movement to her left and turned her head.

Crossing the lawn at the far side of the house, away from the main show, were Tommy and Park-Coombs. Tommy was waving his arms at her and trying to draw her attention. Clara had a hunch there was something wrong in the way he was desperately trying to draw her gaze to him. She hurried down the steps and walked swiftly towards them. She did not want to run as that might attract unwanted attention.

"Clara, thank goodness we found you," Tommy said, sounding out-of-breath. "We have another body."

Chapter Twenty-Five

They escorted her to the corpse of the unfortunate gardener. Inspector Park-Coombs gave her a condensed version of the events of the last couple of hours, skimming over how he had hurt his back. They reached the greenhouse and Clara peered through one of the smashed side panes.

"Fred Bottle," Park-Coombs said miserably. "I feel terrible that is about all I know of the fellow."

"You were not to know this was going to happen," Clara reassured him. "No one could know."

"The inspector is certain the gardener knew something concerning the incident at the house and was going to mention it to him," Tommy added.

"Those damn women interrupted just at the vital moment and accused him of being a dog thief," Park-Coombs growled. "Had I not pulled my back... oh, who am I kidding? I let him go thinking there would be plenty of time to find him later. I was not really considering the significance back then."

"He cannot have known about the murder," Clara

speculated. "No one outside of us and the Trelawneys do."

"And the killer," Tommy reminded her.

"And the killer, which I doubt was this gentleman," Clara glanced at the corpse once more. "I don't suppose this fellow had ever set foot in the house beyond perhaps the kitchen. He looks like one of the old-school of servants who have a strong sense of what is right and what is not. He would consider it unthinkable to roam about Mulberry Hall, even to commit murder."

"Not that he had a motive," Tommy said. "I don't think dog shows appealed to him."

They all fell silent again as they stared at the dead man. He looked so much older and frailer now he was dead, rather like a bundle of sticks and straw someone had dressed in old clothes. Clara wondered who there was to mourn him, who should they inform of his sad demise?

"He saw something. I am sure of it," Park-Coombs repeated the refrain that had been haunting him since Mrs Cobb and Beryl had scared off the gardener in the first place.

Clara took a look around their location, leaning towards the greenhouse and attempting to get an idea of what precisely the gardener could see from his hiding place. After a moment she made a decision.

"I am going to scramble inside," she told the men.

"Mind yourself on the edges of the metal frame, they are sharp as anything," Tommy told her.

Clara ducked down and squeezed into the ruins of the greenhouse. It was awkward as she was attempting not to stand on the poor gardener or in the puddle of blood that oozed around him. She felt rather as if she should apologise to the corpse, which was ridiculous, but the apology was almost on the tip of her tongue.

She managed to slot herself into the greenhouse without disturbing the body and then she took a good look at the view from the spot. Standing up she could see quite a lot, as the weeds had been pruned to stop them at about neck height. However, standing up also would mean that anyone glancing over could see the gardener, or at least his head above the brambles. For someone who was meant to be hiding away, that did not seem logical.

Clara next crouched down, again being very careful of the corpse. She placed herself as best she could in the position she imagined the gardener would sit in when having a quiet smoke or taking a rest. There was a patch of ground just before the old workbench that bore a slight indentation, indicating someone had spent a lot of time sitting there. Clara was a few feet ahead of that spot, but it gave her a broad view of what the gardener could see when sitting down.

The brambles cut out most of the garden at this level. She could no longer see the lawn with the show tent and when it came to the house, she could just see the first floor and the attics, when she looked up beyond the tops of the brambles. This did not bode well for Park-Coombs' theory that the gardener had witnessed something; there appeared, at first glance, to be no means of seeing anything.

Clara paid closer attention to the weeds and brambles within her eyeline. Though at first glance they appeared to form a solid web of greenery, as she studied them more intently, she realised she could make out gaps amid the branches and tendrils where you could look through and see elements of the world outside. It was when she turned her head slightly to the left that she realised there was a gap perfectly aligned with the corner of the house, giving a prime view of the bathroom window and the bush outside where the hammer had been dumped.

Clara sucked in her breath. The gardener, quietly sitting here, would have been an unseen witness to the disposing of the murder weapon. He could not have known the significance, but he must have realised it was odd. Clara stared at the window, thinking again how Mrs Trelawney had seen no one enter or leave the house and all the windows and doors, except for the kitchen door, were locked. But they were locked from the inside, which meant someone going into a room could unlock them and push them open. The windows had bolts that went up into the frame and fixed them in place, and yet, when O'Harris had gone to look out of the bathroom window, it had no longer been bolted. If the killer had climbed out of the bathroom window to make their escape, it would explain one element of the mystery of how they were not seen by anyone.

Only, someone did see them, someone who did not appreciate a murder had been committed, but who would have been concerned about what they saw. And what could the gardener do about this information? Speaking to the Trelawneys would naturally reveal his secret and he was not keen to do that. It had been sheer luck he had encountered Inspector Park-Coombs and realised that here was a person he could tell about what he had seen, and who might be able to do something about it.

The gardener probably presumed he had witnessed a burglary, or something along those lines. He could not have realised how serious a thing it was, or how dangerous it would be for him to be a witness. Well, none of them had thought of that.

Clara stood up again, cramp beginning in her legs as they protested at being forced into a crouch for so long.

"There is a gap here, through which the gardener had a perfect view of the bathroom window," Clara explained to the others. "I imagine he saw at the very least the dumping of the murder weapon, but it is possible our murderer clambered out of the window to escape and he saw that too."

"The window is rather small," Park-Coombs protested, a spasm in his back reminding him that such activity would be out of the question for him.

"We have already considered that the killer may be a woman. I postulate that I could climb out that window. It would not be easy, but when you are panicking after killing a man, well, you can do remarkable things."

"True," Park-Coombs scratched his chin. "This makes it even more frustrating that the man did not tell me what he saw."

Tommy had a worried look upon his face.

"If the gardener was hidden from view all this time," he said, "then how did the killer realise he had seen anything at all? Inspector, you have told no one other than us that you thought the gardener knew something, haven't you?"

Park-Coombs frowned for a moment, trying to recall if he might have blurted out that information to Mrs Cobb and her friend. He had been rather vulnerable with his sore back and might have spoken in haste. He finally shook his head.

"No, I am sure I did not."

"Then how could they possibly have known?" Tommy said, greater anxiety creeping over him.

"Hey! What are you doing?"

The shout came from several feet away, outside the overgrown section of garden. They all looked over sharply and saw Dominic Wood loitering just at the edge of the weeds.

"You have been in and out of that ruined greenhouse like wasps around a jam jar," he added. "What is it all about?"

Clara now noticed in alarm that Melissa Painter had wandered over to see what was going on and other people were beginning to show interest in them. Clara was not ready to reveal the corpse of the gardener, which would inevitably lead to the corpse of Nigel Love. She glanced at the inspector urgently.

Park-Coombs rose to the occasion in only the way he could. He had spoken at enough public meetings to know how to bluster and bluff his way out of a problem. You aimed to give enough truth to make things sound believable without actually revealing what you were doing. He wandered now in the direction of Dominic Wood.

"I am Inspector Park-Coombs of the Brighton Constabulary," he explained to the judge. "I am here as a civilian, as it is my day off. I am showing my greyhound,

Angel."

Dominic Wood glanced at the dog which had gone from high alert to dog-tired in the span of time it had taken the inspector to discover the body and summon Clara. Angel wanted to sleep and was heartily fed up with his day out.

"I judged the greyhounds," Dominic said solemnly. "You were not in the ring."

He folded his arms across his chest to further indicate that he was not gullible and would not be fobbed off easily.

"You are quite right about that," Park-Coombs said. "And the answer ties in perfectly with why I have been hunting around the greenhouse."

"It does?"

"It does. Mrs Cobb, who has whippets, recognised me, and voiced her concerns about a dog thief being present at the show and wanted me to look into it. She thought she had seen someone lurking about this old greenhouse and was convinced they were the thief."

Dominic Wood glanced over at the greenhouse, where Clara remained inside, afraid to move just at that moment. His stern, disbelieving gaze returned to Park-Coombs.

"Go on."

"There was no dog thief in the greenhouse," Park-Coombs answered with utter honesty. "But in the process of clambering inside to examine the location for signs of a thief, I threw my back out and became virtually immobile. I have spent most of the last couple of hours either sitting somewhere to ease my back or walking up and down to try to loosen it.

"It was during one of these walks that I realised I had lost my pipe. With difficulty I retraced my steps to see if I could find it, but without success. Somewhat in desperation, for my wife gave me that pipe, I thought it might have fallen out of my pocket in the greenhouse, but it is impossible for me to go back in there and search for it, so I engaged my friends to assist me."

Park-Coombs waved at Tommy and Clara.

Dominic Wood was still looking uncertain, though he

was hard-pressed to conjure up any other reason for people to be delving about in a ruined greenhouse.

"You can verify all this with Mrs Cobb. She and her friend had to assist me out of the greenhouse," Park-Coombs added. "Naturally, my indisposition forced me to miss my class, which is quite the pity."

The inspector looked down at Angel in a disappointed fashion. The greyhound gave him a baleful look in return, the only thing that he was disappointed about was the fact he had lost a day when he could have been lounging on the sofa in the sun.

"Do you think he would have done well?" Park-Coombs asked, distracting the judge.

Dominic Wood was not entirely satisfied. Something was amiss at the show and it seemed to be revolving around certain people, one of them being the police inspector, but the answer had the air of truth to it, and you could not really argue with an officer of the law.

"You can ask Mrs Cobb, of course, if you don't believe me," Park-Coombs said, judging the amount of displeasure in his tone perfectly.

Dominic Wood backed down.

"No, that seems all in order and it makes sense. I mean, why else would you be lurking around that old greenhouse," he said, laughing lightly. "It has just been a strange day."

Clara was extracting herself from the greenhouse now, with some degree of difficulty.

"It has not been the greatest day for me either," Park-Coombs told the judge. "My wife is going to be furious when she discovers I put my back out on a wild goose hunt for a dog thief."

"I thought for a moment you might be trying to find out where Nigel Love disappeared to," Dominic added, still with that strange laugh.

"Why would I be doing that on my day off?" Park-Coombs asked him. "A person is perfectly entitled to go off by themselves for a bit if they wish. It would be a terrible world where all our movements were constantly monitored. Sounds very un-English."

"You have a point," Dominic smiled, no longer feeling so confident. "I should get back to my ring."

"You didn't answer my question," Park-Coombs stopped him. "How would Angel have done in your ring?"

He proudly motioned to the dog and a look of deep anxiety came over Dominic Wood's face.

"Ah, well…"

"Full pedigree, you know," Park-Coombs said with a flick of his moustache. "Fine example of the breed. Look at those muscles and those ears."

Angel gave Dominic a baleful stare.

"You see," Dominic said uneasily, "It is about the all-round appearance, not just elements of it. I would need to see him trot…"

"I can do that," Park-Coombs insisted, however when he went to stride briskly his back twinged painfully and he came to a sharp halt, cursing under his breath.

Dominic saw his moment.

"Oh dear, you best rest that. I need to get back to my ring. Good day!"

He scuttled off as Clara and Tommy ran over to the inspector.

"You know, I don't think he liked my dog at all," Park-Coombs said forlornly. "What is wrong with Angel?"

He sounded quite hurt. Clara patted his arm.

"That is perhaps not our most urgent problem right now," she said. "We need to find a way to cover up the gardener's body, so no one sees him. The oil cloth Tommy used before does not mask the fact there is a body on the ground."

"Man calls himself a judge of dogs!" Park-Coombs said hotly. "What does he know."

"Come on Inspector," Clara nudged him. "You didn't want to win a class, anyway. That is not why you are here."

"Stupid man," Park-Coombs puttered. "Never mind Angel, the world is full of philistines and imbeciles."

Angel puffed out the edges of his mouth and gave a sigh.

Chapter Twenty-Six

O'Harris glanced at his watch. He had to admit he was rather bored. The others were getting on with solving this mystery, while he was sitting here keeping an eye on two 'patients'. Mr Trelawney he felt sorry for, the man was clearly a nervous wreck and so, in a way, he did not mind being nearby to assure himself the man was all right. He had given the captain a slight scare when he started to twitch as if fitting. O'Harris had leapt up from his armchair to rush to his aid, only for the man to violently sneeze and apologise. He seemed otherwise fine.

Diana Doddington, he felt far less amenable towards. The woman had yet to say anything pleasant to either of them. As soon as she opened her mouth it was to voice some criticism or to complain. She had so far denigrated the weather, the house, the organisation of the show, the quality of the dogs present, Captain O'Harris' choice of shoes and Mr Trelawney's sneezing style. The only reason O'Harris was putting up with her nonsense was that if he spoke harshly and sent her away, it would not only look bad for the show (and no doubt Diana would spread far and wide all manner of lies about it in revenge), but he would also be going against Clara's desire to keep everyone here until the murder was solved.

Thankfully, Mr Trelawney was dozing most of the time and with any luck had not absorbed any of the things she had said.

"You can leave, you know," Diana said coldly to him. "I do not need you and if this duty is taxing..."

"I was merely checking the time to determine at what stage the show is at," O'Harris interrupted her. "Mr Trelawney needs to be present for the prize giving at the end."

This was a lie, but it came out smoothly and it made him feel better. Diana gave him a sour look.

"I dislike being watched over like this," she said. "I am not a child. I am perfectly capable of taking a little rest by myself and, quite frankly, I would prefer the peace and quiet."

They had had this conversation before, several times, in fact, and O'Harris was tired of it.

"I am keeping an eye on Mr Trelawney, because of his head injury," he said for what felt like the fifth or sixth time. "It was a nasty wound."

Diana glared at the unfortunate Trelawney, who had his eyes shut once more and seemed asleep.

"I have never known such a fuss," she muttered.

"Madame, if you are tired of my company you can always return to the show outside. It strikes me you have done very little resting all the time you have been here, instead you have found fault in everything. An hour has passed, and you have seen no benefit from it."

Diana's glare switched to him, but he was too fed-up with her to care. He picked up his book again and ignored her, pointedly.

"This has been a terrible day, terrible," Diana muttered to herself, though she said it loud enough that O'Harris could hear plainly. "No wonder Nigel has abandoned us. Quite the disgrace."

Her constant wittering made it hard to concentrate on his book and his patience was fast running out. It was therefore some relief when Tommy appeared at the door of the drawing room.

"O'Harris, might I borrow you a moment?"

O'Harris had never heard a grander suggestion. He made one last check of Trelawney to ensure he was breathing and comfortable, then he left his book and the frustrating Mrs Doddington to join Tommy.

"Something amiss?" he asked as soon as they were far enough from the drawing room.

"Clara wanted me to fetch you and catch you up on what has happened. Things are getting rather serious."

They had walked into the kitchen as he was speaking. O'Harris glanced around expecting to see Mrs Trelawney. He had a mind to send her to the drawing room to keep an eye on her husband and to get a spot of rest herself, but she was not there. He frowned.

"Is Mrs Trelawney out at the tea stall?"

"No, I walked past it on my way indoors," Tommy answered. He looked around too, now realising what was missing. "Oh no, we have not another disappearance!"

"It is probably nothing," O'Harris said with more confidence than was genuine. "We must not leap to conclusions."

All the same, they were both leaping.

"She has not left this kitchen, aside to go onto the terrace to tend the tea stall all day," Tommy added, his eyes were going about the room as if the woman might magically appear from a cupboard or something. "I really don't like that she is missing."

"We shall conduct a discreet search for her," O'Harris suggested.

Tommy agreed and they both began to take a look around the kitchen for a sign of where the woman might have gone. The surfeit of cheese sandwiches had been neatly arranged on plates and covered with tea towels, and the knife for the butter and the cheese grater had been washed up and were drying on the draining board. It seemed as if Mrs Trelawney had not simply abandoned her work and run off.

"The tea urn has been changed recently," Tommy said, having gone out onto the terrace to look around and see what was happening at the tea stall. "The lady who is tending it for Mrs Trelawney says she refreshed the urn no more than half an hour ago."

O'Harris rubbed his chin thoughtfully.

"That was after Clara had brought Diana Doddington into the house. I have been in the drawing room all this time and heard nothing. Not a commotion nor a shout."

"You are not really considering this is another attempt by the killer?" Tommy asked him incredulously. Then he recalled the dead gardener, and the idea did not seem so preposterous.

"I don't like to think it, Tommy, but supposing Mrs Trelawney remembered something about the time of the murder. Maybe she did see the killer enter the house, but it had slipped her mind. You know how it is when you are not really paying attention to someone. They go by you without you paying heed, only later when you have time to really think about it do you remember."

Tommy's face went ashen at the thought of another victim on their hands. Things were going dreadfully. The killer was running rampant, and they seemed unable to do a thing about it. To say he felt a touch hopeless was an understatement.

O'Harris was surveying the kitchen again, trying to spot something out-of-place that would hint at what had become of Mrs Trelawney.

"There is another possibility," he said quietly.

Tommy's eyes fixed on him. He was ruffling his hair in agitation.

"What?"

O'Harris drew in a breath.

"That Mrs Trelawney chose to disappear, of her own volition, because it was her that slew Nigel Love."

"No!" Tommy gasped and then he ran the idea through his head a little more. "And yet, why, it could have happened."

"It would explain why she saw no one, and how she was able to slip up behind her husband and knock him unconscious. She was in the house at all times, perfectly placed to commit all these crimes."

"What of her motive?" Tommy asked.

O'Harris shrugged.

"We know very little about her, about the Trelawneys in general. What if this whole affair was a massive ploy to bring Nigel Love to his doom?"

"Now that is going too far," Tommy put a halt to that line of thought. "But we ought to repeat this to Clara and I need to show you something else. We have another victim."

"Another?" O'Harris blurted out.

"Yes, and if your theory is correct, then it may be because of his death that Mrs Trelawney has finally run away."

Tommy led O'Harris out of the kitchen and around the house to the secret garden. Clara and Park-Coombs had made a valiant effort to hide the gardener's body using strands of bramble and tall weeds. Though it was not perfect camouflage, a person would have to look closely to notice the oil cloth covering the body. Clara turned from her work as O'Harris arrived.

"How is Mr Trelawney?" she asked at once.

"I think he will be fine. He seems calmer now. I suspect the shock and adrenaline are wearing off," O'Harris replied. "Unfortunately, I have had to leave him alone in the company of that obnoxious woman."

"Diana Doddington? I am sorry I put you in that position. Has she been truly dreadful?"

O'Harris did not think there was a polite way of saying what he thought about the woman.

"She is not easy company," he sighed. "In any case, Tommy says something else has occurred?"

"The gardener is dead," Clara explained. "Or rather, the former gardener. It is all a bit complicated, but the

Inspector is certain the man witnessed something he should not have seen and was killed for it."

"That ties in with what we have just discovered," O'Harris said sadly. "Mrs Trelawney has disappeared. She appears to have gone on purpose. There are no signs of a struggle and I heard nothing while I was in the drawing room. The kitchen is neatly arranged, as if she set it straight before she vanished."

"If the gardener witnessed Mrs Trelawney dropping the hammer, then that was why he was slain," Park-Coombs said thoughtfully.

Clara was thinking hard too, but the information did not make sense.

"No, it is not right," she said. "The gardener witnessing Mrs Trelawney dropping a hammer would seem odd, but not enough to make him consider seeking you out to tell you about it, Inspector. Remember, the gardener had no way of knowing there was a man murdered and he would expect to see Mrs Trelawney about the house."

"Then how do you explain where she has gone?" Inspector Park-Coombs said with a slight hint of self-satisfaction.

"I cannot," Clara confessed. "But to suppose Mrs Trelawney the murderer means ignoring a lot of evidence. For a start, she alerted us to the matter."

"A diversion, covering her tracks and throwing us off the scent," Park-Coombs said.

"All right, but explain why she stayed this long? If it was her intention to leave, why wait until the middle of the afternoon?"

Park-Coombs opened his mouth, but no words fell out. The truth was that did seem odd.

"We have absolutely no motive for her killing Nigel either," Clara persisted. "Everything we have so far learned indicates they were perfect strangers to one another. Why would she savagely bludgeon him?"

"We do have other suspects with far better motives," Tommy agreed.

"Did you check to see if she had gone upstairs to the bathroom?"

Clara looked first at O'Harris, then Tommy and they both became sheepish.

"I must admit we did not think of that," O'Harris confessed.

"We rather got carried away," Tommy added.

"It has been a long day," Clara said to them gently. "We are all overtired and stressed by this affair. Time is running out if we wish to solve this case before the show ends and all our suspects depart."

"I take it the pin we found was a dead end?" O'Harris asked. "Excuse the word choice, that was in poor taste."

"Melissa Painter is wearing her brooch and everyone I have spoken to says the thing looks more like something Nigel would wear than anyone else. It is a cheap thing, rather his style," Clara explained.

"Considering the amount of havoc this person has caused, you would think we might have a few more clues," O'Harris sighed. "They seem to have left no trail at all."

His words sparked a reminder in Tommy.

"Inspector, we completely forgot to tell Clara what we noticed concerning the gardener's murder!" he declared.

Park-Coombs did not follow at first and then understanding dawned.

"Ah yes, the shard of glass!" Park-Coombs said. "I placed it on the workbench."

He moved back and pointed through the metal framework to the large shard of glass that had been used as a dagger.

"It is the murder weapon, pierced the man in the neck and probably severed nerves as well as blood vessels," Park-Coombs explained. The news elicited a grimace from O'Harris. "It was a murder of opportunity and a poor choice of weapon, as it cut the killer as well as the victim."

Clara stepped closer to look at the shard and saw that not only the tip was covered in dried blood, but also the straight edge which the killer would have held.

"The killer cut their hand!" Clara said looking at the glass and a flash of insight came over her. "Caught her hand on a nail, my foot!"

She spun around and met O'Harris' gaze.

"Is Diana Doddington still in the drawing room?"

"That was where I left her," O'Harris said. "But why…"

And then his memory kicked in too.

"The bloody handkerchief and the cut across her palm!" he said. "She sat there, opposite the room where she had killed a man so innocently acting as if she was worried about Nigel!"

"What is this?" Park-Coombs said, struggling to keep up.

"Diana Doddington has been playing us all along," Clara explained. "I don't know why she killed Nigel, but her cut hand is evidence that she struck down the gardener because he must have seen her leaving the crime scene through the window. I have been so stupid."

Clara cursed herself, feeling she had been utterly blind.

"All that pretence about needing to rest, well, she knew it would mean we would take her into the house! She has been trying to get in there and retrieve whatever it is she thinks will incriminate her all day. That is why she has been harassing Mrs Trelawney, and when she could not get past her that way, she tried another tactic, saying she felt unwell."

"That explains why she has been constantly complaining about me being in the room with her," O'Harris added. "She acted as though it made her uncomfortable. What she was really frustrated about was that she could not get to the bathroom!"

"And now she is alone," Tommy said in a solemn voice.

"Come on!" Clara cried. "If we hurry, we can catch her in the act of trying to get into the bathroom, and then we can see how she tries to explain that!"

Chapter Twenty-Seven

They rushed inside, aside from the inspector who hobbled as fast as he could. Angel walked along elegantly beside him, barely breaking into trot. They raced through the kitchen, O'Harris noting that Mrs Trelawney was still absent, and headed into the hall. Turning right they were in the corridor that led to the locked bathroom and they saw Diana Doddington attempting to break into the bathroom with the key she had stolen from Mr Trelawney. She was so absorbed in trying to get the door open, and failing, she did not realise they were there until it was too late.

She glanced up guiltily when she finally heard the sound of their feet and sprang back from the door, but it was no use, she had been seen.

A breathless Park-Coombs pushed to the front of the little group and leaned against a wall, his back providing fresh torment for him.

"Diana Doddington," he said between gasps. "I am arresting you on suspicion of the murder of Nigel Love."

"I didn't," she said before he could say more. "I would never hurt Nigel."

She had regained some of her composure and her

stubbornness.

"Perhaps then you could explain why you were trying to get into the bathroom," Clara asked, indicating the key in her hand.

Diana stared at her palm, as if the key had magically jumped there.

"Mr Trelawney asked me to," she lied.

"Why would he ask you to go into a locked bathroom?" Tommy asked her.

"He wanted pain medicine, for his headache," Diana said swiftly.

"He sent you to a bathroom where he knew there was a corpse to get him pain medication," Clara stated plainly for her.

Diana's face froze, though her lips were trying to contort into a grimace.

"That is..." she said, desperately thinking. "He forgot about that, because of the head injury."

"Did he also forget to tell you that is the key to the drinks cabinet and not the bathroom?" Tommy asked her.

Diana's eyes dropped to the key and she made a strangled gurgle at the revelation before regaining her self-control.

"I suppose the head injury muddled his mind."

"You are acting extremely calm for someone who has just learned their friend has been murdered," Clara remarked to her, folding her arms, and giving her a hard stare. "You do not even seem surprised."

Diana's mouth gaped open, there was more gurgling coming from her throat as she tried to swiftly conjure up an excuse.

"I feared he was dead," she said at last. "And I was not surprised when you said it. I have been preparing myself for the worst all day. You told me something I had already suspected and so I was not alarmed as such. Though it is a shock, of course it is."

Diana was trying to regain the upper hand.

"Dead? I can hardly believe it! What happened to him?"

"Don't try to fool us," Park-Coombs said, his breathing nearly under control, though his back was a spasming muddle of pain. "I have had a trying day. We know you came into the house and killed Nigel with a hammer."

"No!" Diana said hastily. "Why would I do such a thing? He was a dear friend, a very dear friend."

"We are not sure of your motives," Clara conceded. "But we are sure of the evidence we have collected. You left footprints in the plaster dust when you went to get the hammer. We can compare them to your shoes. There may even be dust left on them somewhere, that stuff gets into all the crevices and cracks, as my friend Annie would tell you."

Diana gaped at them again, but no words of denial sprang to her tongue.

"Then there is this," Clara took the bulldog brooch out of her pocket. "I found it under Nigel."

Diana stared at the pin. Clara had gambled with the brooch, for she was not certain it was the thing the killer had been searching for. She watched Diana's face closely. The woman made no denial, which gave her hope she was correct. Had the pin not been the thing Diana was looking for, then she would have instantly denied it and used that as proof they did not know what they were talking about.

Diana's face fell into a look of misery. The brooch was hers, her expression told them all.

"Then there is that key in your hand," Clara carried on. "Mr Trelawney knew when he pulled it from his pocket and dropped it that it was the wrong key. He told us that. Also, he told us that it had been stolen from him when someone hit him over the head. The only way you could have that key is if it were you who attacked him."

Diana wrapped her fingers around the key miserably.

"The final proof, as if we needed such a thing," Park-Coombs took up the train of the conversation, "is that bloody cut on your hand. You told Clara you got that when you were retrieving Brutus from the shed, when in reality you cut your hand when you stabbed the unfortunate gardener to death with a shard of glass."

Diana's head shot up and she stared at him wide-eyed, they needed no further proof that their assumption was accurate.

"Yes, we have found the gardener," Park-Coombs said, his voice cold. "The poor soul bore you no grudge, did not even know you, but you murdered him."

Diana blinked at them; she was fast losing her ability to stay calm. She gagged on her denial attempts, then whimpered to herself.

"This has been a very terrible day," she moaned, crumpling up and sagging her shoulders.

"I think it is time you told us everything," Clara said to her. "There is no point denying things or holding back. We know what you did and there is more than enough proof to convict you."

Diana winced at the truth of Clara's words. Her eyes scanned around for a way to escape, then she noticed the door to the drawing room and made a bolt for it. Clara sighed in annoyance. O'Harris and Tommy raced around to the second drawing room door that led onto the main hall, there was no other way out. The drawing room's third door merely led to another room and then back onto the same corridor where Clara and Park-Coombs remained waiting.

They heard a squawk of fury as Diana was confronted by the two men, then there were footsteps in the drawing room. Clara and Park-Coombs went to join them.

Mr Trelawney was just coming awake to the situation. He had finally fallen into a deep sleep but had been disturbed by the commotion.

"What is going on?" he said in a dazed fashion.

Clara was relieved to see that Diana had caused him no further harm, had instead simply waited until he was suitably unconscious before slipping out to attend to her task.

O'Harris was holding Diana by her arm and showing her to the sofa where she had sat earlier. Tommy was guarding the far doors. Park-Coombs pulled the other door closed, and as there was a key in the lock, he turned it, sealing the door, and then pocketed the key. He moved to the third set of doors and did the same.

Diana slumped onto the sofa, finally defeated.

"Now, no more nonsense," Clara told her firmly. "Why don't we begin by you explaining to us how you slipped into the house unnoticed?"

Diana shrugged at her.

"Mrs Trelawney is far from observant and she has been wrapped up in this whole affair. I simply walked through into the house when she was busy in the pantry looking for tea leaves," Diana said with a sneer.

Clara felt this was quite believable.

"You followed Nigel inside?" she said.

"No," Diana said, pleased she could correct Clara. "I was here already. I came inside to use the bathroom."

"Your intention, then, was not to kill Nigel," Park-Coombs frowned.

Diana became haughty, some of her arrogance returning as she saw they had not guessed the full truth.

"My intention was to use the bathroom. Until that point, murder had never entered my mind," she said coldly. "Nigel came into the house shortly after, to use the bathroom himself. I was just leaving, and we met in the corridor," Diana pointed her finger in the direction of the hallway, "I had not seen Nigel since Easter. We had had a falling out back then, he was determined to hold a grudge on the matter. That was the way Nigel was."

"A falling out?" Clara asked. "Over what?"

Diana sighed to herself.

"Nigel was in my ring that day, showing Brutus. The dog had a rather obvious limp and I simply could not place a dog that was lame. I picked one of Melissa's dogs instead. Nigel protested, said there had been nothing wrong with Brutus before he entered the ring and accused Melissa of tampering with his dog. It was quite the spat and the officials had to be called. Melissa was tossing threats at

Nigel and he was calling her and her dogs all sorts of names. It was not good sportsmanship, but it was Nigel's nature."

Diana shook her head.

"After things cooled down, I approached Nigel to see how he was, and he said some horrid things to me. Accused me of being bribed by Melissa, questioned my ability to judge. Until that point, we had been friends, close friends," Diana said, and her voice trembled with emotion. "I thought there was a connection between us. I do not get along with many people. I do not have many friends. Nigel had meant the world to me."

"He broke your heart when he turned on you," Clara said quietly.

Diana did not say anything, but her lack of a denial was revealing enough.

"After he was attacked, I tried to show my support to him. He said some terrible things to me, things that could not be taken back. He said he never wanted to speak to me again," Diana sniffed, but she would not allow tears to fall. "When we met in the corridor today, months later, I thought he might have had time to calm down and realise how awful he had been to me. Instead, he started saying the same things again. I was so hurt, so upset and suddenly I was so angry at him. I wanted to make him feel like I did. I wanted to make him realise he could not treat me that way and get away with it."

Diana paused because the enormity of what she had done was slowly creeping over her.

"I was in a state and I could not go back out to the rings like that. I paced about the house to try to calm down, only I was getting angrier and angrier. Nigel was saying he would put a formal complaint against me, and we all know he has influence because of his connections. I started to understand why Melissa had spoken to him the way she had, and I recalled that since then he had been much more meek and polite around her."

"Nigel Love was a bully and thus a coward," O'Harris

nodded. "When someone stood up to him, he backed down."

"Exactly," Diana said. "You know, I have never been someone to allow a person to treat me badly. I have always been in charge, in control. Nigel was taking that from me. Suddenly I saw the tools in the dining room, and I had this vague notion of proving to Nigel I was not weak, and he could not threaten me. I retrieved a hammer and then headed to the bathroom. He was still there. I opened the door and he told me to go away, made some comments about my nature that I would walk in on a man in the bathroom. I tried to make him see sense, I wanted to give him the chance to apologise. I reminded him of our friendship, I even pulled out the brooch I had bought that matched his. That was how much I cared for him and liked him. He called me stupid and other names. I told him again to not speak like that to me and threw the brooch at him. He laughed and turned his back on me. I only wanted him to respect me again. I only wanted him to be... well... aware that I would not be treated that way, that I could stand up for myself. Melissa had done it, so why not me?"

Diana looked at them, desperate for understanding.

"I struck him with the hammer. I never meant to kill him. I was just so angry."

Diana sagged.

"I panicked when I realised he was dead. Brutus was just stood staring at his master, then looking at me. I had to get us both out without being seen, so I opened the bathroom window and lifted Brutus through it before I followed and dropped the hammer in the bushes. I did not know what to do with Brutus. I walked out into the trees, trying to think of something and then I came across the old shed and saw that I could hide him there until I could retrieve him. After that, I went back to the rings to carry on judging."

"How did you discover there was a witness to the crime?" Clara asked.

"I heard people discussing that an old gardener had witnessed something and wanted to tell the police," Diana said. "I was in the showing tent and they were outside, on the other side of the canvas, talking about it. I started to panic again. I had already failed to find my brooch. I could not afford a witness too. I had to kill him. It was just luck I saw the old man by the greenhouse and realised how he had spied on me. I crept up on him and used a piece of glass to stab him in the neck. Somehow it was not as difficult as killing Nigel. My only regret is that I cut my hand."

Diana scowled at her wounded palm.

"You never would have realised, otherwise, would you?"

Chapter Twenty-Eight

Since discretion was still important and the inspector preferred not to create pandemonium at the show, the revelation that Diana Doddington had murdered Nigel Love was best kept quiet until everyone had gone home. Word was sent to Arnold Jessop that Diana felt too unwell to continue and he must persist with the reserve judge. If Arnold suspected there was more to that statement than they were saying, he had the sense not to mention it. Diana was to remain locked in the drawing room with Park-Coombs and Mr Trelawney until such a time as the police could be properly summoned.

That left Clara, Tommy and O'Harris to make sure the show carried on smoothly. The biggest concern they had was the disappearance of Mrs Trelawney. O'Harris explained all this to Clara as they strode back into the kitchen and looked down towards the lawn and the people going about the task of showing off their dogs without a care in the world.

"When is the last time either of you saw Mrs Trelawney?" Clara asked them.

"When I left to look for the inspector," Tommy explained. "That is over an hour ago."

228

"Considering recent events, it troubles me that Diana Doddington could have done away with Mrs Trelawney too," O'Harris added.

"For what reason?" Clara asked him.

"Perhaps she saw something she should not have?" he suggested.

Clara frowned. It was possible, of course, the judge had killed two people and assaulted a third, but to ask her directly when she was in the same room as Mr Trelawney was only going to upset the poor man unnecessarily.

"She cannot have gone far," she said, hoping she did not sound desperate for that to be true. "Let's search the house."

They began on the ground floor, taking their time to look everywhere. Most of the rooms were still in a state of repair and were easy to search. They lifted dustsheets to check beneath tables and chairs and opened any cupboard they found. It did not take long before they had concluded Mrs Trelawney was not on the ground floor.

"What now?" asked Tommy.

"We shall go downstairs," Clara said. "Perhaps she went down for more supplies and felt unwell."

"She did look peaky the last time I saw her," O'Harris concurred. "She was pale and clearly living on her nerves. I wanted her to rest."

"Maybe she took your advice and went up to the bedroom to lie down," Tommy said with sudden insight.

They wasted no time heading upstairs and checking the master bedroom, which was the only unlocked room on the first floor, discounting the bathroom, and the only one with a floor that was safe enough to take furniture. It proved empty. They checked the upstairs bathroom for thoroughness with the same result.

"The basement it is," Tommy declared.

"Thinking of the basement, we ought to check on Brutus," Clara responded. "I mean, he is a horrid dog, but we cannot just forget about him. We should make sure he has food and water, and something to lay down on."

They agreed that this was a task they ought to undertake, even if the thought of it raised goosebumps on the flesh and made a person want to don armour, just in case. They returned to the kitchen and found two bowls. One they filled with water, the other they filled with the leftovers from the tea table, these included scraps of ham, several cheese sandwiches and a piece of cake that had fallen on the floor. It was not a healthy meal for a dog, but it was better than an empty belly.

"Once this is all over, we shall have to determine what to do with Brutus," Tommy said as they headed down to the basement. Unlike much of the rest of the house, the basement was in good repair, its thick sturdy walls still sound and though it could do with a lick of paint, it was otherwise untainted by the decay that had affected everything else.

"I mean," continued Tommy, "someone has to take him on and now Diana Doddington is out of the picture it is up to us to find someone else."

"Perhaps it might be better if the brute was destroyed," O'Harris said bluntly.

Tommy, devoted dog lover, winced at the statement.

"Everyone deserves a second chance," he said, though he was not convinced by his own words. "Even a dog."

"Do we actually know which room Brutus was shut in?" O'Harris changed the subject and glanced around the sprawling basement which looked to him to be larger than the house above, though it probably wasn't. There were several doors and little light, since the only windows were narrow slits set high in the walls.

"We shall have to check every one," Tommy said. "Especially as we are looking for Mrs Trelawney too."

Clara was a couple of steps ahead of them and had come to a sharp stop.

"Wait, do you hear that?"

They stopped and listened. Dimly they heard the soft lilt of someone singing.

"That is a woman's voice," Tommy hissed, hardly

daring to speak above a whisper.

They listened in silence for a couple more moments, then Clara motioned down the corridor. She headed off, following the sound. The singer was doing a fine job of an old Irish ballad, a sad little ditty that made you think of distant times and friends who were no longer around. The sound was getting louder as Clara wound through the corridors and came to a sturdy door.

"Mrs Trelawney?" she called through the door, taking the handle and fulling expecting to find it locked. The door swung open easily at her touch and she found herself in the doorway of a large cold larder. Mrs Trelawney was sitting at the far end on the floor, propped against the wall. She had spread a picnic blanket on the tiles and had brought with her several cushions. Sprawling across her lap was Brutus, looking very content and at peace with himself. He raised his head as Clara and the others entered, but did no more than look at them curiously, before resting into Mrs Trelawney's lap again with a happy sigh.

"Poor thing was fretful," Mrs Trelawney told Clara. "I brought him down some beef tea and some chicken from our pantry. It was meant to be for my husband's supper, but he shall have to manage without it."

"Well, I never," O'Harris said in astonishment at the sight.

"The poor fellow was so distressed when I came in, he was growling at me and cowering," Mrs Trelawney continued. "I put down the bowl and sat to one side and let him eat it. Then I thought to myself I shall sit with him a while, and so I fetched a blanket and cushions and made us both comfortable. I found he likes singing. He is really like a baby."

Brutus gave another contented sigh through his flattened chops and nestled further into her lap.

"Do you suppose anyone would mind if I kept him?" Mrs Trelawney said.

"I doubt it will be a problem," Clara said, thinking that no one else would want to take a chance on the dog.

Mrs Trelawney smiled to herself.

"That is good, that is very good. You know, it is rather peaceful down here. I think I might stay here a while, unless I am needed?"

"You rest here," O'Harris told her firmly. "You have earned a break."

"Oh, thank you," Mrs Trelawney smiled wearily. "I really am quite tired."

They left her with Brutus, the dog clearly having taken to her and she to him. It was not a partnership any of them had expected.

"Seems Brutus' unpleasant demeanour was a product of his master, rather than his natural tendency," Tommy frowned.

"Nigel was a bully and an angry man," Clara replied to him. "I could imagine he rubbed off on Brutus and probably did not treat the dog as well as he should. Now Brutus is with someone kind and gentle, he appears to be flourishing."

They headed back upstairs, the last mystery of the day resolved. They arrived on the terrace in time to see the final rounds of the best of breed classes. There were fewer people now, most having gone home. They saw Alex parading one of his Labradors around the ring and Tommy gave him a round of applause when he won.

Arnold Jessop joined them on the terrace steps.

"A successful day," he said conversationally. "All things considered. Might I ask if the matter of Nigel Love's death has been resolved?"

"It has," Clara informed him.

Arnold nodded his head.

"I thought as much. You all seemed calmer suddenly, as if a burden were off your shoulders. Can you tell me who did it?"

"Diana Doddington," Clara informed him, seeing no reason to hide the truth. "That is why we sent a message she was unwell. She is currently under house arrest in the drawing room until the show is over, then the police will come and take her away. It shall all be very discreet."

Arnold whistled to himself.

"Well, well," he stared across the lawn as the last couple of classes finished. "Wise decision on your part. I can see this becoming a regular event, you know. If the Trelawneys are amenable."

Clara could not say if that would be the case or not, the Trelawneys had been put through the wringer that day after all.

"Well, time to wrap things up," Arnold strolled down the steps. "Good show, all things considered."

The show was at last at an end and none too soon to Clara's mind. She had not discovered the appeal of dog shows and had found the whole event quite stressful, though of course that was in part due to trying to solve a murder. She would be glad to get home.

When the grounds were at last clear, Park-Coombs telephoned to the police station and gave instructions that the coroner's van should come to collect two bodies, while the station's solitary police car was to come and collect a killer.

Mrs Trelawney had emerged from the basement with Brutus trotting by her side. The dog seemed glued to her leg and he was no bother to anyone, as long as they did not try to prise him from his new mistress. Mr Trelawney still seemed dazed by events, but a chat with Arnold Jessop about the success of the show, and an examination of the takings from the day had brightened his spirits no end. He was already considering a repeat event in autumn.

Nigel Love's body was finally removed from the bathroom on a stretcher. It was not a moment too soon, for it had been a hot day and the bathroom had been stuffy. Clara wondered if the Trelawneys would ever get the smell out of the room.

The gardener was also removed. Clara felt sorrier for that poor man than Love, he had certainly not deserved his fate. She felt quite sad as he was taken away, an accidental victim in the midst of it all.

Tommy was looking even more morose. He was holding himself and Park-Coombs personally responsible for the man's death. If they had not carelessly discussed the gardener when stood behind the show ring tent, then Diana would never have learned he was a witness. He thought himself a fool of the worst kind, for he had caused a man's death by his mistakes.

"Are you all right?" Clara came up to her brother and placed a hand on his arm.

"I am angry with myself," Tommy told her. "I shall be fine."

They watched the gardener being carried away on a covered stretcher in silence for a moment.

"Don't beat yourself too hard over this. It was a mistake, but you will learn from it," Clara said.

"I cost a man his life."

It was not easy to deny that.

"It was unintentional," Clara added.

Tommy shook his head.

"You cannot make it better, Clara, I just have to live with what I did."

He shrugged her off and walked away. Clara did not follow him, she sensed he wanted to be alone.

It was much later that they arrived home. The glorious summer's day was turning into a fine summer's evening and Clara was considering the possibility of dinner in the garden, if they could persuade Annie. Tommy was still sombre, but there was nothing she could do about that.

They walked into the house and entered the kitchen. The first thing they noticed was the kitchen table, it was barren, nothing sitting upon its surface. These last weeks it had been constantly adorned with a wedding cake as Annie endeavoured to ice it perfectly. To see the table empty was something of a shock.

"Hello, how did you get on?" Annie appeared through the back door.

Tommy looked at her suspiciously.

"You seem happy," he said.

234

"You sound surprised," Annie remarked back.

Tommy bit his tongue on a response as he could see he was waltzing into deadly territory.

"Have you finished the wedding cake?" Clara asked, a touch timidly. She was sure something was amiss, but like Tommy was nervous of saying too much.

Annie paused and gave a fierce glance at the kitchen table.

"No," she said firmly. "I realised something after you two had gone and my thirteenth icing attempt went particularly badly."

"You did?" Tommy said uncertainly.

"Yes," Annie said stoutly. "I realised that our wedding is not about a cake. It is not about food at all, or what people think of it. It is about us, me and you, Tommy. It is about us sharing vows that shall unite us forever."

Annie took a deep breath.

"I realised I can sometimes be... difficult."

"You Annie?" Clara spluttered, while at the same time Tommy said.

"Not you Annie!"

"I can become obsessional about my cooking," Annie continued, ignoring them. "And I am not always a pleasant person to be with when I am obsessional. I want to change that. I want to be a better friend to you, and a better wife."

Tommy grinned.

"You are already perfect, Annie," he assured her.

Annie snorted at him.

"You really talk rot," she scolded him.

Tommy's grin grew broader.

"Then, if you are not making the wedding cake anymore, who is?" Clara asked, finding the empty kitchen table rather disconcerting.

"I have commissioned a baker," Annie said proudly. "And while I have given them very specific instructions, I shall not raise a murmur if the cake is not quite as I envisioned."

Clara said nothing, though Tommy almost choked

235

behind her as he heard this. They would wait and see on that one.

"What about the cake you had already made?" Tommy asked.

"I have sent it to a local charity that feeds the poorest. They shall distribute it as a treat to the most needy. I felt I was looking at things all the wrong way. Just to have such a fine cake is a gift that some shall never receive."

"Very noble, Annie," Clara smiled at her, wondering how long this new, gracious Annie would last. "I was wondering about dinner in the garden this evening?"

The glare she received told her that she was expecting too much, too soon. Tommy chuckled.

"Come on, old thing, I'll set up the table outside and once we are settled, Clara will tell you how she solved a murder today."

"A murder?" Annie said aghast. "You only went to a dog show!"

Clara pulled a face.

"Yes, well, you would be surprised how tempers flare at these sorts of things!"

Printed in Great Britain
by Amazon

80183013R00140